A SPINSTER FOR THE VISCOUNT

SAVING THE SPINSTERS
BOOK THREE

JACKIE KILLELEA

PROLOGUE

1817, England

Jane couldn't help humming as she strolled the weathered path toward the ruins on the outskirts of her family's country estate, the tune light and merry. Picnics never ceased to excite her. She held a woven basket at her side, awkwardly tilting her body to the left in order to make carrying it easier.

Mrs. Mollith, her family's beloved cook, had certainly ensured that not one person in a party of ten would go hungry. The problem was, there were not ten people, never had there been a hint of ten people, and the basket was rather heavy to be lugging across uneven fields. As if to prove her point, the toe of her kid boot connected with a rock, causing Jane to stumble—the basket dragging her off to the side before she straightened and fixed her pale-green cotton skirt.

"Dratted stone," she muttered, glancing behind her at her golden-haired maid, Abigail, who averted her gaze with a hint of amusement playing on her lips.

No mere pebble would ruin Jane's mood, not when she had

a picnic with Laurence to look forward to. He'd become her closest friend ever since they'd met during the start of the London season five months earlier. After her first four unsuccessful seasons, she'd never expected to meet someone who was interested in getting to know her. But now their every conversation bolstered her heart, and Jane had begun to think of her future in a new light. She wouldn't be alone—an unwanted spinster being passed from family member to family member. No, there was a very good chance she'd be a wife. A partner—indeed, perhaps even today.

Jane called to her maid, "Oh, do not hide your laughter, Abigail, for we both know my pride has received greater damage."

Abigail chuckled, eyes brimming with mirth. "That it has, miss."

Jane's arm began to ache, and she moved the handle to her other arm. She licked her lips at the thought of the goodies within the burgeoning basket as her stomach gave a quiet rumble, impatiently awaiting its due.

"Are you certain I can't help ye with that, miss?" This was the second time she'd asked, though Abigail was familiar with Jane's stubborn tendencies.

"Thank you, Abigail, but I can manage." She threw the maid a gentle smile over her shoulder, then beamed at the bright summer day and the verdant fields before her. She inhaled the fresh midday air, sweet with the scent of apple blossoms as she walked alongside her family's orchard, the blooms decorating the ground with hues of pink and white. A sudden breeze whispered around her, and she took a moment to watch as some petals alighted from the safety of their wooden perches and danced in the air before floating to the soft earth.

Up ahead, the smoke-stained ruins came into view, the darkened stones of the long-decrepit chapel in sharp contrast to the beautiful day. If her mother were with her, she would say it was a scar on the estate lands and wrinkle her nose in distaste. Jane, however, thought the structure beautiful in its own way, despite her mother's misgivings about it.

The chapel had been built in 1607, a small chapel even then, and a fire had ravaged its walls in 1723. No attempts to rebuild it had ever come to fruition, something Jane was not terribly saddened by, given that she'd always enjoyed climbing around the stones as a child and imagining that she was an adventuress who'd stumbled upon something incredible.

As she approached the structure, Laurence appeared from behind one of the crumbling walls, a broad grin on his handsome face. He wore a slate-grey coat and buff pantaloons, a snowy cravat tied around his neck in the latest knot. His riding boots were spotless, as they always were. Jane's heartbeat quickened at the sight of his neat black hair and shining eyes. She couldn't see the color from this distance, but the deep blue hue of them was ingrained in her mind.

He was the man she wished to spend her life with—the man who she was hoping would soon ask her to marry him. She stood on the tips of her toes and raised an arm in a wave, only for the wind to pick up once more and blow her bonnet askew. She quickly straightened it, a self-conscious heat coming to her cheeks as she moved forward.

"My dear Jane, you look absolutely lovely! Quite the rival for the day itself." Laurence dipped his head when she came to a stop before him.

Her face heated even more. Lawks, she must be as pink as the apple blossoms.

"You look quite well yourself, Laurence." She returned the compliment as Abigail wandered away to give them privacy. What a dear she was.

Jane followed Laurence behind the wall to find that he'd spread a worn blanket on the ground in a flat area of the ruins. Jane placed the basket down before seating herself. She arranged her skirts around her legs as Laurence sat beside her. Opening the basket, she began pulling out cold meats and cheeses, large hunks of bread, blackberries, and confections of all sizes.

A rumble of laughter from beside her drew Jane's attention to Laurence, whose shoulders shook slightly. He met her gaze with lifted eyebrows. "Mrs. Mollith never ceases to amaze me with the sheer amount of food she can fit into a basket."

Jane's mouth quirked up to the side. "Indeed. It seems she added a few items that were unnecessary, as well." Jane grinned as she pulled a large wooden spoon from the basket. "I suppose she'll be looking for this."

Laurence guffawed and popped a blackberry into his mouth. "That seems likely."

Jane plucked a piece of cheese from a plate and nibbled it for a moment. She paused. "How's your father? Is his health improving?"

Laurence's lips pulled down into a frown as he absent-mindedly rolled a blackberry between his thumb and forefinger. "Unfortunately not. None of the herbs Dr. Williams has been suggesting have done anything to ease his cough, and he grows weaker by the day..." The silence hung for a moment before he spoke once more. "I'm not sure I'm ready to take his place...to be the next Lord Arcot..." The uncertainty in his expression made Jane's heart ache.

She reached out and placed a hand gently on his forearm, causing him to glance over at her. "I'm sorry, Laurence. It must be terrible to be in such a position. I do believe, however, that should the worst occur, you will make your father proud. After all, you've spent many years anticipating your future role as baron, and from what I've seen, you're ready to assume it."

Laurence ducked his chin. "Thank you, Jane. I wish I had the confidence in myself that you have in me." As Jane removed her hand from his arm and took another small bite of cheese,

Laurence changed the subject to a more pleasant topic. "Are you going to the Wrenthams' ball tomorrow?"

Jane stifled a groan. "My parents insisted." There was seldom a day she didn't have an event to attend or visit to make, and now that she was on her fifth season without a match, her parents were increasing their efforts to see her married. Jane had considered herself to be firmly on the shelf, a certain spinster at three-and-twenty—although—she did have one man in mind, now that he'd been introduced into her life...

Laurence raised his eyebrows at her over a biscuit. "Well, while you are busy dancing the quadrille, I'll be busy looking for a lovely lady to court."

And just like that, the air was whisked from Jane's lungs.

Laurence continued, oblivious to her shock. "My mother believes it's time for me to find a wife." He sighed. Suddenly, he smirked, but the way the corner of his mouth turned up made her uneasy. "Perhaps I'll be fortunate enough to be introduced to Miss Eugenia Castleborough. Have you met her? I've heard she's a diamond of the first water." He turned his inquiring gaze to Jane, who had just lost her appetite.

Her mind spun as she thought over all of her interactions with Laurence. Jane had believed he'd held an affection for her as she did him—after all, they spent so much time in each other's company, and he looked at her often with some sort of intense emotion. Though now...now...

"Jane?"

She flicked her gaze back to his face, stuttering as she attempted to form a response. "I-I—Well, I do not—She is—" Jane inhaled a quick breath and released it to regain control of her voice—and thoughts.

Laurence crossed his arms.

Jane took another breath, this time to fortify herself for what she was about to say. She had to know. She'd been so certain all along of his feelings, only patiently waiting for his profession. "I thought... That is to say...you've been so attentive, and we spend so much time together..."

She swallowed the lump of hesitation in her throat. She would have to say it. "Truthfully, I have come to have affection for you, Laurence, and I believed you reciprocated it. Am I mistaken in my belief?"

A terrible moment passed as silence filled the space between them, Laurence staring at her with his mouth agape.

The next moments had the potential to break her.

Laurence covered a cough with his fist but couldn't cover the laughter that followed, a cold sound she could hardly hear past the pulsing beat of her heart. "You almost fooled me there, Jane. The serious expression on your face...very convincing, but it'll take more than that to trick me." He waved his hand in the air.

Jane's heart thumped painfully, then not at all. "I'm serious Laurence. I—It wasn't a joke. I—"

Laurence stopped laughing almost as soon as he'd begun. "You mean to say that...that you believed I...loved you? *You*?" A crease formed between his brows, and a frown pulled on his lips.

She held her breath.

"Jane..." He paused, that intense look coming to his eyes once more. She'd thought it was affection—perhaps even love —but she recognized it now. Pity.

"Surely, you must understand that this is a surprise to me," he continued. "I thought when we first met that you were someone I could pass the time with at dull events. I was certain that a spinster with five seasons to her name would not dare raise her hopes at the attention of a future baron." He grimaced, looking away. "After all, haven't you evidence enough of your...deficiencies? I mean—before I met you, no one was asking you to dance..."

The blood rushing in her ears drowned out the sound of his

voice as he explained how he'd used her, making her light-headed. Her throat closed.

"You know how I've been averse to marriage, Jane. Dancing with you at events helps to keep the matchmaking mothers and scheming daughters at bay. They believe there's some sort of understanding between us and leave me alone. You get to dance a few times, as I know you enjoy doing, and I get to attend events without being pestered by young ladies. Surely, you understood?"

Her cheeks were aflame, burning with shame and embarrassment. She stood from the blanket with weak knees, brushing her skirts with trembling hands. She had to get away from here before her tears fell—before they made known to Laurence just how high her hopes had been.

"I-I see," she croaked, the lump of emotion in her throat threatening to choke her, "that you've used me most abominably, Laurence."

He stood as well, his shoulders set. He opened his mouth. Before he could utter another word, she turned on her heel and fled back the way she came, leaving the basket, the food, and Laurence behind. She clutched her skirts, barely seeing where she was going. She only caught a glimpse of Abigail scurrying after her before the tears fully clouded her vision, streaking down her cheeks as she ran from the man who'd just broken her heart.

CHAPTER 1

THREE MONTHS LATER

*J*ane clasped her hands in her lap, her knees pulled up toward her chest. She fought the urge to continue her fidgeting as she reclined in the window seat. She and her aunt had only arrived at Lord Sperrin's house party an hour before, and her nerves were already creeping up on her.

Lady Sperrin had placed her in this comfortable room with pale-yellow walls and a quilted bed with a flowing white canopy. A mahogany table with tapered legs sat on the opposite end of the room with a mirror above it, a cream-colored basin on its polished surface. The mirror reflected the vision of a writing desk in the same dark wood as the dressing table, with gilded handles and a full supply of paper and ink.

Despite her lovely surroundings, she looked out the window and sighed, drawing her aunt's attention from across the room.

"Dear Jane, you look as though you've been sentenced to hang."

"I almost feel as though I have." Jane sighed once more and rested her cheek in her hand. An isolated estate wasn't exactly where she wished to be, and yet, here she was. Not only was it isolated...but full of strangers.

Aunt Agnes propped her hands on the hips of her dark-blue traveling dress and pursed her lips. "You know, I was just as wary of the *Ton* at your age. People in high society have never been easy to please. They always seemed to inspect me and find me lacking in some way."

"In what way could they have found *you* lacking?" Jane's aunt was anything *but* with her dark-green eyes and willowy figure.

"I was a rather terrible dancer, believe it or not. They called me 'tortoise-foot,' for I could never move my feet fast enough in the dance line. I wasn't agile either."

Jane leaned back at her aunt's confession. "This is the first I'm hearing of this. 'Tortoise-foot'? That's not a very clever name."

"Yes, well, it was good enough." Her aunt shrugged. "But that's besides the point. My reason for telling you this is because I want you to know that I'm aware of the Ton's cruelties." She stepped over to the window and took a seat beside Jane. "I know how you feel."

Jane shifted to make room for her aunt. Her shoulders relaxed a bit as she smelled the pleasant rose perfume that accompanied the woman. Jane gave a huff. "My every minor flaw is magnified in their eyes. They overlook me, at best—my five unsuccessful seasons can attest to that."

Jane was all too familiar with empty dance cards and dull evenings spent sitting alone whilst watching others converse and make merry. Her friends had all married and moved to estates across the country. They were no longer there to speak with her during the events she found so intimidating, nor could they encourage her now that they were miles away, with children and busy lives of their own to manage.

Feelings of her inferiority were forever her shadow, and with every passing season that she remained unmarried, they further cemented themselves into her conscience.

"Quite a few have overlooked you, and there will be quite a few more. Such is the nature of our society. Many parade around with their chins held abominably high and wear their hauteur as an accessory, but you must understand that not all act in such a way."

It was true that Jane had seen many members of the *Ton* act with kindness and generosity, and some had gone to great lengths to help those less fortunate. She had always attempted to see the best before being shown the worst, though that task could prove difficult.

"I know, Aunt. I...I...think what troubles me now is the unknown. I've no idea who is attending this party besides you, and there are certain people I'd rather not interact with again. For all I know, Laurence could be downstairs at this very moment." Jane's mind reeled at the idea. Had he been invited? Why had her parents sent her here, anyway? They'd mentioned something about suitors and a prize, but she had a difficult time remembering their exact words.

Aunt Agnes reached out a slightly wrinkled hand to pat Jane's knee. "As far as I'm aware, Mr. Revil is not acquainted with Lord Sperrin. It's unlikely he'll be here."

"What if he is?" Her voice wavered.

Instead of answering her question, Aunt Agnes said, "He broke your heart—that I know. Do not spare another thought for him. I told your parents I'd find you a worthy husband, and so I shall."

Jane groaned and buried her head in her knees. "You'd have to be a magician to procure a man that would love me, Aunt. I thought Laure—Mr. Revil was that man, but..." The pain of the last three months ached dully in her abdomen. It had subsided, for the most part, but thinking of him was apt to bring it back. She'd been so foolish.

"Come now, Jane." Her aunt spoke in a reproving tone. "Enough of this. Mr. Revil is a cad."

Jane raised her head from her knees, in shock at her aunt's language. "Aunt! He—"

"—is not who you thought he was. Not who he acted as," Aunt Agnes concluded. "When your uncle and I met, I wondered why a man like him would speak to me—it seemed like a dream...but it was not. I'd been so used to the Ton's cruel words that his kindness was almost surreal. Your uncle didn't care that I was 'tortoise-foot.' He loved me for me. While I worried, in the beginning, that he was playing some terrible trick...perhaps he'd lost some bet...he wasn't and hadn't. I was blind, Jane. I'd been in a cave so long that it took me more than a few moments to adjust to the light. Of course, we married, but it would have been a shorter courtship had I allowed myself to be vulnerable. Be vulnerable, Jane. Don't let Mr. Revil's actions alter your future decisions."

"What if my heart can never be whole again? Perhaps I'm doomed to live as a spinster for the rest of my days." Jane shrugged.

"You don't mean that." Aunt Agnes shook a finger.

"I wouldn't mind...not if it meant avoiding the pain of future heartbreak."

Aunt Agnes reached out and tucked a dark-brown curl behind Jane's ear, bringing her other hand around to cup Jane's cheek. "Think on my words, dear. Spinsterhood is for some, but I do not believe for you. If your uncle were still alive, he'd say the same thing."

After a moment, her aunt stood from the window seat and brushed out her skirt. She crossed the room to the door, saying over her shoulder, "He'd also call out that blackguard, Mr. Revil."

Her aunt left the room, pulling the door shut behind her with a small click.

Jane turned her head to the window once more. Her uncle was the exception to the rule. While her aunt may not have been a proficient dancer in her youth, Jane had heard enough stories from her parents to know her aunt had been exceptionally beautiful. Jane scoffed. Aunt Agnes still was. Jane didn't have that advantage. She rested her head against the cool glass of the windowpane.

An expensively dressed woman alighted from a carriage, her nose pointed toward the heavens. Jane wrung her hands as the woman glided to the front entrance, her parents trailing a little way behind her. As they moved from her view, Jane tried to build up her courage and persuade herself to exit her chambers.

She shouldn't be a ninny. All of the guests here might be pleasant company, after all.

Another carriage came trundling up the gravel drive. As it rolled to a stop, the crest adorning it gleamed in the sun's bright rays, though it was one unfamiliar to her. As she was the daughter of a baron, she knew several families of the Ton, yet she had never been very good at remembering family crests— something her governess had often scolded her about as a child.

The footman pulled down the steps, and the occupant of the carriage stepped out. The midday sun glinted off a man's pair of leather boots before revealing the man himself, who grinned at his footman and clapped him on the shoulder. Jane lifted a hand to her chest. Such familiarity with servants was uncommon in society.

The man strode toward the entrance, a sort of subtle confidence in his gait. She couldn't see his facial features clearly at this distance, but he appeared to be preparing for something. His movements were somewhat rigid as he strode toward the door in his dark-brown traveling coat and beige pantaloons. She wasn't sure why, but the man piqued her curiosity. Once Jane had lost sight of the intriguing man, she stood.

"Maybe this house party won't be so horrible, after all."

~

*L*ord Henry Lendin, the third Viscount Harroway, adjusted his cravat for the second time that morning as he stared at the imposing estate before him, its wings reaching out like an embrace. Its sand-colored stone would have been intimidating had he not visited multiple times as a child. It was difficult to believe that only a few hours before, Henry had left his estate in Berkshire and set off for Wiltshire and Lord Sperrin's sprawling grounds after so many years of absence.

What disease of the mind had convinced him that attending a house party would be enjoyable? Perhaps it was the possibility that he might actually win the prize Lord Sperrin had spoken to him about—the jewel of Parcathia. According to the man, all guests had a fair chance at winning the jewel as they were given clues toward the jewel's location throughout the duration of the house party. Whoever found the jewel first kept it. While Henry's lands were in reasonably good shape, any extra money could help with the running and improvement of them.

Exhaling a huff of breath, he released his cravat. While he greatly enjoyed laughter and lightheartedness, Henry had never warmed to the conceited nature of some of his acquaintances. His parents had taught him from a young age to appreciate what he had and to help others when he could, no matter their status in society. He knew others who had been taught the same as well—one of his best friends, Edmund Colhampton, otherwise known as the fifth Duke of Albemarle, shared his beliefs and had been brought up similarly.

And yet, there were also those who looked down their noses at those in the lower classes on a regular basis. These types of people were the ones he was wary of and the cause of his growing dread, for the prize—the lauded jewel—would draw them here. Those hungry for wealth and status.

Was he so different?

He swallowed the lump in his throat, eyeing the front steps. He would enjoy himself, surely. The party would be a nice way to pass a few weeks in a relaxing manner. Maybe he'd even meet the woman he'd marry.

Henry stifled a stilted laugh at his own thoughts, his mother's words from the day before echoing in his head. *"There are many unattached women at house parties, and it's high time you find a wife."* She hadn't minced her words, and though Henry was loath to admit it, she was right. He had begun to find himself dreaming of a day when he'd have a loving wife and happy children. The pull hadn't been so strong in his younger years. With the absence of his father, he'd been so focused on learning to manage his own estates. But now that he was five-and-twenty, he felt it keenly.

As Henry entered the foyer, the walls tastefully decorated with colorful paintings in gilded frames, the refreshing scent of citrus filled the room. Crimson carpet covered a small part of the white stone floor, the light-filled room a stark contrast to the dark mahogany doors. Memories from his childhood encircled the Maypole of his mind, each ribbon of thought winding around another. The last time he'd been here, his father had been alive.

Henry pushed the ache away. This visit would prove to be a welcome respite from the grief and overwhelming responsibilities that had lately been thrust upon him. Whatever guests this house party included, they were his friends. People he had known all his life.

"Lendin! It's so good to have you here." Lord Sperrin clapped him on the shoulder. The man's graying head of thick chestnut-colored hair was styled in a neat manner, his clothing in an older style that belied his age.

"It's good to be here. I must thank you again for inviting me." Henry bowed over Lady Sperrin's hand and grinned at the gracious woman. Her hair, unlike her husband's, was still the same blond color it always had been. Only small wrinkles around her mouth told of the years that had passed since Henry had been a boy. Her motherly look of affection further eased his wary mind.

"Nonsense, Lendin!" Lord Sperrin's voice rang through the hall. "You are always welcome here. You should know by now that you are like a second son to us. With how often your parents and yourself used to visit, it's almost more unusual for you to be absent."

Henry gave an appreciative hum and mentioned their actual son. "How is Thomas, anyway? He's at your estate in Cornwall, isn't he?"

Lord Sperrin shared a glowing look with his wife. "He's very well. He's expecting his third child next month. From what he's written, I don't believe the estate is nearly as dull as it once was."

Henry grinned again, thinking of his old friend running after a mob of children. Thomas had never been one for peace and quiet and was surely encouraging his children in all of their endeavors, whether that be catching frogs or stealing biscuits from belowstairs as Henry and Thomas had once done.

"That's very good to hear. Now, Sperrin, I fear I look the worse for wear after my travels. Would you mind terribly if I retired to my room to make myself more presentable?"

"Oh, certainly, my boy." Lord Sperrin gestured for the butler and gave an amiable nod. "Wheaton, please escort Lord Lendin to his chambers. We can't have our guests run away upon being introduced to him."

Henry laughed in good nature. "I think it more likely they would run before introductions were made."

Lord Sperrin gave a hearty laugh as Henry followed the butler, calling out as they strode away, "Dinner's at five of the clock, Lendin."

Henry chuckled to himself, his short meeting with his friends having already affirmed his earlier thought of enjoying himself at Lord Sperrin's estate.

Henry followed the middle-aged butler down a hallway with wood-paneled walls, the dark oak polished thoroughly. Light flooded through windows placed at intervals along the corridor, the curtains drawn open to let guests look out upon the lush grounds. Every turn unveiled a new feast for the eyes —every hall filled with paintings and decorations from his hosts' extensive travels. Blue floral vases and silk tapestries in one, another with wooden masks and a stuffed boar. There were items from what seemed like every continent.

At length, the butler stopped in front of a door. He opened it and gestured for Henry to step inside. As he did so, the grey-haired man spoke. "I hope everything is to your liking, my lord. Is there anything else you need at present?"

The space before him was tastefully furnished and incredibly clean.

"Thank you, Wheaton, it is. There is nothing else I need."

The man bowed, giving a polite click of the heels before quickly leaving the way he came. Wheaton had always been a proper sort of butler. Henry didn't think he'd ever seen a surprised expression on the man's face. Given Lord Sperrin's eccentric home, this in itself was a surprise.

Henry's valet, Notham, had already unpacked his trunk and

was presently setting the last of Henry's shirts into the armoire, located in the corner of the room.

"Thank you, Notham." Henry nodded in appreciation.

A garment in one hand, the man closed the armoire doors and smiled. "'Tis nothing, my lord, and might I also inform you that I succeeded in removing the stubborn dirt stains from your waistcoat?" The man held Henry's favorite waistcoat before him, looking rather proud of himself.

Henry stepped forward to get a better look at the garment. "You never cease to amaze me, Notham. Your skills know no bounds."

Notham had definitely had his fair share of work with all of the scrapes Henry had gotten into in the past—and his latest hadn't been any different. A few days previous, Henry had been visiting his estate's tenants after a storm had swept through. He'd wanted to speak with the families, as he'd expected a few minor repairs may be in order. What he hadn't expected was that his tenant's eight-stone Bullmastiff, Barley, would be so excited to see him that he'd leap up on his hind legs and push Henry into the mud. Henry's lips pulled up at the memory. Barley had always taken a liking to Henry, probably due to Henry nearly always bringing him a scrap bone from the kitchen when he visited.

"Thank you, my lord. Would you be liking a bath?" He raised an eyebrow knowingly.

Henry looked down at himself and chuckled. "Do I really look so travel worn, old fellow?"

Notham's greying head tilted slightly. Finally, his mouth also pulled to the side in a crooked grin. "Do you really want my answer, my lord?"

Henry only shook his head with a laugh. "I'll have one." Regardless of the more pompous guests that could be in attendance at this party, if he was to have a chance at finding the love he so desired—a wife, as his mother wanted—then he'd have to look in fine fettle.

CHAPTER 2

The evening of her arrival at the Sperrin house party, Jane brushed her hands down her pale-blue dress as she walked down the hall from her room, the delicate silk soft beneath her fingertips. She'd wanted to wear darker colors as she no longer felt like a debutante, but her parents had stood firm. In their view, she was still just as fresh as any other bloom of a young woman—no matter that she'd spent four seasons alone and her fifth practically courting a man who, as it turned out, had only been spending time with her because she was a distraction. While she appreciated their sentiments, she had forced herself to bite her tongue. Jane knew of no flower in their climate that remained naturally in bloom for five years.

She stopped in front of her aunt's chambers, knocking lightly on the door. It quickly swung open and revealed Aunt Agnes in all her glory. Her aunt's beauty had not seemed to fade with age, as so many others' did. Jane was reminded of it every time she glimpsed the woman. She was mischievous, had a confident set to her shoulders, and a look in her eyes that Jane knew only too well.

Their past conversation had not been forgotten, as Jane had hoped. Jane sighed—inwardly, this time. Arguing with her aunt would be futile, for her aunt's expression told of plans having to do with her only niece—plans that Jane was not informed of, nor would she be.

"Good evening, my dear niece. I see you're dressed for dinner, and I suppose you've come to inquire if I am as well?"

Jane forced away her trepidation and looked on her aunt affectionately. She truly loved Aunt Agnes dearly, even though she was wary of the woman at times. "Yes, Aunt. Are you?"

Her aunt stepped into the corridor, closing her chamber door behind her. Her greying auburn hair had been pulled into a bun at the base of her head with little braids swirling around it from either direction. Jane dearly wished she'd been born with that beautiful color of hair, but all she'd gotten was a dull brown color—somewhere between the shade of an acorn and a pinecone.

"I am, and I am determined tonight that you shall not be overlooked. Have I mentioned that I love that color on you?" Though her aunt clearly wanted to distract Jane from the first part of that statement, it was not to be.

An uneasiness arose inside of Jane once more, and she absent-mindedly twisted a curl around her finger. Aunt Agnes was a stubborn woman, and once she'd set her mind to do something, she'd follow through with it.

"Aunt?" She spoke with a questioning tone. Perhaps she was making Aunt Agnes's statement out to be more than it was meant as. At her aunt's slight hesitation, Jane had her answer.

"Dear Jane, worry not. I believe you'll have made a match by the end of this house party. Mr. Revil's actions were... distasteful, to say the least, but you really mustn't let one man's actions keep you from finding another." Aunt Agnes wrinkled her nose.

This second reminder of Laurence's betrayal stabbed her heart, but her aunt left her to her own thoughts as they headed for the drawing room—thoughts that had just been thrown into turmoil. She tried to calm her nerves as they descended the grand staircase and walked down the hall. Whatever her aunt had planned for her, it wouldn't be terrible. Jane hoped, anyway.

"What are your plans for the jewel of Parcathia?" Her aunt leveled her gaze at Jane.

Jane knit her eyebrows. "The what?"

Aunt Agnes made a *tsk*ing sound. "Don't tell me you've forgotten already. It is the second reason we are here."

"I fear you'll have to remind me."

Her aunt gave a huff. "All of the guests will be searching for the coveted jewel. At the end of the house party, one guest will be given the jewel to keep, and only the Lord knows the price of it."

Well, this was news. "When does the scavenger hunt begin?"

"Within the next few days, I believe. Perhaps even tomorrow. We shall see. You can be assured that each of the guests will be doing their utmost to win it."

As they arrived at the drawing room doors, Aunt Agnes paused just outside. "Be yourself, Jane. Leave the rest to me." She straightened her shoulders, her tone one of concern. "And do not fall for any falsehoods." With that, her aunt gestured for the footman to open the door, leaving Jane with no other option but to follow.

She stepped into the colorful room, and all at once, Jane was thrown somewhere in between England and India. The room with its mixture of rich Indian silks in vibrant oranges and pinks and straight-legged settees and chairs with muted blue cushions was empty except for their hosts. On Lord Sperrin's arm perched a large parrot——an unexpected sight, indeed.

Though their hosts had been speaking, their conversation paused when the footman announced her aunt and then Jane.

Lady Sperrin beamed at them. "Agnes! Miss Talbot! How lovely to see you both. We were wondering if you might be absent this evening, given your weariness from travel."

Aunt Agnes beamed. "Oh, Mary, you know how much I've been wanting to see you. It seems it was ages ago that we last met in person, and Jane, of course, is eager to meet the other guests. No amount of fatigue could keep us away."

Jane forced herself to nod in agreement and smiled, trying to tamp her nerves down as she bobbed a curtsy alongside Aunt Agnes.

"Well, we are both very pleased that you ladies could join us this evening." Lord Sperrin bowed.

Jane couldn't help but eye the parrot, its cerulean wings folded against its sides. They contrasted with its mustard-yellow abdomen in a most pleasing way.

"Oh! I've been remiss in my introductions. This"—Lord Sperrin gestured to the parrot—"is Gerald. He is the finest macaw in all of England."

As though agreeing with this statement, Gerald croaked, "Spinach."

Lord Sperrin raised an eyebrow at Gerald. "Spinach, eh? Someone's been listening to Lady Sperrin's dinner menu."

Jane stifled a laugh. "He's beautiful. I've never seen a bird as colorful."

Lord Sperrin admired his pet. "Indeed. We picked up Gerald on one of our trips to South America. He was being sold at a little outdoor market—cramped in a small cage with rusting wires. Lady Sperrin and I were quick to remedy the situation and took him home. He is an Englishman at heart."

Gerald croaked once more, this time only a mumble of indecipherable sounds.

Five minutes of polite conversation later, a young woman in

a pink dress who seemed familiar entered the room along with her parents. Introductions were made, and Jane curtsied again.

"It's a pleasure to make your acquaintance, Miss Wildon."

"And yours, Miss Talbot." The woman smiled, and it seemed genuine. Her blond hair was drawn up into a knot at the base of her head, and two lone curls framed her face. "I must say, Miss Talbot..." She clasped her hands in front of her and shifted with an uncertain expression. "It's nice to see a familiar face here. I was worried I might not know anyone."

Jane cocked her head to the side. "Pardon me, Miss Wildon. Have we met previously?"

Color suffused the young lady's face. "Not formally, no. I've seen you at a few events, that's all."

At her words, Jane remembered. Jane and Miss Wildon had often shared a commiserating look from opposite ends of a ballroom—both wallflowers, it seemed.

"Oh, Miss Wildon, how could I have forgotten? It's nice to finally know your name."

Miss Wildon brightened. "Likewise. Do tell me about yourself, Miss Talbot. Do you live in London?"

"I do not, thankfully. I can only abide so much of the bustle. It can quite overwhelm the senses."

"I completely agree." Miss Wildon brushed a hand down her skirt. "Dorset is where I live, and I find I'm much better suited to it."

As this conversation very much suited Jane. Miss Wildon did not hold any of the disdain so many others of society did.

Jane caught Miss Wildon eyeing Gerald. "What do you think of Lord Sperrin's macaw?" she asked.

"He's quite large, but I like him very much. I have a canary at home—his name's Heath. Birds rather fascinate me, I must admit."

Soon, more guests began to enter the room. Jane and Miss Wildon were still in conversation—Aunt Agnes having joined them—when Mrs. Wildon called her daughter away to introduce her to a fellow guest, apologizing for the interruption.

Lord Sperrin approached Jane and her aunt, Gerald now absent from his arm. "Pray tell, have you yet been introduced to Lord Lendin?" He gestured to the man standing a few feet behind him, a pleasant expression on his handsome face. The intriguing blond man she'd seen arrive earlier from the window.

Jane's heart beat a little faster.

Aunt Agnes answered for them both. "I don't believe we have, my lord."

"Then let us right that terrible wrong. Mrs. Westby, Miss Talbot, let me introduce you to Lord Lendin, the Viscount Harroway. Lord Lendin, please let me introduce you to Mrs. Westby and Miss Talbot."

Lord Lendin stepped forward as he was introduced and bowed over each of their hands. "It is a pleasure to make your acquaintance." His kind brown gaze eased the tension in Jane's shoulders, though his rich voice momentarily took her off guard.

"Likewise, my lord," Jane murmured.

As the group waited for the rest of the guests to arrive, Aunt Agnes fell into conversation with Lady Sperrin, leaving Jane to converse with Lord Lendin. What topic might be of interest? She had never been very comfortable speaking to people besides her family and friends, and try as she might, her very English mind kept defaulting to the weather.

"Lord Sperrin mentioned that you were the first guests to arrive today. Pray tell, where did you travel from?" The courteous question paused her frantic search for a topic.

She responded with a smile, reminded of her home with its rolling hills and lush countryside. "We traveled from Somerset, my lord. And yourself?"

Lord Lendin clasped his hands behind his back, and his

countenance seemed to warm—almost as though her answer surprised him, though she wasn't sure why. When she'd first seen him arrive, she hadn't been able to tell quite how handsome he was. Now that they were in close proximity, his boyish grin sent Jane's heart fluttering.

"I've come from my estate in Berkshire. I'd not long to travel, fortunately. I find I'm not very fond of traveling great distances by carriage." He leaned closer, as if about to impart a secret, and Jane's stomach did a strange flip. "When I was a boy, I accompanied my father to London. It was meant to be a simple trip, and I was as excited as any young boy would be— I'd never been to London before—but, as it turns out, a fierce storm was making the same trip and soon caught up with us. The coachman had to pull off to the side of the road, for he could hardly see his own hand in front of him."

Jane listened intently, drawn into Lord Lendin's story. As he spoke, his eyes turned a deeper shade of brown—something like a dark cup of tea...or chocolate.

"All around us, the wind howled, and each crack of thunder rattled the carriage. Our coachman was doing his best to keep the horses calm, but I was certain that—at any moment—they would bolt and take us with them. My father remained unconcerned throughout the ordeal, never showing a hint of fear."

At this, Lord Lendin looked sheepish. "I wish that I would have reacted the same. The storm passed eventually, as all storms do, although my fears did not pass so easily. They have mostly abated over the years, yet every time I find myself in a carriage on a rather gloomy day, my heart does not fail to beat slightly quicker—nor do I feel quite at ease."

As he finished his story, Jane couldn't help shaking her head. "Why, Lord Lendin, after an ordeal such as that, I would find myself reluctant to enter a carriage at all."

He nodded in agreement. "And I was—at first—but my

father told me something that changed my mind. 'The cards do not always fall as we expect them to, but, through failures and successes, we must play again.' I know there is always a possibility of a storm—even in unassuming skies—and so I do not let my past fears hinder me."

"Well, even if you hadn't a frightening experience as a boy, I would still agree with your dislike of traveling in a carriage. Being confined to one for days on end is not my idea of enjoyment." She laughed.

He grinned, a chuckle escaping him. "And what do you find enjoyable, Miss Talbot?" He raised his eyebrows.

"I'm afraid I'm not quite certain what I find enjoyable anymore, my lord." With her parents' constant discussions on finding her a husband and various attempts to do so, there hadn't been many opportunities for leisure. She bit her lip. "Truthfully, my days have lately been so busy with parties and events that I haven't had the time to even think about what I'd like to do, should I have a moment to do it."

Lord Lendin dipped his head. "Not even an idea?"

Jane twisted her mouth to the side. "I used to enjoy playing the pianoforte, but doesn't everyone? So no, not really."

Lord Lendin crossed his arms over his chest and studied the ground intently. Had she said something wrong? A few moments passed before he met her gaze again. "Then, to quote Lord Sperrin, 'let us right that terrible wrong.'"

"I'm sorry. I do not follow your line of thinking."

"We are both currently guests at this house party, and what better place to find enjoyment than at a beautiful estate in the countryside?" He rocked on his heels, propping his hands on his hips. "I will be your companion in that pursuit, if you allow it."

"What do you mean, sir?" Surely, not what she thought he did...

enry hurried to explain. "You, Miss Talbot, have just shared that you don't quite know what you find enjoyable, and I think that is terribly depressing. I cannot imagine living without joy in life. Reading, fishing, riding, fencing...the things I take pleasure in. So if you'll accept my offer, I would like to help you rediscover the joys you've forgotten."

Henry hadn't the slightest idea what so drew him to Miss Talbot. Perhaps her beauty? Or her soft voice? Her lovely laugh? Likely, a combination of them all. When he'd entered the drawing room and seen her speaking with her aunt, she'd seemed shy, though he'd assumed that was a facade as he'd so often found it to be among ladies of the *Ton* who acted so in order to attract suitors. But then she'd smiled—a smile so genuine that it couldn't possibly be false.

Miss Talbot crinkled her eyebrows. "But we've only just met, my lord. Wouldn't you rather spend your time with someone you already know? A friend, perhaps?"

He inclined his head thoughtfully. "Lord Sperrin has informed me of the other guests attending this house party, and they are but acquaintances. My only true friends here are Lord and Lady Sperrin, and I mustn't distract them from their hosting. Additionally, I may be bold in saying so, but I believe we will be fast friends. So...what say you?" Had he even breathed between any of those sentences?

Miss Talbot looked wary, shooting a glance at her aunt. Strangely, though Henry had only just met Miss Talbot, he dearly wanted her to agree to his plans. She stood before him for a moment in silence, looking deep in thought and tapping her foot lightly on the floor before she regarded him again. The din around them increased in volume.

She opened her mouth, but before she could speak, their conversation was interrupted by the announcement of the arrival of other guests. Some with kind faces, many without. One, in particular, searched the throng of people in the drawing room...until her gaze landed on Henry.

He inwardly groaned. Not her. Lady Caroline, daughter of the Earl of Wessex.

Too late to hide.

CHAPTER 3

As soon as Lady Caroline had been announced, the elegant blonde whom Jane had noticed arriving earlier in the day strode to Lord Lendin's side with a purpose, all but pushing Jane out of the way.

"Lord Lendin." Lady Caroline's curls bobbed with her perfect curtsy. "Why, I haven't seen you since last season." The woman completely ignored Jane—something Jane was quite used to.

"Lady Caroline," Lord Lendin replied in a bland tone. "Let me have the honor of introducing you to Miss Talbot. Miss Talbot, please meet Lady Caroline."

Jane flicked her gaze up from the drawing room's maroon carpet before curtsying to Lady Caroline, who stiffly nodded in return. "It's a pleasure to meet you, Lady Caroline." Jane spoke the words quietly, already somewhat wary of the woman.

"Yes." The woman's disdain-laced response caused a muscle in Lord Lendin's jaw to tense. Lady Caroline took no time in shifting her attention back to him, a pretty pout crossing her face. "It's a shame it's been so long. This house party is certainly fortuitous—and what fun it will be to be in such a competition."

Lord Lendin's mouth turned down at the sides, though the woman seemed not to notice as he replied with a bland, "Certainly."

When dinner was announced, Lady Caroline placed her hand around Lord Lendin's arm, and he shot Jane an apologetic look as the pair walked into the dining room. Jane tamped down her disappointment and raised her brows as Aunt Agnes walked over, a dark-haired man following behind her.

"My dear, this is Mr. Langley, son of Baron Langley. This, Mr. Langley, is my wonderful niece, Miss Talbot."

He bowed as Jane curtsied, a dark curl falling over his forehead.

"A pleasure." He spoke in a polite tone, offering his arm to her.

She placed her gloved hand around the sleeve of his expensive-looking jacket, and they walked into the dining room, only silence between them. The space was large and stately, with heavy wooden chairs lining the long table in the middle of the room. The furnishings were more masculine here, though Jane admired the dark wood molding, tall windows, and an even higher ceiling. The silver utensils reflected the light that a few perfectly placed candelabras provided, and the white linen tablecloth was entirely without an errant mark.

Jane was seated in between Mr. Langley and a Mr. Beaton, the former maintaining his silence throughout the meal and the latter speaking almost unceasingly. All the while, she snuck glances at Lord Lendin, who seemed to be having as good a time as she, which wasn't saying very much. He nodded absently to something Lady Caroline said, looking for all the world as though he'd rather be elsewhere.

Jane refocused her attention, trying to listen to whatever Mr. Beaton was saying. He had already made clear his opinions on the weather, the theatre, and various vegetables, as well as spoken quite fondly of his hounds, who—he'd told Jane—were housed on the grounds of his estate of Penderton. Now, his voice rang out again.

"And Mrs. Whittleby said that she'd never seen someone behave as such, and we both agreed that it was incredibly distasteful. I could hardly sleep that night, the memory of it haunting me so. To think, that a person could possibly mistake their pudding spoon for their soup spoon! It's disgraceful."

Jane had to hold in her laughter as Mr. Beaton finished his rant. He turned his head to look at her for a response, and she put on a serious face.

"How terrible, indeed, sir. You must be very brave to attend this house party, knowing that something like that could happen again." She made her voice as solemn-sounding as she could.

Mr. Beaton continued. "Truth be told, I almost declined Lord Sperrin's invitation altogether, though the chance of winning the jewel was too much for me to pass up."

As he spoke to the woman on the opposite side of him, Jane was granted a moment to rest, her lips quirking up at the absurdity of Mr. Beaton's reaction to such a simple mistake. She met Lord Lendin's eye, and the two shared a commiserating smile.

It seemed to Jane that many hours had passed before dinner was over and the ladies retired to the drawing room, leaving the men to discuss politics and other topics over glasses of port wine. This room was decorated in a more feminine style, with light-yellow walls, an apricot settee, and pale-pink cushioned chairs with small golden stripes. A large window at the back of the room showed the slowly darkening sky. The sun had already dipped below the horizon.

A massive bookshelf sat against the left wall, and a few ornately carved tables on the opposite side of the room. What caught Jane's attention most, however, was the vast array of curiosities scattered about, including a statue of an elephant on the mantel and stone carvings of flowers and monkeys in a cabinet.

As they entered, Lady Sperrin clapped her hands. "Since we're all getting settled in this evening, this is the perfect opportunity for us to listen to and enjoy our fellow women's many talents. Would anyone like to play a piece on the pianoforte, or perhaps sing a song or two?"

Lady Caroline immediately spoke up. "I would love to sing."

Her mother furiously nodded her head. "My Caroline sings like an angel. I've never heard another match her."

Her daughter piped up once more. "And I can accompany myself."

Lady Sperrin's tone was kind as she gestured toward the pianoforte. "Then I'm sure we'd all be pleased to listen."

Lady Caroline stood from the settee and strutted over to the well-cared-for instrument, taking a moment to flip through the stack of music that lay there before grabbing a piece and seating herself on the carefully polished bench.

Jane found a seat next to her aunt and clasped her hands in her lap, curious as to how the woman would sound. Jane, herself, had only ever been adequate with playing. Lady Caroline gave a smirk before her fingers descended onto the keys and she opened her mouth to sing—and what a song it was.

Aunt Agnes stiffened as dissonant chords and off-key singing filled the room. Lady Sperrin appeared as though she were trying to enjoy the music—and failing. The others wore shocked expressions. Jane was equally taken aback at the sounds that assaulted her. The war that Lady Caroline had waged on the ears of those within the room seemed to go on for some time.

"'Then I shall leave and we will meet there again, under the shade of the poplar tree...'" Lady Caroline ended the song with a flourish and looked up smugly from the pianoforte before standing and curtsying, giving an unusually pointed look at Jane.

Lady Sperrin clapped politely along with the rest of the group. "Well, I certainly have never met her match." The woman adjusted the sleeve of her gown. "Thank you, Lady Caroline. Would anyone else like to play or sing?"

Another girl stood up and played on the instrument—Jane could only just remember her name as Miss Appret—her music healing the ears of her audience. Jane soon lost herself in the piece. The gentle ascend and descend of the notes eased the tension in her shoulders caused by the time she'd spent interacting with those who deemed her unworthy of notice. Mr. Langley had certainly deemed her as such, seeing as how the man had hardly spoken one word to her over the course of dinner.

Whilst Jane was no great musician, she certainly knew how to enjoy music. She was so caught up in it that she found herself taken off guard when her aunt volunteered her to play next. She fluttered open her eyes and pierced Aunt Agnes with a look meant to communicate her nervousness, yet her aunt just gave an encouraging nod. Jane stood slowly from her seat and reluctantly made her way over to the pianoforte, leafing through the sheet music before choosing a piece she knew and seating herself on the bench. She wiped her sweating palms on her skirts before settling her trembling fingers upon the cold ivory keys, a lump in her throat.

She'd never felt comfortable playing in front of others, though she loved the playing itself. And while her parents had ensured that she'd been taught to play the pianoforte from a young age, she hadn't been afforded the time to properly play since after her first season and subsequent failure at securing a husband.

Jane began to play, fumbling over the keys as she read the notes before her. As she did, a terrible sense of loneliness settled in her heart, aching and throbbing in a steady rhythm. She walked through society as a ghost. She just wanted to be seen. Heard. Her parents had never seemed to really listen to what she wanted, and the *Ton* never truly saw her.

What cared she for a jewel? She just wanted a friend.

As memories of lonely evenings and disinterested looks flooded her mind, her fingers pressed harder and flew over the keys, keeping time with her racing heart. She wanted a life of her own, a love of her own. She wanted to be appreciated. Understood. She had thought that Laurence knew her—truly knew her.

There must be someone who will understand me. There must be someone.

Her energy drained, her fingers slowing as reality crashed into her once more. Jane exhaled as the last chord rang out, the catharsis resonating in her bones. When she looked up from the music, she froze.

The men had joined the ladies in the drawing room.

Heat rose to her cheeks at the sight of all of them facing her. She stood carefully from the bench, limbs not wanting to move. Suddenly, the room erupted in a cacophony of clapping. Aunt Agnes stared at her. Lord Lendin stood at the back of the room, an unreadable expression on his face. Miss Wildon grinned and clapped with fervor. Jane swallowed and bobbed a quick curtsy before scurrying back to her aunt and pressing into the cushion beside her.

The applause died down and Lord Sperrin spoke. "What marvelous talent our guests have. Now, the night is young, and I propose we continue the evening's entertainment with a few rounds of cards."

Lady Sperrin joined her husband and had the footmen arrange tables and chairs for multiple games. Some guests grouped together and began cheerful games of whist, others conversed with their acquaintances. Jane remained seated with her aunt, unsure of what to do.

"Your playing was beautiful, my dear, absolutely beautiful." Her aunt winked at her.

Jane's heart settled within her. "Thank you, Aunt, and thank you for volunteering me. I wouldn't have done so without your pushing, and I believe it did me good to play again."

Aunt Agnes patted Jane's hand. "It's a shame you haven't in so long."

True. Now that she was out from under her parents' watchful gazes, she could take the time to do the things she really wished to. It had felt absolutely freeing to play again.

Perhaps she should agree to Lord Lendin's plan, though were his intentions true? Aunt Agnes had told her to be wary, after all. Why was Lord Lendin so keen to help her so soon after they'd met? Did he have some hidden motive related to finding the jewel? What if—

Her aunt gently nudged her with her elbow. The very man she was thinking of stood in front of them, hands clasped behind his back and a soft smile on his face. Her heart gave an extra thump in her chest as if to remind her of its presence.

"Care to join me in a game of chess?" he asked.

Jane looked to her aunt.

Aunt Agnes made a shooing gesture. "Go on. I was about to speak to Mary, anyway."

Jane's smile grew as she stood and faced Lord Lendin. "I'd love to, my lord."

He grinned and offered her his arm before escorting her the short distance to the chess table in the opposite corner of the large room. He pulled out her chair for her before sitting himself, a knowing expression on his face. "Mr. Beaton seemed very taken with you at dinner."

Jane covered her mouth to stifle a giggle before moving her

pawn one space forward. "I wasn't aware until this evening that a person could have such strong opinions on onions."

Lord Lendin's eyes gleamed with mirth. "At least he didn't mention his aversion to strawberries." He grimaced, moving a knight in front of the row of pawns.

Jane laughed freely this time. "Strawberries! Truly? What a fruit to dislike. I could picture currants, perhaps, or even blackberries, but I've never met a person who would turn their nose up at a summer-ripened strawberry." She moved another pawn forward to give space to her rook, trying to come up with a plan of attack.

Lord Lendin laughed quietly. "My thoughts exactly, Miss Talbot. I can remember quite a few times when I snuck down to the kitchens to steal one of Cook's strawberry tarts. I've yet to meet a person who makes them better than she." He moved a bishop out from behind the pawns, another piece for her to keep watch of.

"And how were your dinner companions, my lord? Do they also believe that beets should be eaten three times a day?" Humor laced her question.

"Alas, I didn't get the chance to ask them. I do know, however, that Lady Caroline has just been to London to acquire a new wardrobe, that she prefers sapphires to diamonds, and that she refuses to visit the poorhouse. In fact, I distinctly remember her saying, 'those wretches are bound to turn my skin yellow.' I'm not sure how she believes the poor souls will accomplish that."

Jane's shoulders shook from laughter. "It seems as though we've both had enlightening conversations this evening."

Lord Lendin chuckled. "Indeed, we have."

He moved forward his knight, sending Jane into action.

She plucked her queen from where it had been and moved it so that it was in direct sight of Lord Lendin's king. "Check, my lord."

He studied the board, drumming his fingers on the table as he deliberated. "Your pianoforte playing is exquisite," he remarked matter-of-factly, moving his king out of the path of Jane's queen.

Her face heated. She wasn't used to such open praise or, really, any at all. "Thank you, my lord. I'd quite forgotten how much I love to play the instrument." Jane moved her bishop forward, regarding the other pieces on the board.

He quirked his lips up. "It appears you're already rediscovering the joys of life, Miss Talbot." He picked up his rook and placed it a few spaces forward.

"Yes." She tipped her head. "Though I do hope that you still intend to help me find the other joys I've missed." She moved a pawn as he stilled, tearing his eyes from the board to look at her directly.

"So you agree with my plan, then?"

Jane bit her lip for a moment. Would this plan be her downfall? A man like Lord Lendin would be easy to fall in love with. Her withered heart would all too easily welcome the sunlight that was Lendin's attention, and the fruit it bore would surely rot when no one claimed it.

Jane's heart could not bear to be broken again when she hadn't yet finished picking up its pieces. Ever since the incident with Laurence, she'd learned to temper her hopes with a much-needed dose of reality, but would that provide sufficient protection when faced with someone like Lord Lendin?

It had to.

She didn't answer his question, instead asking one of her own. "Are you certain you wish to spend your time here helping me? I wouldn't want you to regret your proposed idea, should I accept. After all, wouldn't you rather spend your time looking for the jewel?"

"Have no fear in that regard, Miss Talbot." His declaration

seemed earnest enough. "I can look for it and help you at the same time." A grin came to his face as he captured her rook.

Jane swiftly moved her queen back into sight of the king, pinning the piece in place.

"Checkmate." Jane grinned triumphantly and looked from the board to Lord Lendin, who laughed good-naturedly.

"Congratulations, Miss Talbot. You are truly a woman of many talents."

Heat rose to Jane's cheeks. "Thank you, my lord."

Lord Lendin's eyes reflected his curiosity. "So are you amenable to my plan? I assure you, Miss Talbot, I am aware of the...peculiarity...of my suggestion. It is..." He drew his mouth to the side.

"Odd?" Jane supplied. "Strange?"

Lord Lendin seemed to take these adjectives into consideration. Finally, he settled on, "Unusual." He gave her a crooked grin that awakened the butterflies in her stomach. "But I've never believed in being usual, at any rate."

Jane raised an eyebrow. "Might I have the night to think about it?"

Lord Lendin's smile remained. "Certainly. Take as much time as you need to decide."

He wasn't pushing her to be in his company, though his congenial nature made her wish to be. Would every minute near him make her heart flutter in the same way it currently did? If so, she was in trouble.

CHAPTER 4

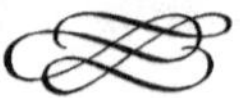

That night, Henry lay in bed, the pale moonlight flooding his chambers from the windows. A warm feeling spread in his chest as he remembered the game of chess he'd played with Miss Talbot. She'd been a skilled player, blocking his every attack whilst making pleasant conversation. And before that, she'd played the pianoforte with such passion. Henry had been in awe, listening to the beautiful music emanating from the instrument—music filled with such emotion. Many musicians simply played what was written without adding any depth or feeling. Miss Talbot was different. She seemed to put her heart and soul into every note.

Henry's mind was filled with unanswered questions. Why hadn't she been enjoying what she'd been doing? What was her family like? Why was she yet unmarried?

Every time he spoke with Miss Talbot, it was as though he was pulling the end of a ball of yarn, unraveling it. Tomorrow...

His eyelids began to close, and he gave in to sleep's gentle pull.

ane stifled a yawn as she entered her room. She'd already been weary from travel, but the rest of the evening had served to tire her even more. Lady Caroline had glared at her for almost the entirety of the night, and Jane's playing of the piano in front of the fellow guests had taken much energy.

Abigail was setting Jane's nightgown on the bed as she walked through the door. "Good evening, miss."

Jane closed the door behind her and started pulling pins from her hair as she walked to her dressing table. "You know you needn't have waited for me, Abigail. I can undress myself, and you have an early morning tomorrow."

Abigail waved her hand. "Nonsense, miss." She followed Jane to the dressing table and swatted her hands away from her hair, continuing Jane's work at the pins. "How was your evening, miss?"

Dinner had been a rather miserable affair, but playing the pianoforte had renewed her interest in that instrument—and, of course, she'd spoken with Lord Lendin, as intriguing a man as any she'd ever met.

Finally, she settled on, "Enjoyable."

Abigail raised an eyebrow in the mirror. "Although?"

"Although...tiring. And confusing."

"Confusing?"

Jane sighed. How to explain? "Lord Lendin proposed—"

"Proposed?" Abigail's hands stilled.

"Not marriage," Jane explained, tamping down her maid's excitement. She told Abigail of her and Lord Lendin's conversation and his subsequent suggestion that he help her find what she enjoyed once more—at least for the next three weeks. After Jane's explanation, both of Abigail's eyebrows were raised.

"What an odd proposal."

Jane tilted her head to the side. "It is—but very kind, don't you think?"

"Yes. Will you take him up on his offer?" The maid set the pins down and picked up a hairbrush from the table.

Jane blinked at her reflection in the mirror. She hadn't yet made up her mind.

Spending so much time with Laurence—Mr. Revil, rather—she'd been made to think he was partial to her. Would the same thing occur if she were to spend the next three weeks in the company of Lord Lendin? What if Lord Lendin was only feigning helping her in order to sabotage her chance at finding the jewel of Parcathia?

"I don't know," she replied as Abigail began to carefully brush out her long hair. After that, she helped Jane undress and put on her gown. Jane quickly washed her face, the cool water relaxing her tumultuous thoughts.

Picking up the basin of water, Abigail spoke a quiet, "G'night, miss. Sleep well." Then she was off to her own bed, closing the polished wooden door softly behind her.

A candle was already lit on the bedside table, so Jane blew out the candelabra near the door, creating shadows. She stepped over to the comfortable bed and crawled beneath the covers, wrapping herself in a cocoon of quilts and sheets.

If she said yes to Lord Lendin's plan, she'd have to be careful—no, not careful...wise. Perhaps both.

Jane would not fall in love if she were to go along with Lord Lendin's plan. She simply wouldn't allow it.

~

*H*enry awoke the next morning, eager to begin the day. He glanced out of his chamber windows at the sprawling grounds. Verdant fields stretched out to meet the forest in the distance beneath skies that were grey but not ominous.

Notham entered with a basin of water, quietly humming a happy tune. "Ah, my lord, you're awake." He clicked his heels together. "I thought you might soon be."

"Good morning, Notham." Amusement colored Henry's voice. "You are correct, as always. At this point in my life, a person might presume that I would be used to your perfect timing, yet I must admit that I continue to be amazed by your constant state of readiness for whatever I might ask."

Notham placed the basin down in front of the mirror before opening the armoire and selecting a few items of Henry's clothing. "I do try my best, my lord. If only I could predict when you might muddy your boots—on that day, I suppose you must call me Nostradamus."

Henry laughed at this quip as his valet pulled two waistcoats from the armoire. "I suppose I shall, old fellow. And I think I'll wear the maroon today."

With the help of Notham, Henry was soon ready. Before he could open the door to his chamber, a folded piece of paper slid underneath. He bent down to pick it up and unfolded it, reading the scrawl written upon it.

You'll find it where the butterflies.

His first clue regarding the jewel's location. Butterflies. Outside, then. Better to look later when the sun was higher in the sky. He pulled the golden watch from his waistcoat pocket and flicked it open, inspecting its face.

Nine o'clock. Perfect. He moved down the grand staircase and strode down the hall, taking a wrong turn before pausing at the morning room's door. Considering it was the day after many guests had traveled, it was to be expected that few were awake at this time, but thankfully, a handful of people were in attendance. Henry stepped in and made his greetings.

The room was filled with light, with many windows lining

the walls. A long table was set in the center with chairs enough for all of the guests, and one wall hosted a side table covered with various silver trays. Though the room was beautiful itself, the side table was what truly held his attention. Beckoned by the delicious smells, he walked over and filled a dish with eggs, toast, kippers, and other delectable foods, the sumptuous repast making his mouth water. He settled at the breakfast table, pouring himself a cup of tea before digging into the glazed ham that filled one section of his plate.

Gerald perched in the corner of the room on a side table, a lump of egg in his clutch. Henry raised an eyebrow.

Two ladies sat at the opposite side of the main table, excitedly chatting and picking at their plates. A Miss Clarke and Miss Wildon, he believed. A few places down on his right sat Mr. Langley, whom Henry had only met a few times previously. The man had always kept to himself, though he was polite when he did speak.

The last guest was one that Henry had just recently been introduced to, a Lord Windham. Henry had not spoken much to the man, but from the short amount of time he had spent with him, Henry had deduced that the man was insufferably arrogant. Fortunately for Henry, the man seemed completely occupied with his newspaper this morning.

As Henry continued to eat his breakfast, Miss Talbot stepped into the room, radiant in her pale-pink day dress, a cream-colored ribbon around her waist. Her hair was tucked into a low knot at the base of her head, two curls left hanging by her forehead to frame her face. He immediately stood from his chair—perhaps a bit quicker than the other men—though he was pleased to see his friend, after all. She smiled shyly and greeted the rest of the guests before focusing on him. She walked toward where he was standing.

"Good morning, my lord."

He returned her smile. "Good morning, Miss Talbot. I must

say that I am pleased to have your company this morning. I feared you might take breakfast in your rooms, given yesterday's wearying travel."

"On the contrary, my lord, I find myself quite refreshed." Miss Talbot's tone was cheery. "Furthermore, I've always been early to rise."

Henry followed her to the sideboard and picked up a plate for her, filling it with a little of each of the food items there as he spoke. "Then you are in fine company, Miss Talbot, for I am an early riser, as well. There is something about the morning air that calls me to wake."

Now, it was her turn to follow him as he walked back to the place he'd been seated.

"I must admit that I am somewhat surprised at that, my lord," she replied with some amusement, "for I once heard of a viscount that never rose before the noon hour."

Henry placed her plate in front of the seat next to his and pulled out her chair for her, sliding it toward the table as she sat.

The footman stationed at the side of the room gave a rather disapproving look at Henry, but Henry could only give a wide stare and shrug at the man while Miss Talbot spread a napkin over her lap. He seated himself beside her and picked up his fork once more, spearing a piece of ham with it.

Miss Talbot glanced at him playfully as she spread strawberry preserves on a slice of toast. "I believe you overestimated my appetite, my lord."

Henry grimaced at the sight of her plate, only now realizing the amount of food he'd placed on it. "It appears I have." A mountain of eggs was on the verge of collapse, about to collide with the tower of kippers he'd stacked next to it. The thick slice of plum cake he'd set across from these was threatened from the downfall.

Henry took a sip from his teacup and gently set it back on

its saucer, the beige liquid inside trembling for a moment before settling to display its previous calm surface.

"In addition to me being an early riser, I also think I know one thing which you might enjoy." His tone was confident.

She chewed thoughtfully and swallowed her bite of toast, her head tipped slightly to the side. "Oh? And what might that be, my lord? I still haven't agreed to your plan, you remember."

Henry grinned and skewered another piece of ham with his fork. "Joy can also be found in suspense, Miss Talbot."

She laughed and took a sip of her own tea, drawing Henry's attention to her mouth for a moment. He quickly focused on his plate instead.

"Fair enough, my lord. I suppose I'll just have to trust you. I've nothing planned to entertain myself today, so a surprise sounds like just the thing. I've thought about it, and your plan intrigues me."

Henry raised an eyebrow, his heart beating fast with sudden hope. "Does this mean you agree to it?"

~

Jane's mind was in conflict, half of her adamant that this plan could only lead to further heartbreak and upset while the other half strove to convince her that Lord Lendin's plan was harmless.

She had to make a decision. She was no more sure after receiving her first clue this morning—something about butter-flies—but now the time had come that she had to answer him.

Lord Lendin was surely different from Laurence. Laurence had spent time with her because she'd been a distraction, but Lord Lendin seemed to really *want* to help her. He *looked forward* to the challenge of helping her rediscover those things that made her happy and—from what Jane had seen of him— he was truly a kind person. Besides, Lord Lendin was higher in rank than Laurence. Surely, that was enough information to steel her heart from him, as there was even less of a chance that he'd harbor any affection for her. Could she trust herself to remain unaffected in his company?

In addition, rediscovering the things she enjoyed would distract her from thoughts of Laurence. And house parties were meant to be fun—so would it be so terrible to accept?

$$\approx$$

*M*iss Talbot tilted her head to the side, and Henry's heart seemed to still. Why did he feel as though so much depended on her response?

After a few seconds, she nodded. "Yes."

Henry beamed at her, his pulse increasing. "Your trust is in safekeeping, Miss Talbot. Will you meet me in the library in three hours' time? Your aunt can play the role of chaperone, if she wishes—and be sure to bring your bonnet."

He could hardly wait to begin.

CHAPTER 5

Jane left the breakfast room, a spring in her step. She'd made her decision, and now the excitement had begun to set in. As she turned right down the hall, someone called her name—followed by the sound of quick footsteps on the carpet behind her. She looked over her shoulder. Had Lord Lendin forgotten to tell her something about their meeting?

"Miss Talbot!" Lord Windham called, his dark hair falling over his forehead as he approached her. He wore an expensive blue coat and cream-colored waistcoat, a white cravat tied around his throat in a complex knot. Why had he followed her from the breakfast room?

She turned to face him and bit the inside of her cheek. She'd only met the man the previous day. Indeed, she hadn't believed he'd recall her name should they be in company again. "My lord?"

The corner of his mouth raised. "I couldn't help but hear of your agreement to Lord Lendin's plan in the breakfast room. I beg you to put my curiosity to rest, Miss Talbot. What plan is it that you agreed to? Something regarding the jewel, perhaps?"

His brown eyes bore into hers, but unlike the warm-toned brown that comprised Lord Lendin's, Lord Windham's were dark. Cold. They reminded Jane of the dirt atop a freshly covered casket. She inwardly shivered.

I'm being ridiculous—the color of a person's eyes does not reflect their character.

"If you must know, Lord Lendin offered to help me rediscover the things I once found enjoyable—as well as discover the things I never knew were. That is the extent of the plan. Our conversation had nothing to do with the competition." Jane crossed her arms.

To her surprise, Lord Windham's smile widened. "That is truly a relief, Miss Talbot. I'd feared Lord Lendin had convinced you to elope, or something similar."

"Elope?" Jane swallowed hard at the mere idea. "Certainly not, my lord. Why would he do that?"

"You must have an idea, Miss Talbot, surely? If you were to find the jewel and then elope with Lord Lendin, all of your possessions would become his—including said jewel."

Jane's breath stilled in her throat. Was that why Lord Lendin wished to help her? To get close to her so he might double his chances of taking the jewel?

"I do wonder, Miss Talbot—are you amenable to the idea of courtship?" Lord Windham pointed his chin up, tugging at his lapel.

No one had ever asked her that question, and her mind was already spinning from Lord Windham's words about elopement. Jane had no idea where this conversation was headed, but it had already taken an unexpected turn. "I...am...my lord."

"Very good." He took a step toward her, not so close as to make her uncomfortable but close enough to be heard while speaking quietly. "Perhaps, then, you'd like to walk in the gardens with me?"

Jane's shoulders tensed as her eyebrows moved closer

together. Was this relevant to his question of marriage? "Erm—I—Now?"

"But of course. There's no time like the present, as they say." Lord Windham continued to stare at her, awaiting a response. "Please, say yes, Miss Talbot. I'm sure it will be a lovely morning —and you're quite the rival for the day itself."

Those words sounded familiar, but Jane couldn't remember where she'd heard them. How should she react? She'd only been at Lord Sperrin's house party for a day, and already, she had received the attention of two lords—she, who'd spent many a ball without a single partner. Could it be the work of her aunt? Surely not—as it was still early for her machinations to come to fruition. Jane attempted to go over what she knew of the man in her head, and this was when she realized that she scarcely knew Lord Windham at all.

Her parents' words whispered in her mind. *Do try to meet a husband, dear. The more time that passes you by, the more the likelihood of you marrying decreases.* Her parents had attempted to be encouraging, but they weren't very skilled at it. Nevertheless, their words had stuck with her and were that which drove her to answer, "I'd love to, my lord."

~

*L*ord Windham allowed Jane a moment to get Abigail, and then they were out the back door and into the garden and the summer sun's rays. He offered her his arm, and she took it with hesitance.

"What lovely weather." Jane admired the garden with its exotic blooms, tempered only by the native flowers scattered here and there. Some emitted a bitter sort of smell, but others enticed her to wander closer.

"Indeed." Lord Windham glanced at her as they began

down a stone path through the middle of the garden. He cleared his throat. "I hear you're from Somerset, Miss Talbot."

She hummed in pleasant surprise. "I am. Have you ever visited Somerset? It's quite beautiful. My family lives in the north of Somerset, near the oce—"

"I have. Yes, beautiful. I know of a breeder there who produces fine horseflesh."

Jane raised her eyes heavenward. "I can only thi—"

"Lowston's the name. I bought a gelding from the man a matter of months ago. A fine beast."

Jane clenched her jaw at his second interruption. "What's the gelding's name, my lord?"

"Nero." He gave a smirk. "I've always admired that man's leadership during the Roman empire."

Perhaps she'd made a mistake agreeing to walk with Lord Windham. "Where are you from, my lord?"

"Hampshire." He picked a piece of lint from his arm, a proud lilt to his voice. "The most pleasant county in all of England. I have an estate there called Clarin Manor. My lands are expansive, and I house my hounds in a kennel next to the manor. I love to hunt, you see—I shot two-and-thirty pheasants this year, and the season ended in February!"

How sad to hear about two-and-thirty of those graceful creatures being killed, but they'd surely been made good use of. "Your tenants must be very pleased."

Lord Windham scoffed. "My tenants? Heavens, no! Whatever pheasants my cook cannot roast go to the hounds."

Jane's fists clenched at her sides. She shouldn't run to conclusions. Perhaps his tenants were not in need of the extra meat, anyway. At least the hounds were getting it, if no one else.

"Have you any brothers that hunt, Miss Talbot? Your father, perhaps?" He raised a questioning eyebrow.

"I have no siblings, my lord, and my father does not hunt."

Her father had always disdained the sport, considering it brutish.

"Pity." Lord Windham *tsk*ed. "Pray, do you know anything about these butterflies?" He swatted at one as it crossed his path. He'd apparently received the same clue that she had, that morning.

"I do not know more about them than any other creature."

The walk and subsequent conversation lasted for fifteen more excruciating minutes that finally ended when Lord Windham escorted Jane back inside. The rear of the house was darker than the front—there were less windows there—but the corridor that led inside from the garden was just as pretty as the foyer.

Eager to flee from Lord Windham, she stepped through the wooden doors and onto the forest-green carpet, her footfalls muffled as she took a few steps past a statue of a deer-like animal with spiraling horns. Before she could escape, he grabbed her hand and brought it to his lips. He planted a kiss on the back of it and raised an eyebrow at her.

"Perhaps I might escort you in to dinner this evening?" Not waiting for a response, he gave a wink and turned from her, striding down the hall toward the east wing of the house.

"Impossible man." Jane huffed and attempted to unclench her hands as she headed in the opposite direction.

"Was it that bad?"

She startled as a warm voice sounded from behind. She spun to face a tiger posed to strike, fangs bared...and Lord Lendin standing beside it. The tapestry had been woven by a master's hand, for the tiger looked as vivid as any drawing she'd seen. Jane raised a hand to her rapidly beating heart and exhaled a breath.

"My apologies." Lord Lendin scratched the back of his neck, a sheepish expression on his face. "I happened to be in the hall when you and Lord Windham entered."

At the mention of the man, Jane's irritation rekindled. Lord Lendin must have taken notice, for he raised an eyebrow.

"I take it your walk was not as enjoyable as you'd hoped." He leaned against the wall behind him.

She crossed her arms over her chest and sighed. "It was not. He talked unceasingly of…of…himself!" At this, she threw her hands out to her sides. "Every time I spoke, he interrupted, directing the conversation toward his own interests. It was exhausting, truly." She joined him at the wall, resting her back against it in the space next to him—the space not occupied by the tapestry, that was.

"I feared that might be the case when I first met the man— quite the saucebox." Lord Lendin wrinkled his nose. "I do hope your walk hasn't soured the desire to meet me later."

"Not at all, my lord." She straightened. Their meeting was something she was looking forward to. More than she probably should be.

"Very good." He rolled his shoulders, stepping from the wall. "I've some important matters I must attend to at the moment, but I assure you that I won't be late."

Neither would she. Indeed, her stroll with Lord Windham had made her anticipate her time with Lord Lendin even more —a most dangerous turn of events.

～

A few hours later, Jane descended the main stairway with her aunt, who was only too eager to play chaperone. "Aunt, you needn't be so excited." A tinge of exasperation colored her voice. "Lord Lendin and myself are only friends, and he is simply trying to help me enjoy my time here."

Aunt Agnes shot Jane an arch look. "You may believe so, yet I imagine that you aren't looking enough into his actions. You're a pretty thing, you know, with a good head on your shoulders. It isn't difficult to see why Lord Lendin might wish to spend more time with you."

Jane groaned inwardly, swinging her bonnet by its ribbons as they walked down the hall. Her aunt didn't understand that Lord Lendin was different from other gentlemen of nobility. He was only being nice—unless he truly was using her as Lord Windham had suggested.

They arrived at the oaken doors to the library, and Jane grasped one of the shining brass knobs and turned it clockwise. As she opened the door, she drew in a quick breath at the grandeur of the room before her. Shelves upon shelves of books lined the papered walls, and the welcoming smell of them immediately greeted her nose. A magnificent stone fireplace was set into the far wall, its hearth unlit, given the heat the mid-July sun had been providing. Centrally placed cushioned chairs and settees awaited those who wished to bide their time in this haven.

Lord Lendin sat in one of the moss-colored chairs, his golden waves of hair mussed and a heavy tome in his hands. Paper rustled slightly as he turned a page. She was only a few meters away when he finally noticed her approach, her aunt not far behind. His mouth quirked up, and he snapped the book shut as he stood, bowing. "Miss Talbot, Mrs. Westby, I thank you for agreeing to meet me."

"I am curious as to what you have planned." Jane spread her arms out.

Lord Lendin flashed a grin. "Your curiosity will soon be put to rest. Come with me." He picked up something from behind the chair—a basket.

Jane raised an eyebrow and took the arm he offered, the fabric of his tailcoat soft beneath her fingertips. Aunt Agnes trailed them, offering them as much privacy as she could whilst still fulfilling her chaperone duties.

Lord Lendin led them to the foyer. There, he paused to

allow Jane time to put on her bonnet before he nodded to the butler and they exited the front of the house. She breathed in the fresh air, happy to be outside where she could feel some of the sun's warmth on her skin and hear the clear chatter of birds.

As a child, she'd always preferred the out of doors, often causing distress to her nurse and parents who chased after her. A small smile came unbidden to her as she thought of the days when the hem of her skirt would get muddied and she'd try to tell time by the movement of the sun.

Lord Lendin peeked over at her. "What thoughts have brought your smile to light, Miss Talbot? If you don't mind me asking, that is."

She shook her head. "Not at all, my lord. I was thinking of the enjoyments I used to have as a child. You may find it hard to believe, but I was rather free-spirited then."

He looked reflective for a moment. "Actually, I don't find that hard to believe at all. While we've only known each other for a short amount of time, there have been moments when I've seen that carefree spirit within you."

They continued to walk the grounds as she pondered this, moving away from the manor with footsteps padded by the lush grass beneath their feet. At length, they came to a worn dirt path, half hidden by the surrounding foliage. Lord Lendin made sure to keep her steady on the uneven ground as they tread through the dense woodlands—an action that made her heart lift in her chest ever so slightly. Good thing they had worn their walking boots. Oddly, her aunt seemed to have no problem with the rough ground, stepping over roots and around stones while humming to herself.

Perhaps there was more truth to the name *tortoise-foot* than others had known.

Lord Lendin's strong arm allowed Jane to focus on the beautiful scenery. Trees with aged bark towered proudly on all sides, their leaves vibrant green. Soft moss coated parts of the ground near their roots, and lichens dotted their trunks, worn as though they were patches earned over time.

Signs and sounds of life were everywhere. Here, the sweet song of a thrush, there, the rustle of bushes as squirrels playfully chased one another. Up ahead, a rabbit scurried across the path, stopping for a moment to wiggle its nose before continuing on to run whatever errand it had to accomplish.

"It's so beautiful here."

Lord Lendin glanced at her, an eager grin on his face. "You haven't even seen the best part yet, Miss Talbot."

He embodied good cheer. Excitement fluttered in her stomach. She had no idea where they were going, yet she somehow knew she would love it.

They walked for another minute before an opening appeared ahead. Large clumps of greenery ruled the area, spread across the clearing. The late-morning sun shone down, illuminating the red berries that decorated their runners. A grin came to Jane's face as she took in the glorious sight.

Strawberries.

CHAPTER 6

As Miss Talbot turned her lovely gaze to him, Henry quite forgot how to breathe. Her lips were lifted in an expression of glee. Her eyes shone with excitement, a light brown that reminded him of honey. Her cheeks were aglow with an eager flush. The light dusting of freckles on them made them all the more charming. Dark curls peeked from beneath her bonnet. Time seemed to slow as he took in her bewitching visage.

"Are you two picking strawberries today? How lovely!" Mrs. Westby clapped from only a short distance behind them, breaking him from the daze he'd been in.

He looked over his shoulder at the woman. "We are. Last night, I asked Lord Sperrin if there happened to be any strawberries around, and he was happy to inform me of this patch. He also said we can enjoy as many as we want as long as we bring back this basket full so his cook might make a batch of tarts. Mr. Beaton will be disappointed at dinner, I'm sure."

Henry walked with Miss Talbot toward the bushes while Mrs. Westby settled herself in the grass beneath the shade of a nearby birch tree. Miss Talbot dropped her hand from Henry's arm and moved a few feet ahead, inspecting the plants. It was strange, but he keenly felt the absence of it. He placed the basket on the grass and joined her.

She turned to grin at him. "My, but these look absolutely delicious."

Henry removed his gloves, for Notham would certainly have a few remarks if he stained them. Miss Talbot did the same and dropped hers near the basket before bending and plucking a ripened berry from its stem. Her eyes closed as she took a bite of it. A look of pure contentment crossed her face.

"I had worried, Miss Talbot, that you might find picking strawberries to be dull...but I see now that I was mistaken." He scratched the back of his neck, his tone full of amusement.

"Not at all, my lord—and they are just as delicious as they look! I suggest you try one." She laughed and popped the remaining part of the strawberry into her mouth.

Henry dropped to his knees beside her. He picked one himself, biting into the red fruit and tasting the sweet and somewhat tart flavor that he so loved. "As a child, I'd sneak away from my tutor and hide near a strawberry patch on the border of my estate."

Miss Talbot chuckled. "Your clothing must have been dreadfully stained."

"It was. I'd spend what little time I had there eating the berries. Alas, it was never long before I was found. That was known to be my hiding place of choice."

"We've never had strawberries on our grounds."

They both reached for the same berry, their fingers connecting in a gentle collision. A jolt of energy shot through Henry's hand as her soft fingers brushed his knuckles, the touch like the flutter of a butterfly's wings. Miss Talbot's breath caught in the space somewhere just behind his left ear. He was ever aware of her nearness.

She pulled her hand away in haste, reaching for the berry

beside it instead. She plucked it from the stem and gave Henry an uncertain smile as she dropped it into the basket, her cheeks becoming the color of the ripe berries before them. Her face remained so close to his own, her exhale fanned his chin.

Henry spent the next hour picking berries alongside Miss Talbot, placing the majority of them into the basket and every once in a while eating a particularly ripe one. Soon, they'd filled the large basket Lord Sperrin had given Henry, and their fingers were stained a bright red.

The sun had broken through the grey skies, and the day was becoming warmer. The bush they had last been picking from happened to be shaded by a large alder tree. Henry removed his coat and sat down. He leaned against the cool bark of the trunk.

Miss Talbot placed one last berry in the basket before wiping her hands on the grass and joining him beneath the tree, arranging her skirts around her as she sat. Just across the clearing, Mrs. Westby also leaned against the trunk of a tree. Her bonnet shaded her face as she read the pages of a small novel.

A contented sigh escaped Miss Talbot. "Thank you, my lord. That was very enjoyable, indeed."

He angled toward her. "I'm very glad to hear it, Miss Talbot."

She chuckled softly, a melodic ring to the sound. "As I previously mentioned, I was quite the carefree young girl when I was a child. I've always loved to be in nature and would take whatever opportunity I could to run away into the lands surrounding our estate. I spent much of my time walking along fallen tree trunks, attempting to catch frogs by the nearby creek, and even climbing a few trees." She rested her head back against the smooth bark of the alder.

"Climbing trees and catching frogs?" Henry laughed. "Our childhoods were more similar than one might imagine."

Miss Talbot's mouth twisted, revealing an endearing dimple Henry hadn't noticed previously. "Yes, and though I've never had any siblings, I did rather well on my own." She clasped her hands in her lap, raising a brow. "Do you have any siblings, my lord?"

A smile came unbidden to his face as he thought of his family. "I have a younger brother of two-and-twenty—George —and a younger sister of twenty, Phoebe. George has always been mischievous, frequently causing my parents grief, and Phoebe...quite the opposite. I remember a time when my brother was but nine years old. He'd broken our mother's favorite vase. Phoebe was only seven, but she spared no time in scolding him for it. George was never so careless as to repeat his mistake again."

"And have their temperaments remained as such?"

Henry chuckled. "Yes," he replied, his tone reflecting his affection for them. "George gets into scrapes on a weekly basis and causes much grief for my mother. Just the other day, in fact, he brought a wild goose into the foyer, causing quite the commotion."

Miss Talbot dimpled again, and she covered her mouth to stifle a laugh as he continued.

"Phoebe, on the other hand, causes my mother much grief in a different way. She abhors going to balls and is incredibly stubborn, often secreting herself away with a few books until one of the servants manages to find her."

Miss Talbot met his gaze, smiling brightly. "It sounds as though there's never a dull moment with siblings."

They sat for a few moments in companionable silence, enjoying the beauty of the day and the pleasant company. How odd, to feel so comfortable in Miss Talbot's presence. Henry still didn't know her very well, and yet he was able to relax in her company as though they'd known each other for a long while.

On the way back to the manor, Henry held the basket of strawberries in one hand, his other arm claimed by Miss Talbot. Her aunt followed behind them once again, content to let them lead the way back. Henry watched the ground in front of them for any uneven patches or rebel stones. Their gloves were now back on, hiding the berry-stained fingers within.

"Tell me, Miss Talbot, who taught you to play chess?" Henry asked.

She turned her head slightly to look at him, her berry-tinted mouth pulling up at his question. "My father." She moved her gaze forward once more. "He's always been fond of the game, and so was only too eager to teach me. We used to play in the evenings, my mother reading aloud by the fire." A wistful look crossed her face. "That was before my first season. After that, all of my evenings were occupied by balls and dinner parties, and there was no longer time for it." Miss Talbot's bonnet partially concealed her expression, but her tone had sobered.

He hesitated for a moment before deciding to speak. Perhaps she'd confide in him. "Is that why you aren't quite sure what activities you find agreeable?"

She looked at him once more. "Yes." She sighed. "With the start of my first season came the end of all else. Gone were the quiet evenings at home and small family outings. The time which I had once spent reading in the library was then occupied by fittings at the modiste's or rides through Hyde Park during the fashionable hour. At first, I attempted to resist the change, weaving in a few minutes here and there for myself. Soon after, I realized that it was futile to do so and resigned myself to days that seemed without end and nights that were all too short. Since then, things have remained the same for five long seasons. I have yet to secure myself a husband—and so the cycle continues."

Henry ached to help her in whatever way he could. The

way he saw it, Miss Talbot was not living—only existing, and that was unacceptable. Here was this lively woman, once carefree and happy, now forced to act on others' whims. She was a beautiful marionette, pulled from one event to another without cease, and Henry wished to help her cut her strings.

"Surely, you must've attracted suitors, at least?" He inclined his head.

She only shook hers. "None of the serious nature, unfortunately. Through my seasons, I've come to realize that I'm utterly invisible. Gentlemen seldom ask me to dance, and matrons' glances pass over me as though I am naught more than an open field."

To say that Henry was surprised would be an understatement. Though she'd had multiple seasons, he'd assumed that she must have garnered a great deal of attention, given her pleasant countenance and elegant beauty. Her gentle voice already made Henry loath to be out of her company. Her amber gaze was warm and inviting, and she had a kind, if somewhat shy, smile that had drawn him in when he'd met her and which continued to do so every time she revealed it. She wore no mask of pretense. She was all...truth.

"There was...someone..." She swallowed. "I'd thought him interested, but I was mistaken."

"Oh?" He raised an eyebrow, a discomfort in his stomach at her words. He couldn't make sense of the sensation.

"Indeed. His name is Mr. Laurence Revil. Have you met him?"

The name sounded only vaguely familiar to Henry. "I cannot say I have. What happened—er—if you don't mind telling me, that is..."

She bit her lip. "Mr. Revil...I met him in my latest season. We'd spent much time in each other's company, but...a few months ago, he—he—well, I, rather, well..."

Henry hurried to ease her anxiety. "If it discomforts you, you needn't tell me, Miss Talbot. I quite understand."

"Oh, it's no trouble, really. A few months ago, we met for a picnic on my family's grounds. I...made the mistake of revealing my affection for him. I believed it to be reciprocated, but he assured me—quite adamantly—that it was not. We spent so much time in each other's company, you see...I believe my heart was eager to stifle my head." She gave a deprecating half smile and looked at the path ahead.

"I have long suspected that those comprising the *Ton* are blind, and this confirms it."

Miss Talbot raised one eyebrow ever so slightly. "Forgive me, but I miss your meaning, my lord."

Henry released a soft, scoffing breath. "If I may be so candid, Miss Talbot, I do not believe anyone could find you invisible, and this Mr. Revil you speak of—he seems a most miserable character. Certainly befogged, anyway, considering he so missed what was right in front of him. You are not plain in the least...and are unequivocally genuine. Therefore, I am forced to come to the conclusion that the *Ton* is blind."

A light pink blush appeared in Miss Talbot's cheeks. "Y-You are much too kind, my lord." She ducked her chin.

"I only speak the truth, Miss Talbot," he responded earnestly, flashing her a grin to lighten the conversation before changing the subject. Despite this, he couldn't make heads nor tails of Mr. Revil's actions. To snub such a woman as Miss Talbot, who had been so open in her admission of affection, seemed unfathomable.

The rest of the walk back to the manor passed all too quickly, and they soon arrived at the front doors of the estate. Wheaton welcomed them back as they entered the foyer. The man gladly took the basket of strawberries from Henry, promising with a gleam of excitement in his eye to deliver them to the cook belowstairs.

Miss Talbot divested herself of her bonnet, letting the garment hang by her side from its ribbons. She glanced at her aunt—who'd caught up with them by now—before bobbing a curtsy to Henry. "I suppose I should attempt to rid my fingers of their red hue, my lord. Thank you, truly, for planning the lovely outing. It was enjoyable, indeed." She held him in place with her grateful gaze.

He swallowed, his throat dry as he bowed. "It was my pleasure, Miss Talbot."

She nodded her head lightly before turning and following her aunt up the main staircase, looking over her shoulder for a moment before continuing on.

When they'd disappeared from his vision, Henry exhaled, alone in the foyer. No doubt, the foolish Mr. Revil now regretted spurning Miss Talbot. If Henry didn't miss his mark, she would make a match by the end of the house party. Was he ready to throw his name into the hat?

CHAPTER 7

That evening, after dinner concluded, Jane sat in the drawing room with the other women, attempting to read a book she'd picked from one of the shelves. It appeared that Lord and Lady Sperrin were avid readers, and Jane was glad for it. She nestled farther into the cushioned chair she had settled herself in and turned a page, her mind occasionally drifting from the written words before her. She paused her reading, her lips pulling up as she thought on this evening's repast.

Tonight, she'd been seated between Lord Lendin and Mr. Langley, and the former had been a delightful dinner companion. She'd feared that Lord Windham would escort her in to dinner, but that man had been waylaid by Miss Parblot on his way into the drawing room. Jane had only met the young woman on the previous day, but it was clear to her that Miss Parblot was determined to marry—and well.

Jane inwardly thanked her for her assistance, for she'd enjoyed dining with Lord Lendin. They'd discussed a variety of things, from favorite colors to their respective estates. The topic of onions had not been brought up once, and Jane had felt comfortable throughout their conversation. On her opposite side, Mr. Langley had remained mostly silent, only asking a few questions and making polite remarks, which Jane had been content with. It appeared she'd mistaken his quietude the previous evening for a rude demeanor when, in truth, the man was only given to shyness.

Jane flicked her gaze back to the book she was reading, but only a few moments passed before she was distracted again. Bright pink fabric clouded her peripheral vision. Lady Caroline had seated herself in the chair nearest Jane and was adjusting her skirts around her. Once she was satisfied with how they looked, she turned her head toward Jane, a calculating smirk on her porcelain face.

"Dear Miss Talbot, how lovely your gloves are." The woman almost purred like a cat.

Jane glanced down to her white kid gloves. An uneasy feeling stirred in the depths of her stomach at this odd start to a conversation as she brought her gaze back up to Lady Caroline. "Thank you."

The woman leaned closer to Jane as though to impart a secret. "You know, Miss Talbot, I do not believe I remember seeing you this season."

Jane eyed her warily. "Perhaps we were at different events. I was in London for the season, I assure you."

The lady's jaw jutted and she tittered. "Oh, but of course you were! You *have* been for the past—how many...six seasons?"

Jane's cheeks burned. "Five."

"Oh, my! But how could I forget? Do forgive me." Lady Caroline covered her mouth with a hand. "After a woman has two seasons, I can never keep track." She giggled. The sound grated on Jane's ears. "I wonder why you've not made a match... but then brown hair is not currently in style, is it?" She gestured to Jane's curls with a raise of her eyebrows.

Her shoulders stiffened. Irritation welled up inside Jane, and she struggled to keep her expression impassive. "I suppose not."

Unfortunately, Lady Caroline wasn't done. "And those freckles." She *tsk*ed. "What a shame." The woman poured herself a cup of tea from the short table between them and took a dainty sip, running her gaze over Jane. "You might make a match yet, despite your nose. Perhaps Mr. Dobson? I believe his poor wife's just passed."

Jane's temper flared. Mr. Dobson was the five-and-seventy-year-old vicar whom the Sperrins had invited to dinner. And nothing was wrong with her nose!

She took a calming breath, praying to God for peace. Her tongue tended to get the better of her. "Mr. Dobson seems quite nice. You surprise me, however, Lady Caroline, as I thought I heard someone speak of an impending engagement between the two of you." Jane gave an innocent look as the other lady sputtered.

"I would n—certain—nev—" The teacup Lady Caroline was holding rattled in its saucer. Her face reddened with outrage. After a moment, the woman composed herself, an eerily calm look about her. She directed her gaze to Jane's dress, a thoughtful expression on her face. "Your dress has a beautiful color, Miss Talbot. I've always loved that shade of brown."

Jane flicked her gaze to her gown. Unease crept up her spine. "I'm afraid you're mistaken, Lady Caroline, for this dress is a light green."

A malicious glint came to the woman's stare as she moved even farther forward. "Is it?" In the span of a blink, Lady Caroline's teacup turned on its side, the beige liquid that had been within it flying toward Jane. Jane had little time to react, only watching as the tea splashed over her skirt, droplets scattering and increasing the area of staining.

Lady Caroline raised a hand to her mouth, covering a smug

smirk as those near them turned their way. "Oh, my dear Miss Talbot! I'm so sorry!" Her exclamation drew the other women's attention, followed by gasps and murmurs.

Jane clamped her jaw shut and stood, then quickly excused herself. She fled in a storm of disappointment and anger and took the stairs to the guest wing two at a time, Aunt Agnes not far behind. Jane was eager to get the dress off, as any dallying would result in permanent stains. She arrived at her room, throwing open the door and scaring Abigail.

"I'm sorry, Abigail, but, well..." Jane gestured to her gown.

Abigail immediately helped Jane change out of it. "Don't worry, miss. I'll have it right in no time." She scurried off, presumably belowstairs to the laundering room.

Aunt Agnes helped Jane out of her other garments and, with a knowing look, held up her nightgown. Jane nodded. With the help of her aunt, she dressed for bed. She perched on the edge of it, her bare feet on the carpeted floor.

Aunt Agnes sat next to her, raising an inquiring brow. "What happened, my dear? It doesn't seem likely that Lady Caroline would have spilled the entire contents of her teacup, nor does it seem likely that the entirety of those contents would end up on your gown."

Jane grimaced. "She sought me out under the guise of making polite conversation. Believe me, Aunt, it wasn't nearly as polite as you might imagine. She didn't quite like my response to one of her remarks and used her tea to show it. I seem to be some sort of threat to her, but I have no idea why."

Aunt Agnes patted her hand with affection. "She seems to have set her cap at Lord Lendin. Perhaps she wishes to defeat the competition."

Jane's eyebrows raised as she flicked her gaze to her aunt. "Competition? Me? If anything, I'm more of a spectator." Jane scoffed and met her reflection in the mirror across the room.

Aunt Agnes pierced Jane with a look. "If anything, my dear,

you're the main attraction. We've only been here for a few days, and yet most of your time has been spent in the company of Lord Lendin."

Heat rose to her cheeks as she protested. "He's only helping me, Aunt. And while he is different from other members of the Ton, I don't see why he should be so interested in me. After all, there are many beautiful women here to catch his eye. Miss Apprett, Miss Parblot, Miss—"

Her aunt hummed in disagreement but stood from the bed, shooting Jane a parting glance. "Get some rest, my dear. Who knows what mischief tomorrow will bring. Besides, you'll need your sleep if you're to interpret the next clue and seek the jewel."

That was true. With all Jane had done today, she hadn't even put a thought toward the clue she'd received this morning. If she was to be successful in the hunt, she really ought to start—well—hunting. From now on, she would do so every day she could. That was, if Lord Lendin didn't decide to take up the rest of her time at this house party. Though, would that be so bad?

~

*H*enry entered the drawing room with the other men the evening after strawberry picking, his eyes immediately seeking Miss Talbot—only, she wasn't present. He frowned before he noticed her aunt sitting on the settee. Henry strode over to her and bowed.

"Good evening, Mrs. Westby. Might I inquire as to the whereabouts of your niece?" Henry could have sworn that he saw the woman smile but, with a blink, it was gone, leaving him to assume he had imagined it.

"Unfortunately, Jane decided to retire for the evening after a mishap with Lady Caroline."

This confused Henry even more, a hint of concern sprouting within him.

"A mishap? Is Miss Talbot well?" He attempted to keep the anxiety from his voice as his chest tightened.

Before Mrs. Westby could respond, Lady Caroline was there at his side, batting her lashes.

"Are you speaking of Miss Talbot? I'm afraid I spilled my tea earlier, and it stained her gown. I can be ever so clumsy!" She tittered, keeping her gaze on Henry. "Mrs. Westby, do say that Miss Talbot is much recovered from the incident, as it would greatly ease my troubled mind."

Mrs. Westby gave the socialite a reproachful look which Lady Caroline missed while she inspected him. "She is well, I assure you. She has experience with uncoordinated persons."

A flash of anger crossed Lady Caroline's expression before she rebuilt her facade, smiling once more. "Delightful." There was an edge to the word.

Henry redirected his attention to Mrs. Westby. "I'm glad to hear the mishap was no worse than a few stains, though her presence is missed. Please give her my regards if you happen to see her."

Mrs. Westby returned his smile, a gleam in her eye. "Thank you, my lord. I will be sure to do so."

Henry bowed again, this time to both women, before stepping away to seat himself in a maroon-cushioned chair by one of the windows. The sun had disappeared by now, with the moon taking its place, illuminating the estate in a silver veil. The moonlight peeked through trees, between blades of grass and behind rocks, searching. Searching for something, but what?

Unlike the moon, Henry knew what he was searching for.

He was at an age now where he should be looking—was looking—and though it was dreadfully romantic of him, Henry wanted a love match. They did occur, however seldom. He had seen the love his parents had shared, and he yearned for that same thing.

He'd spent countless events dancing every set and joking with his partners, but he'd never felt that spark of a connection. Many times, his partners weren't interested in anything beyond his title or the weight of his coin purse, only attempting to convince him of an affection that wasn't truly there.

Henry caught a movement reflected in the candlelit window. He turned to face whatever had caught his eye, immediately regretting that decision.

"Lady Caroline." He massaged the back of his neck. "I thought you were still speaking with Mrs. Westby."

An unnatural-sounding laugh escaped her mouth, her blond ringlets bouncing as she lightly shook her head. "Oh, I'd much rather speak with someone whom I know better." A flirtatious tone tinted her words.

Henry coughed, hiding a chuckle at her absurd statement. He'd only encountered Lady Caroline twice before, and while he knew a bit about her, she'd never inquired about *him* whatsoever. He doubted very much that she knew him at all. Lady Caroline didn't wait for him to respond, instead seating herself in the chair opposite Henry's and signifying the start of what would be a very long evening, indeed.

CHAPTER 8

Jane tied the ribbons of her bonnet, adjusting the straw garment in the looking-glass of her room. It had been a few days since the tea incident, and no more mischief had occurred since. Lady Caroline hadn't sought her out—nor even spoken a word to Jane—for which Jane was grateful. She sincerely hoped that would be the end of it.

The guests of the house party had visited the local parish on Sunday, and Jane had enjoyed speaking with the local townspeople. After witnessing an elderly couple's affectionate glances and subtle gestures, Jane's heart yearned all the more for a love of her own. She'd pushed it like a flower bulb into the ground, covering it up with earth and tamping it down with her foot. She had to be more careful with what hands she placed her heart into.

The group had visited the village on Monday. Lord Lendin had accompanied Jane and her aunt to a small bookshop, located right next to a bakery. The smell of books and freshly baked biscuits had mingled in the air, and Jane had enjoyed searching for titles she'd not yet read. Lord Lendin had bought a book on philosophy, and Jane had purchased a few novels before they'd popped into the bakery for some almond cakes.

Jane's mouth watered when she remembered how they'd tasted. They'd been sweet, yet not too sweet, and had a delightfully crumbly texture. Between the books, cakes, and company, Jane had wondered if she'd somehow found herself in heaven.

Each day brought with it another clue—another piece of a poem that directed the guests toward the jewel of Parcathia's location. So far, the directions read:

> *You'll find it where the butterflies*
>> *And stones speak with the stones.*
>> *Where tears are shed as time goes by,*

Today's clue had read, *Lament of broken bones.* Could that mean the jewel was buried in a cemetery? Perhaps near some ruins where stones had fallen and a battle had taken place?

"Ready, miss?" Abigail raised an eyebrow.

"I am." Jane gave a nod and smoothed out her lilac day dress, her mind still full of ideas of where the jewel might be.

With one last glance in the looking-glass, she strode out of the room, her maid following not far behind. Lord Lendin had invited her on another outing, and because her aunt claimed a headache, Abigail would have to suffice as a chaperone. Excitement bubbled up within her, taking precedence over thoughts in the competition.

Lord Lendin hadn't ceased to surprise her, in more ways than one. When she'd first met him, she'd seen a carefree and friendly man, yet she now knew there was so much more to him. He was a puzzle as complicated as the scavenger hunt, and Jane looked forward to solving the mystery.

She descended the grand staircase into the foyer, grasping her skirts with one hand. The soft muslin of her day dress was light in her hand, and her sturdy black kid boots peeked out from beneath with each step.

Lord Lendin stood near the door, inspecting a painting of an elephant with his hands clasped lightly behind his back. He looked very well in his cream-colored pantaloons and Hessian boots. His dark-blue tailcoat paired nicely with the earth-brown of his waistcoat.

She stepped onto the carpeted floor, and he turned from the painting, giving Jane a broad smile, which she returned with ease.

"Good morning, Miss Talbot." He bowed.

"To you as well, Lord Lendin." She curtsied. "My aunt has a headache today, so my maid, Abigail, will be our chaperone—if that's agreeable to you, that is."

Behind her, Abigail bobbed a curtsy.

"Certainly." His expression was bright. Jane stepped up to him, and he held out his arm. "Shall we?"

She took his arm gently and flashed him a grin. "Let's."

They were soon on their way, though Jane hadn't the faintest idea as to what Lord Lendin had planned. Fortunately for her, he seemed to read her thoughts.

"I thought we could take a walk about the grounds today. There's a large pond nearby, and Lord Sperrin has informed me it is quite beautiful this time of year."

"That sounds lovely." Jane tilted her head back, allowing the sun's rays to warm her face. That would be the perfect opportunity to find out if there might be any ruins on the grounds—and she'd get to know more about Lord Lendin.

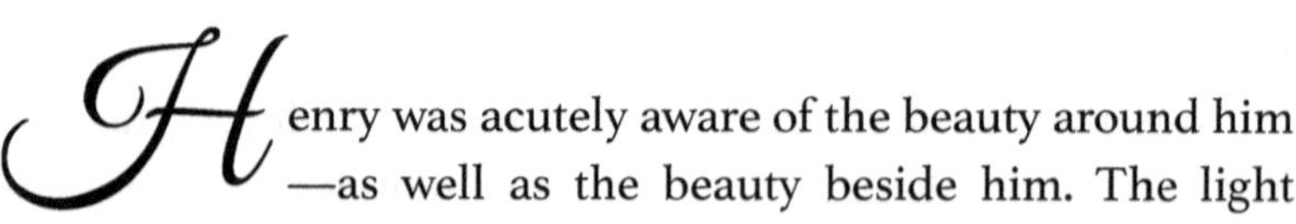

*H*enry was acutely aware of the beauty around him —as well as the beauty beside him. The light rustle of the grass beneath their feet and occasional buzzing of dragonflies filled the peaceful silence between them as he led Miss Talbot toward the pond.

A warm feeling spread throughout him, most likely due to the bright sun. Being in England, one was not accustomed to such warmth. The sensation was unlike anything he'd felt before...but very pleasant.

A blackcap flitted past, its movements quick and easy. Miss Talbot placed her hand on top of his arm, joining it with the other one. "I'm curious, Lord Lendin, what your favorite bird is."

He hummed in thought, taking a moment to deliberate before meeting her walnut-colored irises. "I've always enjoyed the mellow call of the dove. Yet herons are so graceful in their careful movements. I suppose one of the two," he said, inclining his head toward Miss Talbot. "Is there a bird especially high in your esteem?"

"Oh, many." Miss Talbot looked ahead, her tone light. "Each has unique qualities and traits." Her grip tightened almost imperceptibly, though she probably didn't even notice. "I believe the wren to have one of the most beautiful songs, however common it may be. It easily hides in the midst of foliage with its brown color, and when it decides to come out and show itself, no one is ever discontented at the prospect of hearing it sing." She wrinkled her nose in an adorably endearing way. "I could not abide a world without such a beautiful sound."

The corner of Henry's mouth tugged up at her expression.

"I find I'm in agreement, Miss Talbot. Every bird has its finer qualities. I have some friends, however, who wish that the wood pigeon would let them sleep a bit longer in the morning." He winked. His friend, Edmund, the Duke of Albemarle, had complained of the birds and their propensity for singing rather early in the morning. While Henry had always been an early riser, Edmund had not.

Henry's remark was rewarded with a laugh from Miss Talbot, a lovely sound—both musical and warm. Her mahogany curls peeked out from beneath her bonnet as she gifted him a wide grin.

Lord Sperrin hadn't exaggerated the beauty of the pond. Wildflowers lined its edges, and honeybees hovered from one blossom to the next. The water was calm, its surface like glass. It reflected the sky and surrounding flora in a beautiful painting of summer.

Miss Talbot gave a contented sigh from beside him, a calm look on her face accompanied by a subtle upturn of her lips. She released him to move toward the water's edge, her dress matching the surrounding flowers. If only he had paint and brushes to capture the view on a canvas.

Together, they strolled the perimeter of the pond, taking their time to enjoy the natural scenery.

Henry plucked a piece of grass and twisted it between his fingers. "I've always loved nature, as well as all of the creatures which inhabit it."

Perhaps it was the fact that he'd spent most of his time in Miss Talbot's company lately, or maybe it was the way she listened so well, always nodding and taking in his words, but Henry felt inclined to share with her what he hadn't told many others. They were friends now, certainly, yet that didn't seem a strong enough word to describe their relationship. The problem was, he didn't know what word was.

She turned her head to him as she waited for him to continue.

"As a boy, I loved to explore the woodlands near Harroway. I'd look for all sorts of creatures. Deer, squirrels, pheasants, rabbits—all were of interest to me." Henry grinned as memories of his adventures flooded his mind. "There was a particular stream not too far into the forest, and I loved to catch frogs and newts there with George. When I was successful in catching one, I'd race to the house to show my parents." Henry chuckled. "My mother had to put on a brave face, for she had no tolerance for creatures of that nature."

Miss Talbot laughed softly at his side. "Your poor mother. Every time you brought a frog for her to see, she had to act unbothered or risk your disappointment in her reaction."

Henry's lips pulled upward as he thought of the interactions in a new light. "I suppose she did. Now that I think about it, many of those smiles she gave when I brought her toads may have been grimaces."

Miss Talbot chuckled. "Such is a mother's love." She raised a hand to her bonnet to keep it in place as a light breeze blew by, but dropped it when the air was calm once more.

They paused in their walk, and Henry took a moment to study a vibrant blue dragonfly, its iridescent wings giving it a fairy-like look.

"I wonder..." Miss Talbot's tone was musing, drawing his attention to her once more. Her expression held a playful gleam, and he couldn't prevent a small smile from coming to his face in anticipation.

"You wonder...?"

"You see, my lord, I used to catch frogs as a child as well, much to my parents' chagrin, and I do wonder who—between the two of us—is quicker at doing so." She tilted her head to the side.

Henry put his hands on his hips, a hint of mischief sparking within his chest. "We are already in competition for a jewel, and now you seek to set up another competition between us? You seek to test our friendship, do you?" He cocked his head, a grin on his face.

She raised an eyebrow and stuck her chin out in an exaggeration of stubbornness. "The best friendships are often stretched thin by fate, only to see if they will become stronger or break, my lord."

"Well, I hate to be the bearer of bad news," he teased, "but I am certain that I can catch one quicker than you."

"Certain? My, but you're quite confident. Shall we put our skills to the test?" She put her hands on her own hips, mimicking Henry's stance.

A few minutes later, Henry's jacket and hat lay in the grass, and his shirtsleeves were rolled up. Miss Talbot had taken off her bonnet, her dark curls shining in the light of the sun. Both pairs of their gloves were also on the ground, as catching frogs tended to get messy.

Abigail had a perplexed look on her face yet made no comment. She only counted down as she'd been asked to. Doubtful she'd expected this to be a part of her duties today. "… two, one, go!"

Henry scanned the edges of the pond, careful not to step into the water. He combed through the grass with his fingers, turning over stones to see if any frogs were hiding beside them.

Ten feet away, Miss Talbot was doing the same thing, a determined and competitive set to her brow. Henry had to pull his eyes away from her and focus on the task at hand. He pushed a patch of grass where the water met land. A dark-brown lump was there, its skin shining with moisture. He grabbed for it, yet the creature was faster than him. It leaped from its spot and splashed into the water, surely eager to tell its friends of the two bedlamites who were terrorizing the frog community.

"Blast." He continued his search. In his peripheral vision, movement came from Miss Talbot's area. He glanced over, only to find her holding a rotund frog in both hands, a triumphant look on her face.

"Pardon me, my lord, but I do believe you've been beaten." She held the frog high for all of heaven to view.

He stood from where he'd been crouching and walked over, steps faltering as he beheld the size of the frog. It was humongous. Henry wasn't sure he'd ever seen one as large. He bowed in defeat, smiling at her grin before giving a playfully distraught look.

"Alas, Miss Talbot, you have bested me. And what am I to do, now that you've proven how terribly unqualified I am at catching frogs? I'll never be able to show my face in Berkshire again!" He leaned back as though wounded, trying—and failing—to keep the grin from his face.

Miss Talbot looked from the frog to him, a contemplative look on her fair face. "I'll keep your secret." Her mouth twisted to the side. "But only because we're friends."

Henry put a hand to his heart. "Thank you, Miss Talbot. Your mercy knows no bounds."

The frog in her hands croaked its agreement, and they burst into laughter, the ridiculousness of it making them laugh all the harder. Finally, Miss Talbot deposited the frog back into the pond, where it gladly disappeared beneath the surface. She brushed her hands together and beamed up at him.

Taking careful steps back up the slope to solid land, she bit her lip. The long grass descended into the water at a modest angle. Miss Talbot was almost past the incline when the mud took its revenge on the trespassers.

Henry's heart stuttered in alarm as her foot slipped, throwing her off balance and sending her careening toward the murky depths. He reached out to grab her arm, but the ground beneath him was not as level as he'd thought, and his momentum only helped with sending them both tumbling into the pond. Before he knew it, the water closed over his head. At least it was warm from the summer sun.

Henry quickly stood in about three feet of water. Miss

Talbot sputtered next to him, and he offered her a hand up. She stood, tugging at her water-heavy skirts that moved like molasses in the mud. Moisture dripped from her curls down her forehead and cheeks.

He was about to ask her if she was all right when, much to Henry's surprise, a burst of laughter erupted from her. Her shoulders shook, and she clutched her abdomen as her melodic laugh rang out. Henry joined in, the absurdity of the situation setting in. Abigail, who had been ready to jump in after Miss Talbot, stood to the side looking both dismayed and amused, her cap in hand.

Henry and Miss Talbot dragged themselves up the slope—successfully this time—still chuckling at what had just occurred. Miss Talbot's bright eyes connected with his as they finally stood on level ground, her gaze somehow warming him even more than the sun's rays. They looked at each other for a moment, only the sounds of the light breeze and busy songbirds filling the silence. A few locks of Miss Talbot's hair that had come free were now plastered to her neck. The dark strands contrasted with her light skin and drew his attention to the gentle slope of her shoulders.

It was then that it hit him how improper it was for him to be seeing her in this state. Her hair was half down and her dress stuck to her legs. His mouth grew dry. She seemed to realize the impropriety of their situation at the same time, for a crimson blush stole across her cheeks. He quickly averted his gaze, swallowing as the back of his neck burned.

Abigail fussed over her mistress, fretting over the drenched dress.

"I—er… Here." He grabbed his coat from where he'd left it and carefully draped it over Miss Talbot's shoulders. She murmured her thanks and pulled the garment tightly around her, looking anywhere but at him.

Egads! What a fetching sight she made.

~

Thankfully, Lord Lendin focused on pulling his gloves on and spared Jane a portion of her embarrassment once their immodest situation dawned on her. His damp shirtsleeves clung to his muscular arms, and droplets of water occasionally dripped from his golden curls, darker now that they were wet. Water glistened on his shaved cheeks and inched down his neck, disappearing into his damp cravat.

He really was abominably handsome. Jane couldn't keep her stomach from flipping, nor her heart from beating at a faster pace. She forced her gaze away and plucked her bonnet from the ground, tying it in place in an effort to hide the mess her hair likely was.

Once they had gathered their belongings, they trekked back to the manor, Jane's heavy gown hindering her movements. They chatted quietly as they walked. The easy conversation once again set her at ease. They entered through the kitchens to avoid being seen by any of the other houseguests, much to the surprise of the servants there.

Fortunately for them, the servants were all incredibly loyal to Lord Sperrin and, because they knew how good of friends he and Lord Lendin were, promised not to breathe a word to anyone about their odd appearance and subsequently odd entrance into the kitchens. Jane and Lord Lendin were ushered to the servants' stairs, and there they took their leave of each other.

"Congratulations again on your win, Miss Talbot. I've never witnessed someone catch a frog as quickly as you did." He bowed to her.

She tipped her head back, straightening her shoulders in an

exaggeration of pride. "If I feel charitable in the future, perhaps I might impart my hard-earned knowledge to you." Her voice was solemn. With that, she strode up the stairs with Abigail close behind, but not before witnessing a glimpse of the magnificent grin on Lord Lendin's face. She chuckled to herself as his quiet laughter followed them up the stairs.

Would it always feel this good to be around him?

CHAPTER 9

*L*ater, the afternoon of his pond outing with Miss Talbot, candles aided Henry's vision as he inspected the green fabric-covered billiard table. Outside, the heavy droplets of rain tapped on the window in spontaneous intervals, the sky a dark hue that foretold more to come. Henry flicked his wrist and pocketed Lord Sperrin's cue ball, sending a crack of noise throughout the room. He was the first to reach the agreed-upon one-and-twenty points.

"A good game, Lendin. Very good." Lord Sperrin shook Henry's hand and placed his billiard mace in a cabinet to the side of the room. Gerald had been perched atop the cabinet for the duration of the game but now stepped politely onto Lord Sperrin's shoulder.

Henry grinned, placing his own mace away. "Indeed. You certainly had the upper hand in the first quarter."

Lord Sperrin hummed in thought. "Perhaps so, though it wasn't to last for long."

"'Very good,'" rasped Gerald, making them laugh.

Henry unrolled his shirtsleeves and slid his arms into his coat, that *vêtement* having been draped over a nearby chair. As he made to leave the room for the library, he was stopped by Lord Windham as he paused his conversation with Mr. Alton and stepped forward.

"Lendin. Fancy a game of brag?"

Henry inspected the man, wariness seeping into him. "I'm not much for gambling."

"Come, now. Alton and I were just about to sit down. We need another." Lord Windham raised a haughty eyebrow and smirked. "Or is it the stake you're worried about?"

Henry clenched his jaw, shoulders tightening. "I'll play."

They sat down at a nearby table. Lord Sperrin decided not to join them but provided the three of them with well-polished counters of multicolored stone and mother-of-pearl before taking a seat at the opposite end of the room. Each man pushed forward a few counters, and the cards were soon dealt by Lord Windham. His was the highest face-up card. He slid the counters toward himself.

"Alton and I were just speaking, Lendin. It appears as though you're looking to get leg-shackled." Giving Henry a smirk, Lord Windham placed five more counters on the center of the table. "I brag." He puffed out his chest like a peacock.

Alton pushed forward his own, but upon this declaration, his head fell. He looked at his remaining cards and gave an irritated huff. "Fold."

Henry matched the *ante* and tossed five counters forward. The polished oak wood was smooth under Henry's hands as he picked up his cards. After taking a moment to look them over, he pierced Windham with a stare. What the others didn't know was that, while he wasn't usually a gambling man, Henry had been to many card parties during his Oxford days—and he'd certainly learned a thing or two while there.

Henry pushed a few more counters forward. "Does it?"

The corner of Lord Windham's mouth turned down. "Indeed. You've been quite attentive to...oh, Alton, what is that chit's name? Miss Talcot?" Lord Windham pushed forward five more counters and took a moment to regard Alton.

Alton, that unfortunate gentleman who was, at this point, a trifle disguised, replied, "No, old fellow, no. 'Tis…" He leaned back in his seat. "Her name quite eludes me. She's often in the company of that tempting armful, Miss Wildon."

"I know she is, Alton, but—devil take it! You're foxed!" Lord Windham grimaced.

"Not so, Windham. A bit bosky and nothing more." Alton reclined in his chair and folded his arms across his chest. "What *is* her name?"

"Miss Talbot?" Henry supplied in a polite tone, sliding some counters into the middle.

Lord Windham's eyes narrowed, and he looked as though he were about to speak when Alton burst out, "That's it! Miss Talbot!" He brought a hand down to slap the table, nearly upsetting the pile of counters in the middle. "Knew it wasn't Talcot, Windham. Quite so."

Henry remained straight-faced as Lord Windham once again pushed a pile of counters forward. Was his hand truly so valuable? Doubtful.

"It matters not, Alton." Windham straightened his shoulders and huffed. "Our Lord Lendin here has been in her company almost every day since this house party began, is my point."

"And if I have?" Henry raised an eyebrow.

"Hoping to give yourself another chance at the jewel, eh?" Lord Windham asked in a condescending tone. "Well, you're not the only one. You should know, Lendin, that the poor chit's set her cap at me—who could blame her, after all? You might try to sway her, but I think there's no turning her head." The man shrugged. "I'm in need of a wife. Perhaps she'll prove entertaining enough to fit the role. My creditors have been blasted insolent ever since I've been in dun territory. I could use the blunt."

The idea of Miss Talbot married to this snake of a man made Henry's blood heat in a most uncomfortable way. Though Lord Windham spoke of Miss Talbot carelessly, what really bothered Henry was his open admission to using her for her dowry and the jewel, if she found it.

"Hold your tongue, my lord." He flicked a few counters into the pile. "You might yet regret your words."

Lord Windham scoffed but didn't reply to this. Instead, he said, "I'll see you, Lendin! Your cards can't possibly be better than mine."

Each of them revealed their hand. Lord Windham held a pair of tens. His face paled as he beheld Henry's pair of aces. Next to him, Alton shook his head solemnly.

"A pair royal! No beating it, Windham. A shame." He offered a grin to Henry. "You've a good bluff, you know. Never suspected it."

As Lord Windham stormed from the room, a sense of unease bloomed in Henry's stomach. Lord Windham was someone he'd have to keep an eye on. If the man was in such a state after losing a game of brag, who knew how volatile he might be when unsuccessful regarding Miss Talbot?

CHAPTER 10

*J*ane melted even farther into the maroon-cushioned chair of the library as the storm rattled the windows the evening of her pond excursion with Lord Lendin. Her candle was the sole provider of light in the room, and it flickered every once in a while. Despite this, she remained cozy—a rabbit in a burrow of her own making. Jane smiled at the thunder as it once more roared through the sky, but that smile disappeared as the library door creaked. Shrouded in darkness as it was, she couldn't tell if it had opened or not. Who would be up at this hour?

At a rustling sound, her heart raced and her limbs tensed. Jane pulled her shawl tighter around her shoulders. "W-Who's there?"

Footsteps crossed the room, and the click of metal preceded the spark of a flame in the hearth. Jane raised her candle in that direction and squinted. A black silhouette came into view. What on earth?

The silhouette moved, a fire now at its fingertips. Her heart raced ever more. It took a few steps forward. She opened her mouth to scream—

"Well met!" Lord Lendin walked toward her, a flickering candle in hand. He'd been lighting it in the hearth. "I thought you would've gone to bed hours ago." He gave a cheerful grin as he sat in the chair opposite Jane, still sporting his dinner attire, much as she did.

She tried in vain to stifle the bout of humor that overtook her, erupting into a fit of laughter and doubling over in her seat. She viewed Lord Lendin through blurred sight, both of his light eyebrows raised.

"Have I missed something?"

Her laughter continued as she shook her head and gasped for breath. "You—you...I thought you were—well—I do not know what I thought you were..." She raised a hand to her cheek and brushed away a tear. "I apologize, my lord, but I quite thought you some sort of apparition. Then, for you to reveal yourself in so cheerful a manner—I must say, it is a relief that you are not a ghoul come to haunt me."

Humor shone in Lord Lendin's gaze. "Are nightly visits from ghouls something that you experience often?"

Jane chuckled. "No, my lord, I cannot say they are."

"I must look very much like one, then?"

Jane dipped her head to the side and peered at Lord Lendin's golden hair and warm stare. His eyes held a brightness that put the flame of his candle to shame.

"I should say the opposite, my lord." Her cheeks pricked with heat.

Lord Lendin leaned back in his chair and rested an ankle on the opposite knee.

"You are too kind, Miss Talbot." He leaned his head back against the chair and raised an eyebrow. "Now—I must inquire —why are you lurking in the library at this midnight hour?"

Jane raised the corner of her mouth in a playful look. "Waiting for unsuspecting lords to walk in so I might turn them to stone in true gorgon fashion."

Lord Lendin let out a guffaw. "A gorgon, indeed? They'd never suspect you, for if *I* look nothing like a ghoul, then *you* certainly look nothing like a gorgon. Regardless, I do hope my presence isn't disturbing your plans."

"Not if you don't mind being turned to stone."

He drummed his fingers on his armrest. "It could be enjoyable."

Jane laughed, straightening in her seat. "And how is that, my lord?"

He shrugged, turning somewhat serious. "There are no responsibilities for a statue. A piece of stone need only be moved from one place to another, and it needn't think about how to get there."

Lord Lendin's jokes and easy smile were an integral part of him, but it seemed they also helped to mask some of his deeper emotions that he wished to keep hidden from the world. There was a look in his eye she couldn't quite put a name to. Loneliness? A man as pleasant as he could hardly want for company. Perhaps he was overwhelmed.

"While I don't have experience running an estate, I imagine that the prospect of doing so must be daunting."

Lord Lendin's mouth twisted—almost bittersweet—and he looked past her shoulder into the darkness. "My father died two years ago. It is not the prospect that is daunting anymore but the actual effort."

Jane leaned forward. "I'm terribly sorry, my lord. To have lost someone so dear must have been...simply awful. And to have such responsibility suddenly thrust upon you..."

"Thank you, Miss Talbot. It was difficult adjusting to the absence of my father—it still is, truthfully. At times, the weight of my responsibilities is a chain around my neck. It grows all the tighter when I remember my father is not on a trip. He will not return. I struggled most grievously in the months that followed his passing, though the burdens have grown somewhat lighter in the years since." He blinked, seeming to shake himself from a reverie. "I apologize for waxing on. There are days when I feel that weight more palpably than others."

Jane shook her head. "You do not have to apologize, my lord."

The corner of his mouth quivered up as he gave a disbelieving chuckle. "You're the only person I've told that, you know."

Something inside Jane warmed. "I'm honored."

"Because I'm a lord?" His tone had flattened.

"Because you're my friend." Her stomach flipped under his scrutiny, his eyes as warm as the coals in the hearth. Whatever happened to steeling her heart? Dratted thing! She'd have to build up her defenses.

"You have an effect on me, Miss Talbot."

She fought to hear Henry's unexpected words over the thrum of her pulse.

"I'm able to speak of things in your presence that I wouldn't be able to otherwise. What's your secret? Some sort of gorgon charm?" His warm voice seemed to seep through her skin.

Jane blushed and gave a small smile despite herself. "I've no secret, my lord. I suppose only you have the answer to that."

"Perhaps it's simply your fine character, Miss Talbot. A good character is a very admirable thing." His expression was earnest as he focused on her.

From the library doorway, muffled voices could be heard, growing in volume as they moved down the hallway. Jane raised a hand and shot a nervous glance at Lord Lendin. Though the library door *was* open, the room was mostly shrouded in darkness, and they were alone. Should they be found together in such a place and at such an hour...Jane didn't want to think about the consequences.

As the voices continued to grow, Jane stood from her comfortable seat. Henry did the same and ushered her behind one of the dark-green drapes that hung next to a large window while he remained in view. She tucked her skirts close around her and remained quiet. Footsteps entered the room, followed by slurred voices.

"It must be in here somewhere...I just know it. Lendin? Blasted unfortunate running into you here." That sounded like Lord Windham.

"Come now, Windham...'tis—'tisn't proper to greet a fellow like that..." A hiccup followed this statement. Mr. Alton? A curious character—unexpected in action and phrase in all of the interactions Jane had witnessed.

She held her breath, her heartbeat loud in her ears. Lord Windham and Mr. Alton were not as strict as London society matrons, of course, but there was a chance they'd tell fellow houseguests—should they find Jane behind the drapes—-that she and Lord Lendin had been rendezvousing in the library. Thank heavens they sounded foxed.

"—late for you to be in the *library* of all places..."

"Maybe he couldn't sleep, Wind. At home, I like to heat—"

"Alton, you already spoke of—"

"—a pint of milk and then add—"

"—Alton—"

"—an onion—"

A huff of impatience.

"—Alto—the devil—did you say an *onion*?"

"'Tis a good thing, an onion."

A moment of silence followed this odd statement before Lord Lendin's voice sounded. "Right you are, Alton—I couldn't sleep. I wonder what the both of you are doing about, however."

Once again, footsteps drew near and she held her breath.

Lord Windham's slurred voice sounded only a few feet away. "Cards...I believe you owe me a rematch."

Lord Lendin replied, "I owe you nothing of the sort, although I'd be glad to win once more."

Lord Windham snorted—at least, Jane thought it was Lord Windham. "I was feeling unwell then, and that is the only reason for your win."

"If you were unwell *then,* I'd wager you're feeling worse *now.*"

A pause, and then, "So I am. Your company has that effect on a person, you know."

"I'll keep that in mind," Henry replied.

Two sets of footsteps withdrew from the room, and Mr. Alton said quietly, "'Tisn't right, Wind. Not good Ton..."

A few moments after she could no longer hear their slurred voices, the drape was pulled away from her with careful motions. It revealed Lord Lendin's relieved face—a halo around his golden head from the candlelight behind him.

"Are you all right?"

Jane nodded, cool air hitting her face as he helped her out from behind the stifling green velvet. She was certainly flushed —especially as the warmth of his hand enveloped her own. He didn't let go. "Yes. I'm fortunate they missed my feet. I'm not sure the drapes fully covered them."

Henry rubbed the opposite hand over his face. "They were ape-drunk. I'm not sure they'd even remember your presence here in the morning, were they to have seen you."

Jane smoothed her skirts and gave him a hesitant half smile. "There are some gentlemen I've met multiple times at balls, and yet they still go to my mother for an introduction. I suppose that speaks to how memorable I am." She turned her head away, embarrassment creeping up from what she'd revealed. "Thank you for your quick thinking. I believe that's enough excitement for so late—or so early, rather." She curtsied and grabbed her candle from the table. Lord Lendin must have extinguished the flame when the unexpected guests arrived, so she touched her wick to his candle's still-burning flame and looked over her shoulder at him as she walked to the door. "Good morning, my lord."

"I'd remember you." His words paused her at the doorframe.

She looked over her shoulder. "What?"

He had not made a move, still standing where she'd left him with his candle in hand. "I'd remember you," he repeated. "Even if I'd seen you from across the room at a crowded fête for mere seconds—even if we'd met once as children at our parents' behest. I'd remember."

Would he, though? Oh, how her heart squeezed in its traitorous desire to believe him. But long-ingrained mistrust raised doubt. Would he remember her now, after he left this house party?

CHAPTER 11

Two days later, Jane helped Miss Wildon—Harriet, as she'd come to know her—pull her skirt from a bramble as Lady Caroline whined for the umpteenth time, "'Tis so dreadfully long a walk!" The woman huffed in annoyance and stepped over a small stick that crossed her path. "These woods are treacherous, as well."

"We're almost to the ruins." The afternoon sun shining down through the branches highlighted Lady Sperrin's rather brittle smile.

"We only started seven minutes ago, dear," murmured Lady Caroline's mother. "And the ruins are sure to be a beautiful sight."

Harriet thanked Jane as they managed to untangle her skirt and catch up with the others. "I, for one, am enjoying the pleasant weather," she said, linking arms with Jane. "The forest is so pretty in the daytime. The sun shines through the branches, and the birds always sing so sweetly." She shuddered. "The forest at night, however...quite a different story."

Mr. Langley appeared at Jane's side, peeking over her at Harriet. His brown hair looked soft, as did his expression. "The only thing to be scared of in the forest is the people who traverse it."

Harriet bit her lip. "What of the...creatures? Are there dangerous creatures in this forest?"

Mr. Langley opened his mouth to respond, but Mr. Alton's voice rose above the group. "I assure you, Miss Wildon, I will protect you from any foul beasts, should they dare to harm you." He puffed out his chest, and Mr. Langley failed to hide his scowl.

Jane flicked her gaze between Mr. Langley and Harriet. Was there something there?

All that passed for a few moments was the sound of snapping twigs beneath feet and the calling of birds, both near and far. Jane breathed in the scent of fresh leaves as they trekked on, her pale-pink day-dress swishing around her legs with each step.

Where would the jewel be in the tower ruins? It had to be there. Why else would Lord Sperrin have arranged this outing? Besides that, the clue she'd received today seemed pointed. The piece of paper had read, *There is aged rock and metal there.* There would be old hewn stones and the remains of whatever used to be inside the tower—perhaps pieces of iron or other metals. Surely, this was the place the jewel was located.

As Mr. Langley fell behind the group, Jane took the moment to whisper to Harriet, "Mr. Langley seems quite taken with you. I didn't miss that he escorted you to dinner last evening."

Harriet's cheeks suffused with pink over her freckles. "Does he? I must admit that he's been rather attentive these past few days."

Jane hummed in thought and lifted her skirt to step over a decaying branch. "Do you find him agreeable?"

Harriet inclined her head to the side before giving a resolute nod. "Indeed, I do. He's quiet"—she leaned forward, her voice low—"but very thoughtful." A moment more passed before she spoke again. "I suppose we both have been fortunate at this party."

Jane raised an eyebrow in Harriet's direction.

Harriet jutted her chin. "Lord Lendin's been in your company as often as Mr. Langley's been in mine." She nudged her shoulder.

Jane waved her hand to dismiss the idea. "He's only helping me with something. Do you remember the plan I told you of?"

Harriet nodded. "I do, but he looks at you in such a way..."

"If he does, then it's only because we're friends." Jane brushed a wisp of hair from her cheek, tumult rising within her. She didn't want to continue this line of conversation.

"I don't thin—"

Before Harriet could finish speaking, Lord Lendin appeared beside Jane, a grin on his face that made her heart beat faster beneath her ribs.

"Good afternoon, Miss Talbot, Miss Wildon. I'm afraid some of the guests have become quite consumed with the talk of hounds." He gestured toward the front of the group, and Jane followed his gaze to find Lord Windham at the center of the conversation. "I beg you to be merciful and allow me to join your discussion. Please, pardon my interruption. What was it you were saying?"

Harriet took a quick intake of breath, and Jane's heart leapt. Would her friend be able to come up with a believable excuse?

Harriet's mouth opened. "Oh! Of course. I was—erm—just speaking of—of how I...don't think that eel should be served on Sundays."

Jane stifled a desperate laugh as Lord Lendin leaned his head back, looking very much like a person attempting to read a messily written letter.

"Did you say eel, Miss Wildon?"

"I did, my lord."

"And why, pray, do you think it not fit to be served on Sundays?"

"Erm...It reminds me so much of—of...*the evil one,* you see."

At this, Lord Lendin's eyebrows raised. "*The evil one*? Do you mean—"

Harriet put a gloved finger to her chin. "Eel is so unholy, of course—"

Fortunately, the woman was saved from having to explain herself as Lord Sperrin called, "And here we are! This is Cobb Tower. It fell in 1653 and has been this way since then."

Harriet's shoulders eased as Lord Lendin's attention was directed away from her. She shared a relieved look with Jane before the trio moved forward with the rest of the group into a small clearing. Stones dotted the grass, and a half-fallen structure stood as proud as a statue in the middle.

"I'm sure the others will regret having stayed in the manor." Harriet stretched her arms out before her. Her parents, Miss Clarke, Aunt Agnes, and a few others had decided to forgo this day's walk to the ruins, and as Jane viewed the tumbled stones and pondered the ethereal beauty of the area that was reclaiming them, she agreed with her friend.

"Miss Wildon, would you care to explore the ruins with me?" Mr. Langley looked hopeful as he uttered these words.

"I would love to." She glanced at Jane, an undertone of excitement in her voice. Then she took Langley's proffered arm, and the pair walked away.

Lord Lendin shifted beside Jane, holding out his arm. "Will you let me escort you around the ruins, Miss Talbot?"

The corner of her mouth turned hesitantly upward as she placed her gloved hand on his arm. "Certainly." A pleasant haze seemed to descend upon her mind the minute she touched him.

This was the plan she'd agreed to. He was only helping her to find enjoyment. No matter that she tried to convince herself of that, her heart was a traitor. It thumped heavily with each second that passed in Lord Lendin's company.

Lord Lendin was not Laurence, of course—he wasn't using her—but she had to stay vigilant in the fortress she'd built. For even if the fortress was made of stones as large as those that made up the ruins, if the gate was left open, any intruder could waltz in and soundly trounce her heart. She couldn't—wouldn't—let that happen. Not again. The meeting they'd had in the library two nights prior had been far too dangerous already. That look he'd given her had nearly been her undoing...

He led her around a pile of stones, the fabric of his coat soft beneath her fingertips. She peered into a crevice where two stones leaned against one another. No jewel there. "Did you enjoy the hunt yesterday?"

Lord Lendin grimaced. "I fear I'm a bad shot. Whenever we approached a buck, I attempted to fell it. Alas, every shot I took, I missed—allowing the poor creature to get away." He shook his head solemnly until Jane met his gaze and his innocent facade broke. He shot her a wink as a mischievous expression spread across his face.

Jane matched his grin with a disbelieving one of her own. "The others must've been irritated with you."

"Ah, yes." He nodded. "They were. We were—erm—unsuccessful in all of our hunting endeavors yesterday." His deep brown eyes gleamed with mirth and a hint of triumph as Jane laughed aloud.

"You're speaking of the hunt yesterday, Lendin?" Lord Windham called from a separate pile of rocks, moving toward them.

Lord Lendin's arm tensed beneath her hand.

Lord Windham smirked as he continued. "Lord Lendin, I fear, is not a great huntsman, Miss Talbot. Missed every shot, he did! Did you know—he doesn't even have any hounds?" The man guffawed.

Lord Lendin remained as a statue beside her.

"I've no enthusiasm for the hunt either, I must admit." Jane shrugged a shoulder.

Lord Windham's laughter abated. "Surely, your enthusiasm will grow once you witness a real huntsman in pursuit. At Clarin Manor, I hold large hunting parties. I'll make sure that you're invited for the next."

Jane tried not to frown at the prospect. "Thank you, my lord."

"But of course, Miss Talbot. We must only hope that your beauty doesn't distract the others from the hunt." He grabbed her free hand and planted a kiss on the back of her glove before he left to rejoin Lord Alton.

She fought not to wipe her hand against her skirts. Lord Lendin began to lead her again, this time in the opposite direction from Lord Windham.

"I can't make heads nor tails of that man." She shook her head, peering over her shoulder at the arrogant lord. "First, he insults your hunting skills, then he boasts of his own and invites me to a hunting party?"

Lord Lendin glanced at her with a strained look. "The other evening, he spoke of you."

Jane lifted a hand to her cheek. "Did he, indeed? And what about me?"

Lord Lendin took a moment to clear his throat. "He—erm —said you'd set your cap at him—"

Jane gasped. "I haven't done anything of the sort!"

"I'm aware." His lips pulled into a thin line. "But the other thing he said was far worse. He mentioned you might prove a suitable wife for him. Apparently, he's in need of money to pay off his debts, and your dowry appeals to him. He also inferred that were you to find the jewel, he'd seek to marry you so it would—effectively—become his property."

Jane covered her mouth. "I suppose I should give up the

hunt now, then, if a jewel will bring such fortune hunters as he. My dowry's not so great, and I do not know why he should think it so. The insolence of that man!" She scowled, clenching her free hand into a fist at her side.

Lord Lendin dropped his arm and raised a hand to his hat, lifting it to run his fingers through his wave-like curls. The morning sun caught on the strands like golden thread. "I'm sorry to have upset you."

Jane patted his arm. "It is not you who has upset me, my lord. Truly. I thank you for informing me."

He set his hat back on his head and winked. "Your servant, ma'am."

They walked some more, examining the stones and tufts of grass that peeked out from the crevices between them. A bee hummed past near her head, and Jane watched it float away.

"It truly is beautiful here." She turned her head and found that his eyes were on her.

They flicked away, and his Adam's apple bobbed. "Indeed. I must admit that I've been to these ruins before. My parents were close friends with the Sperrins'—my mother still is—and when we'd visit, I'd wander here. Truth be told, this is my first time visiting them since my father's death."

Jane had no desire to seek the jewel anymore. She squeezed his arm. "Will you tell me about your father?"

Lord Lendin nodded, not meeting her eye. When he finally spoke, his voice was quiet, almost far away. "My father was a man of few words, but when he did speak, everyone listened. He was a good man—a good father. He knew all of our tenant's names and all of their children's names. He...cared. He truly cared about everyone he encountered."

Lord Lendin's lips raised, slightly crooked. "I remember a time when one of our tenant's dogs had gotten loose and run into the woods. It was evening and the sun had nearly set, but my father gathered the servants and they, alongside the other tenants, scoured the woods. It wasn't long before they found the creature. It nearly knocked my father over in its excitement." He hesitated. "I don't know how I'll ever manage to fill his shoes. It's been two years, and I feel as though I haven't done anything to better the estate. I can't help but wonder if I'm failing him."

Jane paused and pulled Lord Lendin to a stop as they rounded the upright structure that remained despite the years that had passed, the smell of moss and earth in the air. "It sounds as though he was the best of fathers." She moved her hand from his arm and grabbed his hand instead, gripping his gloved fingers. He turned his gaze toward their joined hands. She lifted their clasped hands upward to get his attention, his eyes on hers again. "That being said, I'm sure he wouldn't want you to feel as though you are failing him."

Henry sighed. "Perhaps not, but that doesn't make it any less true."

Jane dropped his hand. She folded her arms across her chest and pierced him with a stare, her eyebrow raised. "Oh? Then I imagine you've gambled away your family's fortune."

He sputtered. "What? No—"

"Or maybe you've left your tenants to fix their own homes and solve their own pest problems?"

"I haven't—"

"Perhaps, then, you've ruined your reputation and the reputations of your father and your family?"

"No." Lord Lendin released an exhale. "I have done none of what you've just said."

Jane uncrossed her arms. "Then really, my lord, I cannot see how you've failed your family."

"Perhaps...perhaps, I have not—but that doesn't mean it won't happen." Lord Lendin held out his arm again, and they continued walking once more.

"I used to climb to the tops of these piles and declare I was the King of England." He shook his head. "Now I don't feel like the king of anything. What if—what if I *do* fail them? My family?"

Jane tilted her head to the side, the sun's rays peeking past her bonnet and warming her face. "How would you?"

"I don't know." He shrugged. "What if I make a bad investment or our crops fail?" He stopped walking. "Or—"

Jane patted his arm. "Slow your thoughts, my lord." She gave him her most earnest look as she continued. "Is that why the jewel entices you? A sort of net to catch you if all your plans fail?"

He hesitated. "Partially, I suppose."

"Your father taught you many things, and mine taught me a few, as well. My mother told me, when I was a mere girl, that she'd spoken to my father about having a child. She despaired of ever having a baby—they'd been married a few years without any sign of one. He told her then that it was useless to fret about the future, for one never knows what it may hold except the Lord. I believe that to be true." Jane lifted her shoulders. "You needn't fret about possible failure, my lord, for there is an equal possibility of success. It is all in God's hands. It is not for us to worry about."

The tension in Lord Lendin's posture seemed to ease at her words. "I hadn't thought of it like that."

Jane shrugged. "It might be easier said than done, of course, but perhaps that idea will bring you peace. So, whenever you worry, just give that worry to Him. He's glad to take it from you...and far better equipped to handle it."

"Thank you, Miss Talbot."

"You're very welcome, my lord."

He pinned her with a stare. "Henry."

"My lord?" Jane's breath stilled in her throat.

"I'd like you to call me Henry—that is, if you'll agree to it."

Jane nodded. "You may call me Jane, then."

His gaze softened, and a cool breeze sifted through the air. "A lovely name. Jane."

Jane's stomach flipped at the sound of her name on his lips. Her blood seemed to rush through her veins at the pace of a reel. She bit her lip and attempted to tamp down the growing warmth in her chest.

He only said her name. That was all. And if it sounded better coming from his mouth than any other...so be it.

"Are you all right?"

Jane shook her troubling thoughts away, focusing on Lord Len—Henry's concerned expression. She flashed him a smile. Was it convincing? From the way his eyebrows furrowed more, it probably wasn't.

"I am." Instead of giving him more time to look at her, she wrapped her hand around his arm and started forward, content to ignore those troubling feelings.

CHAPTER 12

The very next day, Jane awoke early. The sun was just peeking through the drapes, and her stomach churned in a most unpleasant manner. Dinner the evening before had included something she'd not yet tried in her three-and-twenty years—eel. For as much as they'd talked about eel yesterday, Jane had never had it. Now, she found Harriet was correct. It *was* unholy.

Jane leapt from her bed as the churning in her stomach increased. The movement only worsened it, and saliva began to pool around her tongue. She had a moment to pull her chamber pot toward her before she was casting up her accounts in a rather violent way. She sank to her knees onto the wooden floorboards and clutched the pot close. Sweat beaded on her forehead as her abdominal muscles clenched painfully. Her hair stuck to her face and around her mouth. She attempted to lean back against the bedframe, but her stomach was not done. The saliva began to pool again.

Her bedchamber door creaked open as Abigail entered, yawning. "Miss?"

Jane raised a hand up from the side of her bed, retching once more into the cool porcelain bowl.

"Oh, miss!" Abigail rushed forward to Jane's side, brushing her hair away from her face and rubbing her back. Once it seemed Jane was truly finished, Abigail helped her to her feet and took the pot from her, guiding her back into bed. "Should I call for the doctor?"

Jane shook her head.

"I'll be back in a moment, miss. I'm going to dispose of this and see if I can't get you something to make you feel better."

"Thank you," Jane near-whispered in response, her nose wrinkling from the sour taste in her mouth.

It was a few minutes before the maid returned, a clean chamber pot in hand. She set it on the floor next to Jane's bed and rushed out once more. By the time Abigail returned, Jane's sweat had cooled on her face, and she had begun to shiver in an uncomfortable chatter of teeth and tremble of limbs. Abigail entered the room with a tray in her hands and set it on Jane's lap.

"What is this?" Jane eyed the cup placed in the corner of the tray. In it was a curious green-tinted liquid—clearly a tea of some sort. That, or someone had put grass in a cup of water and given it to Abigail to take upstairs.

"The housekeeper said it was adder's tongue tea, miss, with some peppermint."

Jane thanked her and raised the cup to drink. She took a small sip and grimaced. It tasted like grass, too, although the peppermint was a nice addition.

"Cook had me bring up some broth for you."

"Thank you, Abigail, but I'm really not sure I can eat anything right now." Jane took another sip of the tea and leaned her head back against the solid headboard. Her mouth was still bitter from the unfortunate incident but was made less so from the tea.

"Do you need anything else, miss?"

"No, Abigail. Thank you. Only, tell my aunt of my illness, please—when she awakes."

"Certainly, miss." With that, Abigail left the room, closing the door behind her.

Jane moved the tray to the bedside table and reclined farther into bed. She let her eyelids droop closed, finally succumbing to exhaustion's pull.

When next she awoke, the tray was gone, and a brighter light peeked past the drapes into the room. It left a slanted beam on the floor near her bed. A knock sounded at the door, and Jane rasped, "Enter." Her stomach was as hollow as a rotten tree trunk as she sat up in bed. It gave a weak grumble, though Jane didn't feel like taking the risk of obliging it.

Aunt Agnes swept into the room in a flurry of dark-blue fabric and the scent of rose petals. "My poor dear!" She hurried over to Jane's side, touching her forehead and brushing a few wisps of hair out of her face. "Abigail told me what happened. I do wonder what the cause is."

Jane offered a wobbly smile. "I believe it was the eel."

Her aunt gave a hum. "Yes, that seems likely, although I haven't heard of any of the other guests being ill this morning." She shook her head. "Strange." She took Jane's hand in her own and patted the back of it. "Abigail is, at this very moment, bringing up a new tray for you. I've given your apologies to Lord and Lady Sperrin. Is there anyone else I should be telling of your illness?" She raised a knowing eyebrow as the corner of her lip pulled up.

Jane was too tired to protest. "Lord Lendin, please. He told me at dinner last evening that he'd something planned for us today."

Aunt Agnes moved to the window. "A shame. The day is beautiful as can be." She pushed aside the drapes to flood the room with light and cracked open the window. A warm breeze flowed in, tickling Jane's arm. Her heart sank. It really *was* a beautiful day, and here she was stuck inside.

"Perhaps tomorrow will be as temperate."

Her aunt glanced over to her with a hopeful expression on her face. "That's the spirit, my dear. Perhaps Lord Lendin will not have to cancel your plans, after all—only hold them back a day."

Jane nodded.

"Oh, I almost forgot—this was at your door when I entered. Another clue." Her aunt handed Jane a folded piece of paper, and Jane opened it, reading the words written there in black ink.

With salt of the earth and the kind

What did that mean?

Abigail entered the room the moment after. She held another tray, the same victuals on it as before.

"Good morning, Mrs. Westby. I've brought the—oh, miss! You're awake!" She flashed a grin at Jane as she moved forward. "You look much better, if I may say so. Not as green about the gills."

Jane returned Abigail's bright look with a weak one of her own. "I feel better than I did, as well. I believe my fever has broken. The adder has defeated the eel, in this case."

Aunt Agnes left the room to go inform Lord Lendin and to get her own breakfast, promising to return promptly afterward. Jane forced herself to eat a few spoonfuls of broth, the hot liquid easing her tight stomach. Abigail left to go get her mending, and Jane sighed. She hated being ill, but nothing more could be done for it.

*H*enry entered the breakfast room, finding it almost empty. He'd worn his favorite blue waistcoat and brown tailcoat today, anticipation at spending more time with Jane lightening his step. Mrs. Westby and Miss Wildon were the only others in the room, aside from Mr. Langley. That man occasionally peeked around his paper toward the women as Henry filled his plate with breakfast items. The day was bright—a perfect day to go riding—and the excitement of what was to come made his pulse thrum in his veins.

"My lord."

Henry dropped a piece of ham onto his plate and spun to face Mrs. Westby. He smiled and greeted her. "Mrs. Westby, how are you?" Her turban matched the ocean color of her dress. How would such a color suit Jane? He couldn't help but think any color would suit her very well.

"I'm as fine as can be, although my niece is not." She frowned.

Henry's stomach dropped at her words. "Is Ja—Miss Talbot all right? What has happened?"

Mrs. Westby waved her hand. "Just a minor illness, I assure you. She wished for me to make you aware—she said you'd planned an outing for today."

Henry rubbed a hand down his fresh-shaven cheek. "Indeed. Thank you for letting me know."

"Of course, my lord. I told her that perhaps your plans might be better suited for the morrow." She raised an eyebrow, her expression mischievous.

The tension in Henry's shoulders eased. "I've no doubt of it."

An hour later, Henry strolled Sperrin's expansive gardens, fighting disappointment.

What sort of flowers might Jane like? The topic of preferred flowers had never come up. Birds, yes. Flowers, no. Henry examined the rows upon rows of colorful blossoms, many of which he'd never before seen. All around him, the sweet scents from the blooms filled the air.

These gardens would be quite the competition for a perfumer's shop. A butterfly passed, bringing to mind the first clue to the jewel. The more recent ones complicated matters further. He'd originally believed the jewel to be outside, but what if it was inside? Henry had noticed Jane glancing around at the ruins yesterday, searching, but what if it was nearer than that?

He rounded a corner on the stone path and was greeted by the sight of Lady Sperrin holding a pair of gardening shears, a small bowl beside her.

"Henry," she said with a maternal smile. "What brings you out here?"

Henry returned her kind expression. "Perhaps you might help me with that. Mrs. Westby has informed me that Miss Talbot is not feeling well today, and I'm attempting to determine which flowers she might like in a bouquet."

Lady Sperrin shook her head. "Poor dear. I can certainly help you with that. We've many varieties of flowers—we gather exotic plants on our travels, some of which do very well in our climate. Have you any idea what she might like?"

Henry scratched the back of his neck. "Not really, no. I'm afraid the topic of flowers has never come up in our conversations."

"That's quite all right." She cast her gaze about the garden. "We'll select flowers that remind you of her. What do you think of this one?" She moved toward a vibrant flower with sunset-colored petals.

Henry moved forward to inspect it. "It's very nice, but it's not...her."

Lady Sperrin walked over to the opposite side of the path and pointed at a delicate white flower, the shape of the bloom curved and smooth. Beautiful in a subtle way. If it were human, it wouldn't be aware of its beauty. "How about this one?"

"It's perfect. What is it?"

"A calla lily. Lord Sperrin and I first saw the flower in our travels to Africa. It's very pretty, is it not?"

"It most certainly is."

Lady Sperrin took her shears and cut some of the lilies far down on their stems. "Now, what of the other flowers in this bouquet? What will they be?"

A pale-pink flower caught his eye. "What is this?" He stepped up to it and touched its soft petals. The blush of these reminded Henry of the blush of Jane's cheeks. An enticing hue.

"A begonia. These are originally from South America." Lady Sperrin touched one. "They're one of my favorites."

"Might we add a few to the bouquet?" He certainly didn't want to presume to take some of her favorite flowers from her.

"Of course! There are plenty of them." She took her shears to this plant and carefully snipped a few stems off. She led him a little ways down the path and stopped in front of a group of peach-colored flowers. "These?"

Henry nodded. They were a soft color, mild, like Jane's temperament.

"They're tritonias—also from Africa." Snipping these final blooms, Lady Sperrin handed Henry the bunch of flowers they'd collected. "Would you please give Miss Talbot my regards? I hope she'll feel better tomorrow."

"I will. Thank you, my lady. Truthfully, I hadn't any idea where to start."

She laughed and made a shooing gesture. "You're welcome. Now—go put those in some water before they wilt."

Henry went back inside in good spirits and asked Notham to find a vase to put them in. While his valet did that, Henry had more to do.

On his way to the library, he was intercepted by Mr. Alton,

whose hair was mussed and face bleary. The man near-stumbled from his room and into the hallway Henry was moving through.

"Lendin." He groaned. "What is the time? I fear I've woken rather early."

Henry pulled the watch from his waistcoat pocket and flicked it open, inspecting the face whilst trying to keep the look of amusement off of his own. "Ten-thirty, my good fellow."

Mr. Alton ran a hand through his blond hair, a slightly darker shade than Henry's, and yawned. "Devil take it, I've sleeping to do. Spent too long last night looking for that blasted jewel." The man reentered his room and closed the door none-too-carefully behind him.

Henry stifled a laugh and went on his way.

As he pushed open the library door, he sighed in contentment. This was one place he'd always loved. As he moved toward the shelves on the side of the room, his gaze flitted over tomes of various sizes and shades—some of their spines worn and some pristine. He breathed in that old smell he so loved as he walked farther down the rows. No dust was present here—Lord and Lady Sperrin, it seemed, found the library to be as sacred as he did.

Here it was. He plucked a leather-bound book from the shelf and was on his way in a matter of minutes. Now to surprise her.

~

"Miss?" Abigail peeked past the door of Jane's bedchamber and walked in, holding a crystal vase full of exotic flowers and a book.

"What's all this?" Jane leaned up straighter against the pillows.

"Lord Lendin requested I give these to you." Abigail handed

Jane the vase and set the book on her bedside table. Jane inspected the colorful blooms. They were unlike any she'd seen before. She touched a pink flower which looked similar to a rose but smelled different. The peach-colored blooms were very fragrant and sweet, and the white flowers were smooth to the touch and elegant. She couldn't keep from dragging her fingers over them. Her cheeks warmed. Henry picked these for her?

Setting the flowers in place of the book, she grabbed it and read the spine. *Much Ado About Nothing.* She'd heard of the play before but had never gotten the chance to read it. As she opened the front cover, a piece of paper fell out. She unfolded it and read.

My dear J,

I am so terribly sorry you are feeling unwell. Rest assured, our plans will not be thwarted. If you are better tomorrow, perhaps we might go then. Lady Sperrin helped me to pick these flowers. I do hope you like them—they reminded me of you. While I cannot solely claim the flowers, I can claim the book. I love to read it when I'm unwell and am stuck in bed. If you haven't read it before, it's quite the comedy and will be sure to cheer you. I beg you to feel better soon, for I cannot spend another day listening to Lord Windham's voice. I remain

Ever your dear friend,

H

Jane laughed as she finished the letter, unable to keep the grin from her face. She traced her finger over his masculine scrawl with wide looping letters, her cheeks heating. Henry was so thoughtful. Her heart beat faster just thinking about him. Surprising that he hadn't more friends at the house party if this was how he treated them.

Abigail smelled the flowers. "How pretty these are, miss. You've got an admirer, I think."

Jane cocked her head. "An admirer?" She chuckled. "I assure you, Abigail, that Lord Lendin is nothing of the sort. We're friends—that's all."

Abigail gave a look of disbelief as she raised an eyebrow. "If you say so, miss."

"I can't be too careful after what happened with Mr. Revil." Jane lifted a hand to her cheek. "And Mr. Revil made it quite clear that I've deficiencies."

Abigail opened her mouth to speak, but Jane raised a hand. "I haven't even been asked by a man to begin a courtship, in all of my seasons. If I'm to get a proposal of marriage from anyone, it will be a gentleman's son. Not a lord."

Abigail gave a huff. "If you ask me, that Mr. Revil couldn't see the front of his nose if he had an eyeglass."

"Thank you, Abigail, but I fear he's correct. There must be something wrong with me, for no man—other than my father—has ever shown an interest in what I have to say or do."

"Well, someone ought to wring a fine peal over their heads, if you ask me."

Jane chuckled. "What did I ever do to deserve you?"

She cracked open the book on her lap and began to read. She couldn't look for the jewel in her current state, and she couldn't go on an outing with Henry, but at least she could pass her time in these pages. How long, however, would it be before her responsibilities and worries returned in full?

CHAPTER 13

It was fortuitous that Jane felt very well, indeed, the day after her unexpected illness. She set off with Lord Lendin on horseback, a groom not far behind them. Today, they would have a picnic, but this picnic was bound to go better than the last one she'd had. She shuddered at the thought while her horse followed behind Henry's. Lord Sperrin had been very kind in allowing them to borrow the pair for as long as they needed.

"What a fine day." Henry tipped his head up. "Perhaps even finer than yesterday." He glanced in Jane's direction as she pulled her horse up beside his.

She breathed in the sweet afternoon air. "I believe so. Plum, here, is enjoying herself, and I must say, I am as well." She looked down at the sleek brown-coated creature with her black mane.

Henry grinned. "Just a bit farther, and we'll be there." His horse, Mercutio, seemed to bob his head in agreement.

He led them to a grassy knoll, covered with wildflowers in pink and yellow shades, and stopped, dismounting. "Here we are." He moved toward Jane and held his hand out.

She grasped it lightly but stumbled as her foot caught in the stirrup. She tumbled forward in a most ungraceful manner. One hand grabbed at Henry's shoulder, and the other only caught air.

Henry wrapped his arms around her waist and set her carefully on the ground. "Are you all right, Jane?"

She looked up into his concerned face, her bonnet askew, and her breath caught. Their faces were only inches apart, his arms still settled on her waist.

~

Charming. That was what Miss Talbot—Jane—was. As Henry held her in his arms, he could think of no better place for her to be and no better word to describe her. Her bonnet was tilted to the side, rays of sun dappling the ivory skin of her face. She held her hands near his lapel as a perfect blush crept up to her cheeks.

"Yes." Her voice came out breathless.

He dropped his hands from her waist and took a step back, clearing his throat. "Good. Erm..." The groom that had been following them reined in his horse at a nearby tree. He turned and strode over to the man, his heart pounding in his chest. Something about Jane made him lose all sense. He took the blanket and basket from the groom. "Thank you."

The man—maybe Henry's age—tipped his hat and made himself comfortable beneath the oak tree he had tied his horse to. Back at Jane's side, Henry spread out the blanket and opened the basket, removing the food items within. Lord Sperrin's cook had been very charitable when packing it.

"Strawberry tarts!" Jane grinned in delight as she sat down, arranging her skirts around her. "Though I suppose I should endeavor to eat a sandwich first."

Henry sat next to her and held out a tart. "My dear Jane, there are no rules to picnics."

She grasped it with an eager expression on her face and took a bite. "Mmm...delicious."

She closed her eyes for a moment as though to savor the taste.

Henry grabbed one of his own and bit into it. "Lord Sperrin's cook is a rival for my own, I think."

Jane nodded. "Mine as well. Although, I do have a propensity for indulging in sweet things. My family's cook knows it well."

Henry chuckled and stretched his legs out in front of him, picking up a cucumber sandwich. "Tell me more about your family."

"What about them?" Jane tipped her chin up.

"Anything."

"Well, they are very kind people."

"I do not doubt it," Henry said, eyeing a piece of cucumber and then taking a bite.

Jane shrugged. "They want me to marry well, of course—"

"Of course."

"—but theirs was a love match, you see. They wish for me to have what they have—although I'm unsure of whether they hold onto that hope anymore."

"Why shouldn't they?" Henry plucked a berry from a bunch on a plate.

"I'm no fresh debutante. I—I haven't made a match—never even been asked to go on a ride, except for with Mr. Revil."

Henry wrinkled his nose, a sour taste in his mouth. "Mr. Revil."

Jane laughed, the sound a merry one, reminiscent of a dove's call. "I'm certain he's not so terrible as to warrant that tone."

Henry crossed his arms. "From what you've told me, I'm

certain he is. He led you a merry dance—no man should act thusly."

Jane grew quiet, a somewhat somber look crossing her face. "He disappointed me. That much is true."

After a moment of silence, Henry strived to lift her countenance once more. A picnic was not the place for such a sullen expression. Truly, he wished never to see such a look on her face again, such was its effect on him. "I do wonder..." He repeated the words she'd said on their walk earlier in the week.

A smile curled her lips. "You wonder?"

"I wonder if I could fit more blackberries in my mouth than you." He grinned.

She laughed. "I think you underestimate my abilities, my lord."

Henry pulled the plate of blackberries between them and picked one, examining it between his thumb and forefinger. "I think I could fit...seven-and-twenty."

"Seven-and-twenty!" The exclamation from Jane sounded more similar to a question as she leaned forward to pick up a berry of her own. "We shall certainly see about that." She popped the berry into her mouth and grabbed another.

Henry began doing the same, his mouth quickly filling. Jane's cheeks puffed out like a chipmunk's. There was that brightness in her expression that he'd seen when they'd been catching frogs—a determined contentedness that was unique to her.

A minute later, they both struggled to fit even one more blackberry into their mouths. As Henry tried to shove one past his lips, Jane emitted a strangled cackle, her shoulders shaking with mirth. She grinned, but all she revealed was a mouth full of berries—her teeth out of sight.

Henry couldn't help but grin himself, feeling the juice from the berries begin to drip down his chin as he did so. At this, her smile broadened, and the juice began to drip down hers as well.

He glanced toward the groom to find the man with a bewildered expression on his face—something that made him laugh even more.

Jane valiantly attempted to speak, a hand over her mouth. "Mweye gwa—" She shook her head, laughing all the while, and began again. "Mahweyee gwaa cwany—"

Henry's shoulders began to shake as she tried—and failed miserably—to say something. His purple mouth only set Jane to laughing—or perhaps it was the ridiculousness of their competition—and they were soon doubled over in laughter with tears streaming down their faces and berry juice dripping from their cheeks.

Two minutes later, Henry could breathe once more. Both he and Jane had successfully consumed the berries.

He handed her his handkerchief. "How many berries was it that you fit into your mouth? Perhaps 'gwaa cwany'?"

Jane swiped the handkerchief across her chin and lips, the latter now stained a purplish hue. "What I meant to say was that I got twenty." She laughed. "Only, I couldn't quite move my tongue."

Henry grinned. "Twenty, you say? Then I must apologize, Miss Talbot."

"Oh, indeed?" Jane raised an eyebrow. "What for?"

"For fitting five more berries into my mouth than you." His grin turned sheepish. "Though it appears I overestimated my abilities with seven-and-twenty."

"Congratulations, Henry." Her gaze dropped to his mouth. "I do believe you might soon find that more and more people will be applying your methods in order to achieve the look you've created. Berries to stain the teeth such a hue of purple is a fine method, I think." The corner of her own lips quirked up. "Purple teeth look rather nice on you. Maybe you'll be the next Beau Brummel."

Henry gave a great laugh as she mentioned the famous man

of fashion. "Very clever. And you've even been so kind as to be the first of my followers."

Jane placed her hands over her abdomen and laughed. "At great price to my appetite, as well." Her laughter paused as she gestured toward him. "Those berries have certainly made a mess—or, perhaps it is us who've made a mess of them." She got up on her knees and reached forward with his handkerchief, brushing the fabric over his skin with light strokes.

He froze at the touch, so gentle it was. Her violet perfume wafted over him, in addition to the smell of sunshine and the wildflowers surrounding them. His breath seemed to hold in his throat, chest tight. He looked up into her glowing eyes, her sweet breath upon his cheek, and was transfixed.

She focused on his chin, wiping away what remained of the blackberry juice. "There." She leaned away, though her hand lingered near his face. Jane bit her lip, her expression suddenly worried. "I apologize, my lord. My actions have been bold. I wasn't thinking."

Henry shook his head, eyebrows knitting. Before she could pull her hand away, he captured it in his own and brought it forward, brushing a soft kiss over her knuckles. He thought to do so again, but her quick intake of breath brought him back to the present. He released her hand. "You needn't apologize, Jane. I must admit that any 'boldness' of yours was not in the forefront of my mind. That is—"

"I understand." She laughed, the sound coming out on a breath of air.

But Henry wasn't sure she did. For while her somewhat bold actions had been at the back of his mind, the forefront of his mind was filled with the thought that he'd be content to spend every day alongside her.

But it was too soon to be harboring such affection, surely.

Henry leaned back on his elbow and crossed his stretched-out legs, tabling that thought. Instead, he enjoyed the sunshine on his face.

Jane rested her palms on the blanket behind her back and leaned into them, tilting up her own face to the sun's rays. "Are you often away from your estate?" Her eyelids drooped. She covered a yawn with her bare hand.

Henry squinted. "Not often, no. I visit my friends at their estates, but only on occasion—though I do go to London every season."

Jane regarded him, drawing her mouth to the side. "It's rather odd that we haven't crossed paths there."

He offered a lazy grin and stifled his own yawn. "I'm afraid I'm a terrible dancer. I try to stay away from the crush in a ballroom, should any mamas attempt to have me partner their daughters." He chuckled. "Quite terrible of me—I know—but I think only of their safety."

Jane gave a quiet laugh. "I cannot think you're so bad as *that*."

"Ah, but that's where the problem lies. My dangerous feet cannot be stopped. Their wiles know no bounds." Henry huffed in an exaggerated fashion.

"Really? Let us see." Jane stood from the blanket and brushed off her pale-pink riding habit.

Henry's pulse began to thrum in his ears, and his chest tightened. He swallowed. "I really am terrible at it, Jane."

He traced her gaze to the groom, who now leaned against the oak tree with his head lolled to the side and his hat fallen over his face.

"The groom won't see your dancing." Her voice was reassuring.

If only that were what Henry was concerned about. What was really on his mind was that he'd make an utter fool of himself in front of Jane.

Henry could be elegant at times. Dancing was not one of

those times. But then Jane turned to him with such a compassionate smile, such hope, that he couldn't resist standing from his spot on the blanket.

He wiped his hands together. "Very well, but do remember I warned you."

Jane laughed and grabbed his hand, stepping off of the blanket and onto the soft summer grass. The ground was flat here, so they needn't worry about wayward roots and twisting ankles, at least.

"Have you danced the waltz?" The slower movements of the dance compared to the other ballroom dances made the waltz a safer choice out of doors.

Jane's features softened. "I have."

He took her delicate hands in his own and pulled her toward him until she stood only two hand-widths away. He placed his right hand above her waist, and she placed her right hand in his left, clasped in the air.

Jane rested a tentative hand on his shoulder, her light fingers warm through the fabric of his coat. His heart pounded at their proximity. Her riding habit was soft beneath his palm. She began to hum a sweet tune in three-quarter time.

Taking a quick breath for fortitude, he stepped forward, Jane's feet moving in the opposite direction. She kept her gaze on his, never looking away. Her silent encouragement melted the tension in his shoulders and allowed Henry to move to the music she was humming.

"You're doing wonderfully." She beamed.

To Henry's surprise, he was. Never had he danced so well— not even when he'd taken painstaking lessons with the dance instructor his father had employed. Henry hardly wanted to think of his current success for fear of putting a swift end to it.

Jane continued to hum, and they spun through the wild-flowers at a sedate pace, the field a perfect space with its openness and beauty. The wind carried her hum as it passed, and nearby birds seemed to chirp along to it. Her gaze held him as an anchor held a ship. With those gleaming jewels directed at him, he needn't ever have any fear of floating away.

They slowed to a stop as Jane's song came to an end, the air surrounding them complementing the intoxicating violet scent that emanated from her person. The breeze blew a dark curl into her face, but she moved her hand from his shoulder to brush it away.

"Let me." With the utmost care, he thumbed the curl from her cheek and tucked it behind her ear, his fingers grazing the soft skin of her jaw. She seemed to be holding her breath, then gave a quick exhale as he dropped his hand.

In a moment, she had taken a step back, clasping her hands at her waist. Had he been too bold—done something wrong?

Jane gave a somewhat tight-sounding laugh. "You dance very well, my lord. Indeed, I never would have thought otherwise."

He scratched the back of his head before rubbing a hand over his jaw. "Thank you. It was a pleasure dancing with you. I've never had a better partner."

She gave that tight laugh once more, turning to look away from him.

"Are you all right, Jane? Have I done something to upset you?"

She shook her head, brushing a hand down her skirt. "Certainly not, my lo—you've done nothing to upset me." She sighed, moving back toward the picnic blanket. "Forgive me, my lord—I'm a bit tired."

Henry nodded, unconvinced. "I understand. I'll pack up the basket, and we can be on our way." As he refilled the basket with half-empty plates of sandwiches and fruits, he wondered what had been the cause of her change. Most likely, him. Perhaps he'd been too forward. Too transparent with his feelings.

Was he so obvious? Was his skin so glass-like that she'd seen right through it and into his heart?

He made the groom aware of their wishes to head back to the manor, his thoughts a swirling muddle of emotions and worries.

Jane still bore an uncertain look and a tense set to her shoulders, her posture rigid. Something had occurred—that much was certain.

He had to learn what he'd done wrong so he'd be sure not to do it again.

CHAPTER 14

That evening, Jane focused on the dish in front of her as the other guests talked and laughed around the dining room table. She felt Henry staring at her, but she wouldn't look up. The table was bright with multiple candelabras placed evenly down the center, but the light didn't seem to penetrate Jane's mind. She tried to keep it that way. Thinking was dangerous. It allowed her to begin to explore her emotions, and the emotions of the day—those were even more dangerous.

For now, I'll think of nothing at all. If I do not think, I won't feel the pull to examine my feelings regarding Henry.

Lord Windham sat next to her, and for the first time in their acquaintance, she desired to listen to him spout his haughty nonsense.

"So then I said, 'Sir, you mustn't drink that punch, for you'll find it a bit stronger than usual.' He didn't listen, the fool. He'd had four cups of the stuff within the next half hour and was *in his cups* by the end of the next set."

Jane's fork slipped from her hand as the group listening to Lord Windham's story burst out in laughter. It clattered onto her plate with an off-putting clang. She could practically feel Henry's raised eyebrow from the other end of the table, but she forced her gaze to her left, where Lord Windham was sitting. She'd allowed him to escort her into the dining room this evening, desperate as she was to distance herself from Henry.

The latter had made her feel quite out of sorts during their picnic earlier in the day, and she couldn't risk repeating the "incident" that had occurred a few months prior with Lord Revil. Under no circumstances would she let herself fall in love with Henry.

At her other side, Mr. Langley paused in his conversation with Harriet to glance at Jane in concern. "Are you well? You're rather quiet this evening." This, coming from a man who talked to no one apart from Harriet.

Jane stifled a wry smile and picked up her fork once more. "Thank you for your concern, Mr. Langley, but I assure you, I am well."

He drew his mouth to the side in what appeared to be disbelief, but turned his attention back to Harriet.

Jane poked her fork into a buttered parsnip, though Lady Caroline's grating laugh called Jane's attention to where that woman was seated. She placed a hand on Henry's arm in a familiar manner, igniting a glowing-hot ember in Jane's stomach—a very unpleasant feeling.

She was definitely not going to be addressing that feeling. No, indeed.

Jane nodded her head absently at something Lord Windham was saying but came to regret it when the man said, "Miss Talbot, might you like to visit it with me on the morrow?"

Jane's fork stopped halfway to her mouth, and she turned her head toward him. "Tomorrow?"

"Don't sound so surprised." He chuckled. "There are no guest outings set for the day."

"Erm..." *Think, Jane, think!* "Shall we take a carriage?"

"Certainly not." He narrowed his gaze. "It's much too close to warrant one. I say, Miss Talbot, have you been listening?"

Her cheeks flamed. "I have, my lord—of course! I cannot visit...it...tomorrow." She finally fixed her eyes on Henry, whose head was turned toward Lady Caroline. "Lord Lendin and I are to—to...go fishing."

"A woman? Fishing?" Lord Windham wrinkled his nose in distaste.

"I assure you, my lord, it is all very proper." Her fork followed a slippery piece of carrot across her plate.

"How can it be, Miss Talbot? Fishing is not for the finer sex —not at all. Lord Lendin should know that."

Henry must have heard his name from the other end of the table, for he glanced in their direction, meeting Jane's stare with a raised eyebrow and a hint of concern in his eye.

She tried to be subtle as she mouthed the word *fishing* to him, but his other eyebrow joined the elevated one in a furrow as he mouthed back what appeared to Jane to be *hissing*. With a slight shake of the head, she mouthed the word again. This time, Henry's cheeks reddened to a beet's hue. He lifted a hand to his cravat and pulled at it, averting his eyes.

What in heaven does he think I've said?

Lord Windham snorted from beside her. "A woman, fishing. Ha! Do not tell me, Miss Talbot, that you wish to start riding astride." His tone was more of a question as he smirked her way.

Lady Caroline tittered across the table, then aimed a threatening look in Jane's direction. A chill swept over Jane like a flurry of snowflakes.

"No, my lord." She bit her tongue. It wouldn't do to berate the man at the dining table. Truly, she shouldn't have spoken to him in the first place. And how was she to arrange fishing with Henry? Would he even *want* to go with how she'd treated him?

hen the women left the gentlemen to their port, Henry instantly missed the sight of Miss Talbot. He still had not discovered the reason behind her avoidance of him but aimed to soon.

As the men filtered into the drawing room not long after, with Henry at the back of the line, something behind him caught his attention. Gerald climbed up the white tablecloth. The colorful bird stepped over mostly empty plates and stole a green bean from one of them before flying off with his prize. One of the footmen jumped to try to catch him, but the clever bird avoided capture and exited through a doorway as another servant entered to help clear the table. It seemed Gerald was a bird of many talents.

In the drawing room, Miss Talbot sat in a chair at the corner of the room, a book in hand. As he took a step in her direction, a hand on his arm stopped him.

"Lord Lendin, might I speak with you for a moment?" Mrs. Westby asked, her tone kind.

"Certainly." What would this entail?

She led him to the opposite corner of the room where only Mrs. Hutchins, who was hard of hearing, sat knitting and humming to herself on the settee.

Mrs. Westby faced him, her sober expression relaying the seriousness of the forthcoming conversation. "I do beg your pardon for how bold I'm about to be, but I would like to know what your intentions toward my niece are." She eyed him sternly. "You aren't using her to find the location of the jewel, are you?"

Henry shook his head. "Certainly not!" How could she even suggest such a thing? He opened his mouth to speak again, but she continued.

"I know you aren't like Mr. Revil, of course, but I..." She sighed. "I don't want to see my niece hurt."

Henry nodded. Jane's aunt had watched Mr. Revil take advantage of her. He'd been able to fool them, and Mrs. Westby didn't want it to happen again. "I assure you, Mrs. Westby, that I've no ill intentions toward your niece. She and I have become friends, and I enjoy spending time with her. That being said, I do not believe she holds any affection greater than friendship for me."

Mrs. Westby crossed her arms in front of her, leaning her head to the side, eyes weighing him. "I believe you, my lord— but do not make me regret putting my trust in your hands, for your regret will be far more extensive than my own."

"I will not, ma'am."

She turned toward her niece with an expression of almost motherly affection. "Go ahead, then, my lord."

He bowed, masking the dull prick of pain that poked in his abdomen at the truth of his words. He had been speaking the truth when he'd said that Jane did not hold any affection for him—once or twice he'd thought that perhaps there'd been something of regard in her eyes, but Henry had soon come to realize that his own desires were addling his mind. He made his way over to Jane with these heavy thoughts and sat in the chair across from her, leaning into its soft yellow cushions.

"What are you reading?" He made a quiet inquiry.

She clutched her book tight, appearing almost startled at his presence, but her shoulders eased, and she twisted the book around to show him the spine. "I'm reading about Egypt."

"I see." Henry scooted forward and lowered his voice. "I am sorry."

Jane knit her eyebrows, her honeyed eyes dark. "I enjoy reading about Egypt, my lord."

Henry shook his head, scratching the back of his neck. "No

—I mean—I seemed to have upset you during the picnic, and I—"

"You did no such thing."

"Well, I..." Henry faltered. "Didn't I?"

Jane closed the book and set it beside her, her cheeks reddening. "You did not. Today was lovely. You were so amiable, and the picnic was very enjoyable, indeed. I fear I've behaved abominably, avoiding you as I have since this afternoon."

Henry rubbed his jaw. "Oh." He sat back in his chair. "Pray tell, what was it that upset you, then? Why *have* you been avoiding me?"

Jane cleared her throat and eyed him warily. "I've—well—I upset myself, you see."

Henry shook his head. "How so?" This was becoming more muddled by the minute.

Jane shrugged. "It hardly matters now, but you certainly were not the cause of it." She was being rather vague in her answers, but he wouldn't press her. "I'm sorry for avoiding you. I shouldn't have. After the picnic, my mind was in an odd state."

Henry understood that sentiment—although Jane had been the cause of that, for him. The way they'd danced amidst the wildflowers—

"Henry?" His name on her voice was the sweetest sound he could hear. He looked up from his thoughts to find her staring at him, a tilt to her chin.

"I forgive you, of course." He grinned, her tense shoulders easing at his words.

"Thank you. My actions have been most unfriendly—and after all you've done for me!" She leaned back with a sigh. "What a wretch I am."

Henry opened his mouth to protest this, but she pierced him with her stare, giving him an earnest look. "I appreciate your friendship, Henry. Ever so much."

The corner of his mouth quirked up as his heart sank.

Friendship. "And I, yours." His tone was unwavering, despite the deflation of his spirits.

Was that all he was destined to be? A friend? He was coming to realize that, with Jane, he wanted more. *Needed* to be more to her. They'd only known each other for a week, yet she was already becoming someone irreplaceable in his life. How could one woman so affect him—and so quickly? Henry had always thought love took time to grow, but his heart seemed to be watering the seeds of affection every day. At the rate they were sprouting, Henry's heart might as well have been growing a bunch of carrots.

He feared—very much—that he was falling in love, but he feared even more that it was of the unrequited variety.

CHAPTER 15

The next morning, Jane accompanied Henry down a dirt path leading to the small river that Lord Sperrin had told them traversed his estate, Abigail not far behind. The early-morning sun was just peeking over the horizon.

"When you mouthed that to me over dinner last evening, I didn't think you'd said 'fishing.'" Henry carried a fishing rod in one hand and a metal pail in the other.

Jane adjusted her own fishing rod in her grasp as they walked, tilting her head to the side. "I wondered if that message had become lost in translation. What is it you thought I'd said?"

Henry cleared his throat, his pace seeming to increase. "Never mind that."

As their destination came into view, Jane let the remark pass.

Long grasses swayed along the riverbank, and the dark-blue water shimmered where the sun's rays hit it. Abigail retreated to sit on a shaded patch of grass and viewed her surroundings with an appreciative expression.

"Look." Henry pointed to a kingfisher on an oak branch

overhead, its head angled toward the water as it stood perfectly still. With a quick flick of its short tail, the bird swept down from above and dove into the water, creating a splash in the glass-like waves. A moment later, it spread its turquoise wings and alighted from the water, a small fish in its mouth. Henry squinted. "Unfortunately, I cannot teach you to be as good as that."

Jane laughed, walking to the water's edge to set her net down. "I'm not sure if anyone could be as successful as that."

Henry joined her and laid the pail on the grass between them. He took off his coat and gloves and draped them on the ground as well, rolling up his shirt-sleeves.

Jane also removed her gloves. "So...how does one go about fishing?" She tipped her head up to let the sun's rays shine past the rim of her bonnet. The light breeze fluttered the green ribbons beneath her chin.

Henry pulled a wriggling worm from the bucket. "First, you take a worm and put it on the hook." He did this with his own and then pulled another worm from the bucket and did the same for Jane's. "Many prefer fly-fishing, but I prefer to fish with bait, and the worm acts as that."

Jane nodded, and Henry continued. "Then, you take your line and unwind it a bit from the reel."

Jane followed his example, turning the reel's handle in a counter-clockwise motion. Her line unwound from the bobbin, and the worm dropped to the ground.

Henry grinned as he watched her. "Good! Now, cast your line into the water, like this."

He moved away from her and held his rod with both hands, swinging it toward the river. The hook and worm flew past him and dropped into the water with a plunk. The bob floated up and down in the gentle waves, the little cork not straying far from where it had first landed.

She cast a wary gaze to Henry. "I have a feeling you made that look quite a bit easier than it is."

Henry gave a chuckle, sticking his pole into the dirt so that it stood upright before drawing near. "It'll be easy enough once you practice." He placed his hands on his hips. "You remember how I did it?"

"Yes." Jane took a deep breath. She held the rod at her side and faced the water but paused, looking over her shoulder at Henry. "What if the hook catches on my arm?"

He cast her an earnest look, shaking his head. "It won't. I give you my word."

She bit her lip but turned back to the water, setting her shoulders in determination. She swung her arms as she'd watched Henry do, and the hook and worm jerked from the ground and into the air. They landed nearer to the river's edge than Henry's had, but Jane was pleased with her first attempt.

"Capital!" His face brightened. "You'll be an expert angler yet." Her heart lifted at his joy, as well as her own.

Jane's arms tingled with excitement, and she beamed at him. "Somehow, I cannot believe I've done it."

Henry stepped a few feet toward her, glancing between the river and Jane. "A wonderful cast, to be sure." His eyes were like hot coffee as they met her own.

Jane turned to the water. "What happens now?"

Henry moved back to his own rod and pulled it from the ground, holding it with both hands in front of him as he returned to Jane's side.

"Now, my dear Jane, we wait." He sat back against the sloping riverbank, his legs spread in front of him, and offered her a hand as she found the proper footing and did the same. "We must watch our floats...there"—he pointed—"and see if they dip below the surface. If that happens, we must give a tug on our rod and start turning the handles of our reels clockwise, to wind the line."

"And once the fish is closer?"

"We take the net and capture the fish from the water."

The next few minutes passed in pleasant conversation, Jane enjoying the morning sun and the beautiful day they'd been granted. After about a quarter of an hour, she laughed at something Henry said and started to reply when only one of the floats could be seen above the water. She gasped. "Henry!"

He followed the direction of her gaze and gave a smile. "It's yours! Tug on the line, reel it in, and I shall get the net."

As Henry stood, Jane tugged on the line. Indeed, something much heavier was at the end of it than a worm. She began to reel in it, more resistance tugging on it than she had when unwinding it. The reel pressed into her hand, and the top of the rod began to jerk and bend. The line visible above the surface of the water moved to and fro in awkward and sudden motions.

Jane tugged the reel toward herself, hands gripping tight. She was reminded of a time when she'd witnessed two seamstresses fight over the same bolt of fabric.

Henry returned to her side. "That's it! Just reel a little more, and I'll be able to get it."

She did as he said, her fingers aching from the reeling, and could soon see something moving about at the water's edge, like a large dark blot of ink under the murky surface.

Henry moved toward it, net outstretched. Jane reeled in a little more, and Henry thrust the net into the water and, with a quick flick of the wrist, scooped the fish out. The rod fell from Jane's grip as her hands rose to cover her mouth.

Abigail's stifled cry came from behind. Jane had nearly forgotten she was with them.

Henry grinned and moved closer, the fish flopping wildly about in the net. "You've caught a giant!" His voice was merry.

Jane could only nod her agreement as she took a few steps forward, examining her catch. Its gaping mouth was open, dots freckling its pink sides.

She flicked her gaze between Henry and the fish, the former much more agreeable to look upon. "What is it?"

Henry pushed the net toward her. "A trout." The creature flopped once more, its gills moving in and out.

"It's rather large." Maybe two feet long.

Henry moved toward the bucket. "Indeed. I've only ever caught a few of this si—"

Without warning, the fish gave another flop. Henry's mouth dropped open as the creature struggled free from the net and landed on the ground. It seemed to be aware of how near escape was.

"Oh—" Jane followed the flopping creature toward the water's edge, but the fish thwarted her attempts to recapture it. With a splash, it smacked the surface of the river and sank beneath, its dark shadow speeding away to murkier depths. "Oh."

Henry joined her, net at his side. There was a decidedly doleful expression on his face as he stared at the water. "Your first catch, it seems, has gone awry. I'm terribly sorry, Jane. I should've—"

She touched his arm, giving a quick shake of her head. "For all its efforts, that fish deserves to live, and if you blame yourself for its escape, then—then I will be cross, indeed!"

Henry tried to protest, but Jane pierced him with a look of warning, thinning her mouth into a straight line for extra effect.

The corners of his mouth quirked up, and he chuckled. "Fine—then I will not. I would not wish to arouse your wrath."

"A good decision on your part. Now, there are more fish to be caught, I'm sure." She clicked her tongue. "Where did I leave my pole?"

The rest of the morning went much more to plan than the first half hour, and the look on the cook's face when Henry and Jane brought her their catches was one of excitement, to say the least.

"We've not had fish in nigh on two weeks. Trout is the lady's favorite, ye see, so she'll be right pleased with this."

Jane spoke a bit more with the staff before she made her adieus, Henry following close behind up the stairs from the kitchen.

"Perhaps now, Lord Windham will agree that fishing is a perfectly acceptable sport for the fairer sex to partake in." Henry's tone rang with mirth as they reached the main level.

Jane rolled her eyes at the mere thought of that man. "One can only hope. Thank you for agreeing to teach me how to fish." She glanced at Henry, who grinned in return.

"It's been my pleasure. And it's also been an honor to witness your first catch. To think—I may be the teacher of the next Izaak Walton." He raised his eyebrows in exaggeration, and Jane laughed at his mention of the famous fisherman, the sound bouncing in the hall as they neared the main stairs.

"I'm not so sure of that—not as sure as you, at least—but I will say that you *are* a fine teacher, and not strict and menacing like the governesses of my youth." She shuddered at the thought of her old governess, Miss Barnaby.

It was Henry's turn to laugh. "I shall keep that in mind if I ever need to be employed as a tutor or the like." He waved a hand in front of him and spoke as though reading an advertisement in *The London Times*. "I can see it now. 'A Very Unmenacing Tutor for Hire.'"

Jane snorted, causing Henry's grin to widen. Her heart gave a traitorous flutter at the sight of it, so bright and cheerful as it was. "As much as I'd like to continue this intriguing line of conversation, I must change out of these fishy clothes and into some better-smelling ones before a cat wanders in to bite at my ankles."

Henry grimaced and looked down at his own attire. "Indeed —I should do the same. Might I take you in to dinner this evening?"

A cheeky grin spread across Jane's face. "If Gerald fails to do so, then I suppose you are the next best option."

Henry bowed, a false expression of seriousness congealing his features. "Very generous of you, ma'am."

With that, Jane curtsied and turned, near-skipping back to her room with a lightness that lifted her heart and spirit. Was there anything she wouldn't enjoy with Henry? Come to think of it...would all these activities be nearly as fun without him?

"You seem more chipper today than yesterday, my lord. Have you some idea as to the jewel's location?" Notham peered at Henry from the armoire, holding an emerald-green waistcoat out in front of him.

"I suppose I am, though it has nothing to do with the jewel. Yesterday held doubt, but today holds..."

"Promise?" Notham supplied.

Henry hesitated. "Something of the sort. Perhaps not yet promise, but hope."

"Might I ask why, my lord?" Notham helped Henry into the waistcoat and moved back to the armoire, retrieving a black coat from its confines.

Henry dipped his head, thoughts of this morning's fishing stirring a smile upon his face. "Have you ever met someone who made you feel as though you were on a boat?"

Notham hummed in thought. "A boat, my lord?"

"Yes—as though you were not on solid land—as though the earth were shifting beneath your feet. But then, as the waves seem almost too treacherous to remain upright, this someone looks at you—and everything is perfectly in place, and the waves are mere splashes of an oar, and the boat is just a rowboat, and the sea is only a glassy lake as the sun sets over the horizon."

Notham straightened the lapel of the coat he was holding, his gaze softening. "I think I have, my lord."

Henry slid his arms into the coat's sleeves. "Then you understand perfectly, Notham."

CHAPTER 16

Two days later, Jane held onto a battledore uneasily, turning it over in her grip. The past morning's clue had been *within an oaken wood box,* this morning's clue being *where darkness shrouds it like a mist.* The clues, however, were not what currently occupied her mind.

"I'm not sure about this."

Henry held his own battledore, and the shuttlecock only a short distance away. "You'll do great!" he called back, a grin on his face. He stretched out his arm and dropped the shuttlecock toward his battledore's net, hitting the object into the air. It flew toward Jane, its feathers remaining still as it cut through the space between them. She swung wildly as it came within a few feet of her, but the shuttlecock decided her forehead was a better place to land than the ground. A *thwack* sounded as the feathered weapon came into contact with the space above her right eyebrow, and she scrunched her face up.

"Ouch!" Jane raised a hand to where the projectile had hit, her skin stinging.

Henry ran over to her, concern pulling at his brow. He

reached out as if to touch her arm but dropped his hand. "I'm so very sorry! I—"

Jane began to laugh, lifting her fingers from her forehead. "'Tis nothing, Henry. A bruise might come of it, but I've doubt of even that occurring."

He bent down, picking up the shuttlecock and examining it with a frown. He flicked his gaze to Jane's once more. "You're sure? We may stop playing, if you wish it."

Jane nodded, then shook her head. "No—I mean yes. Yes, I am sure, but I would greatly like to continue our game."

Henry went back to where he'd been standing, once more sending the shuttlecock flying toward her. This time, she was prepared. As the leather-covered cork base neared, she followed its movement with her eyes, striking at a particular moment in its descent.

"Wha-hey!" She cried out in triumph, grinning at the shuttlecock as it arched back toward Henry. He matched her grin and sent it back to her. This time, she had to jump to hit it. She succeeded again, and they continued this volley of hits for some time. Each successful strike of the shuttlecock renewed Jane's exhilaration and energized her limbs. Sweat began to accumulate on her brow and the back of her neck, but she didn't mind, content to continue this game she had never before played.

Eventually, Jane hit the shuttlecock to the far left of Henry. "What shall we play next?" She moved toward him with the joy of exertion and achievement running through her veins.

His hat had fallen off during the game, and his hair gleamed like a guinea under the gray sky's bright clouds. His jacket lay nearby, and his shirtsleeves clung to his arms in a most affecting way. Her heart flipped at the mere sight.

He grinned as he caught his breath, cheeks red. "What other games haven't you played?"

Jane pressed a finger against her chin. "Many, I'd say. Which do you most enjoy?"

Henry propped a hand on his hip and rotated the battledore in his grasp. "I'm quite fond of lawn bowls."

"Perhaps Lord Sperrin has a set we might use."

Henry held out his hand for Jane's battledore. "Let us ask."

Not a quarter of an hour later, nearly the entire party had congregated outside, eager to participate in the game Jane and Henry had proposed to Lord Sperrin. Apparently, Henry was not the only guest who favored lawn bowls. Lord Sperrin rolled the jack across the flat open field beyond the gardens, the small white ball slowing to a stop some twenty feet from the guests.

Jane clasped her hands tighter together. Henry nodded at her, his stance confident. It was easier with just Henry to witness her mistakes, but most of the guests would see if she made them now. *Please, let me not make a fool of myself.*

Lady Sperrin looked over her guests. "Who would like to go first? Might I remind you all that the goal is to roll your bowl the closest to the jack?"

Mr. Langley picked up a bowl, but Lord Windham stepped forward, shoulders raised. "I should like to go first, if no one else desires to."

Mr. Langley propped a hand on his hip, still holding the bowl in the other, but took a step away from the pile of bowls that lay in the grass, his jaw clenched.

Lord Windham selected another bowl and sent it sailing across the lawn, much farther than the jack. "I always forget my strength. Alas—it is my fate."

A noise beside her caught her attention, and Jane turned to see Henry covering his laughter. She chuckled as well but quickly stifled it.

Mr. Langley went next, his bowl curving far nearer to the jack than Lord Windham's had. As he turned back to the guests, he grinned at Harriet, who clapped in a rather more excited manner than the rest of the party. Jane's heart lightened for her. Perhaps her friend had finally found a match.

After Mr. Alton sent his bowl careening out of sight and Miss Apprett nearly lost her bonnet rolling hers, Henry stepped forward from beside Jane, his gloved fingers just grazing hers. A thrill went through her arm, and she fought the urge to shake it. Now was not the time for her unruly heart to act up.

He picked up a bowl, the fabric of his coat stretching over his muscles. A blush stole over Jane's cheeks. Henry eyed the jack for a moment, then swung his arm forward, releasing the bowl. The sphere curved toward the jack in a perfect arch. Finally, it slowed, stopping directly beside the jack.

Henry turned back to the group, eyes wide. Jane clapped alongside the rest of the party. As he stepped back to her side, he seemed to emanate an excited energy. "I've never played so well in my life." He murmured the comment.

She leaned close to whisper, "I think your bowl is even closer to the jack than Mr. Langley's is."

Even now, the man attempted to peer past Lord Windham's hat to the field, squinting against the bright sky. As she turned back to Henry, she realized her mistake of leaning toward him. He looked at her with such warmth, his handsome face just a short distance away from her own. Her breath caught in her throat, and her lips parted. She found that she wouldn't mind very much—indeed, at all—if he were to kiss her.

"I think Miss Talbot ought to go, since she's never played the game before." Lord Windham propped his hands on his hips, breaking Jane from her trance.

She leaned away from Henry and bit her lip, taking a few steps forward. "I suppose..." She stepped with hesitance toward the few remaining bowls on the ground and picked one up.

This isn't too heavy. I can do this. It would only curve a little, which she'd have to keep in mind. She took a deep breath and exhaled, moving to the spot where the others had thrown their bowls—all the while everyone's attention pasted on her. She drew her arm back. A gentle breeze blew by, blowing a curl across her cheek. She brushed it away with her left hand and tossed the bowl forward with her right.

⁓

*H*enry's gaze followed Jane's bowl as it made its way over the grass and began to curve. It looked as though it might stop too far to the left, but it continued to curve until it rested only a few feet in front of the jack. Jane looked over her shoulder at him, her mouth forming an O. The rest of her body stood frozen, even her peach dress holding its exact shape against the steadily building breeze.

He gave her a wide grin and began to clap as her tense shoulders lowered. She offered a half smile and turned around to face the group, curtsying as she did so. His heart did a flip as a surge of admiration filled his chest. She took a few steps in Henry's direction, but Lord Windham stepped in front of her, blocking Henry's view. Henry tapped his foot, crossing his arms. That man was becoming the bane of Henry's existence.

Two more guests threw their bowls, then the bowls were inspected by Lord Sperrin. To everyone's surprise—including Henry's—Henry's bowl was directly next to the jack, with Mr. Langley's only a little behind it in second. Somehow the win felt less than satisfying when, as the group returned to the house for refreshments, Lord Windham commandeered Jane's attention.

⁓

That evening, after everyone had fallen asleep, Henry crept from his room. The corridor was empty. This reminded him all too much of his time spent at Oxford, although his midnight trips then hadn't been for such mundane reasons as this was. He was far tamer of a gentleman now than he had been in his youth, although he still maintained the flame of mischief he'd been born with.

The candle in his hand flickered as he shut his door behind him, his stockinged footsteps muffled on the maroon carpet. The moonlight shone through the windows at intervals down the way with white light spilling through like liquefied pearl. It was a beautiful sight, but he had a pressing matter to attend to. Despite the late hour, he was wide awake. Hunger could do that to a fellow. He frowned. Were the servants' stairs to the left...or right?

Taking a left down the hall, he was met with a narrow set of steps hidden behind a corner wall. He rocked on his heels. His memory hadn't failed him, after all. He descended into the cool darkness, ducking his head so as not to bump it on the way down. His stomach gave a quiet rumble. The strawberry tarts would soon be his. He descended the rest of the steps and moved forward, pausing mid-stride when the clatter of a plate cut the air. He tensed. Was someone in the kitchen already?

He stepped around the corner and poked his head into the darkened room. A lone plate sat on the counter, empty. Beside it was a smoking candlestick. The corners of the room lay in shadow. Nothing else out of the ordinary.

Holding his candle before him, he moved to the back of the kitchen and toward the scullery, from which a quiet rustle emitted. Stepping through the threshold, he turned, nearly dropping his candle in alarm. "You, thief!"

Standing before him in her wrapper with a stricken expression on her face was none other than Jane, half-eaten straw-berry tart in hand. She chewed and swallowed.

"I'm no thief. I didn't steal anything." The brown waves of her hair cascaded over her shoulders like the softest silk as she shook her head. Henry almost forgot about the tarts.

He set his candle aside and crossed his arms, nodding his head at the tart in her hand. "And what about that?"

She shrugged. "I was hungry."

Henry raised an eyebrow. "Then why are you hiding?"

Jane shook the tart at him menacingly. "You gave me a fright! I thought you were a servant or the cook coming down the stairs. What was I to do? I'm not dressed for company."

Henry peered down at her clothing, and his mind caught up with him. He averted his eyes. She certainly wasn't. "I—erm—"

Jane took another bite of the tart, seemingly happy enough to let him muddle through this on his own.

He scratched the back of his head. "I suppose I'll settle for bread."

J ane struggled to take in air at the view of Henry in his shirtsleeves and stockinged feet, his hair mussed. It took her a second for his statement to reach her mind. She handed him what was left of her straw-berry tart, her fingers sticky from the sweet filling. "That's the last one, but I know how you love them. If you came down here for one in particular, then I must share it. It's only fair, as we both gathered the berries."

Henry's gaze was warm as he looked at her, the two of them so close in the small scullery. "Thank you." He took a bite and grabbed his candle from off the table, stepping to the side.

Jane passed him and moved into the kitchen, retrieving her

own sputtering candle. She touched it to the flame of Henry's, and the kitchen was illuminated more. Henry's gaze met hers. His eyes were a swirl of earthy brown tones and rich, warm coffee. As she returned his small raise of the lips, she commanded her heart not to leap.

She had to get out of here.

She bid him goodnight and bobbed a curtsy, fleeing up the servants' stairs and back to her room. Her heart now raced for the victory she'd won. She'd remained unmoved in the face of a man who could never be hers.

She'd been friendly with Henry, yes, but she hadn't pined after him like some lovesick girl. He affected her physically—there was no doubt about that—but surely, that was a natural reaction to his being so handsome and kind. Would any woman be immune to his charms?

Unlikely.

Jane placed the candle on her bedside table. She removed her wrapper, draping it across the chair near the hearth before falling into bed and scooting under the covers.

For the first time in a long time, she need not worry about falling in love with the wrong person. She could school it. She had finally learned! She could continue to be friends with Henry and spend time in his company without the worry of her heart becoming too attached. She could command the traitorous organ now and would only get better with practice.

She closed her eyelids and burrowed further into her pillow, a warmth in her chest. She couldn't be hurt again. Not by Laurence, not by Lord Lendin. So much for her aunt's scheme to match them together.

~

*H*enry finished the tart as the glow of Jane's candle disappeared up the stairs. She never ceased to surprise him. His gaze returned to the kitchen. How warm and inviting it would be during the day. Iron tools hung on hooks near the hearth, and pots were placed on shelves nearby. One of the clues came to the forefront of his memory. *There is aged rock and metal there.*

There was rock and metal *here.* As for the first clue—*You'll find it where the butterflies*—he'd thought that line had spoken of the insect, but what if it really spoke of butter? In kitchens, butter was apt to fly everywhere if something was mixed vigorously enough. And while he'd believed *Lament of broken bones* to hint at some sort of grave, what if actually spoke of the bones within meats cooked within this kitchen? Many animals were brought through here, their bones broken in preparation of being cooked or prepared a certain way.

Henry's heart picked up its pace, his awareness growing. Was this truly the place the jewel was hidden? All was quiet. He was alone. Should he search now?

Yesterday's clue had indicated that the jewel was within a wooden box—oak, to be specific. The tea caddy. Where was it?

He thrust his candle before him and began his search, peering around pans and jars. It wasn't long before he spied the caddy, the ornate edges carved into rope-like curves. He set his candlestick down and held his breath, pulling the caddy toward him. Was this the moment that fate would turn in his favor? He placed his thumb beneath the edge of the lid and carefully pushed upward.

Nothing. He tried to pry it up again, but the lid didn't budge. It was locked. Henry heaved a sigh. Of course it was. Any sensible lady of the house kept her tea caddy locked—the key often worn on a chain around her neck. They wouldn't require him to ask Lady Sperrin for the key, would they? The only other person with a key would be the housekeeper.

He shook his head and slid the box back to where it was originally placed. The jewel couldn't be in there. But, then, where *was* it? After a bit more searching, he decided to head back to his bed, though he'd return another evening. The jewel *was* in the kitchen—that much, he was certain of.

CHAPTER 17

*H*enry was just stepping out of the library to seek out Jane when a commotion came from the foyer. Last night's encounter with her belowstairs had only strengthened his desire to see her. He followed the sound of Lord Sperrin's laughter and voices and lingered in the shadows of the corridor. Who would arrive so late to the house party?

A man of average height grinned at Lord Sperrin, his dark hair styled neatly. "I do appreciate the invite, my lord. I apologize that I couldn't have arrived earlier. My father's health—as you know—is not what it once was, and many of his responsibilities have fallen to me in the meantime."

Lord Sperrin nodded. "I quite understand, Mr. Revil. Think nothing of it. Now that—"

Henry ceased listening to their conversation as he tried to place the name. Mr. Revil...Revil...wait a moment. That was the name of the man Jane had mentioned—the man who'd broken her heart. She hadn't said the words, of course, but Henry had seen it in her small frown and the pallor of her skin. He flicked his gaze back to the man in question. Could this Mr. Revil be the very same? If so, how could Henry prevent Jane from meeting him again and becoming hurt once more?

Truly, what was the man's purpose in coming to the party at such a time? Was he to get the clues they'd received until now all upon his arrival? Did he believe he'd have a better chance at finding the jewel that way? He couldn't have known no one would have found it in the days leading up to now.

The sound of light footsteps came from above as someone descended the stairs adjoining the corridor. Henry took a few steps forward and peered through the rails, catching a glimpse of a lilac-hued skirt and similar-colored slipper. Whoever was stepping down the stairs was about to walk straight into this meeting with Mr. Revil. Henry exhaled in a sigh before straightening his shoulders. Best make it a party.

He strode into the room at the same time the mystery woman stepped from the last stair. He was certainly glad he'd made that last-minute decision, for the mystery woman turned out to be Jane herself. The instant she recognized the new guest, her face turned as white and stiff as the marble statues at the museum in London.

"Jane!" Mr. Revil took a few steps toward her, and she seemed to pull herself from her frozen state, giving a brief curtsy.

Lady Sperrin tilted her head to the side. "The two of you know one another?"

Jane didn't say anything, but Mr. Revil replied, "Indeed. Jane and I are good friends."

Henry frowned. From the way Jane had mentioned Mr. Revil, he had rebuffed her—in some severe way. How could a friendship withstand that?

Henry took a step toward Lord Sperrin, who took his hint.

"Ah, Mr. Revil, have you met the viscount?" Lord Sperrin raised an inquiring eyebrow.

Mr. Revil lifted his own. "Indeed, I have not."

"Then allow me the pleasure of introducing the two of you. Lord Lendin, meet Mr. Revil. Mr. Revil, meet Lord Lendin." Mr. Revil bowed and Henry gave the slightest of nods.

"'Tis a pleasure, my lord." Mr. Revil examined him as he spoke.

The next moment, a whisper of skirts on the stairs drew Henry's notice. Jane had fled the same way she'd come.

~

*L*aurence had come. *Laurence was here.* Jane paced back and forth across the length of her bedchamber, clasping her head in her hands. She'd scurried up the stairs before Henry had been able to talk to her. She couldn't have him asking questions she didn't yet know the answers to— namely, if her heart was affected by Laurence's appearance. Truly, she wasn't quite sure. All she could think about was that *Laurence was here.* At the house party. Where she was also staying.

She flung herself across her bed, the goose-feathered pillows crushing under the weight of her head, so heavy with its torrent of thoughts and emotions. Why couldn't anything be easy? Why couldn't he have stayed at his estate? The Lord knew his family probably needed him there, anyway.

She sighed. He looked the same as he had when she'd left him on that picnic blanket three months ago. His hair was just as neatly styled, and his irises were just as stunning a blue. He'd acted as though he hadn't insulted her—as though he hadn't used her in the most rotten of ways. Her chest ached at the thought of that smile and that exclamation of excitement at seeing her. Could he have missed her? Could he have realized what she meant to him, now that she wasn't in his company? Did she even want him to?

Her eyes stung, and she rubbed her palms against them, curling onto her side. What a mess this was.

A knock came at the door. Jane cleared her throat. "Enter."

Her aunt bustled in and shut the door behind her, placing a cool hand on Jane's forehead. "Lord Lendin made me aware that Mr. Revil is now a guest at this house party."

Jane just groaned in response.

"Indeed, that was my reaction as well." Aunt Agnes sat on the bed beside Jane and patted her arm. "A maid will be coming up shortly with tea, my dear. How are you feeling?"

Jane grunted.

"Do you intend to speak like a cavewoman for the rest of the day, dear? If you do, I'll have to brush up on the lexicon of that language." She tucked a curl away from Jane's face, and Jane turned onto her back to gaze at the ceiling.

"I feel...I don't know what I feel," she said quietly. "Seeing Laurence again is strange. I do not love him as I once did, but there's an ache in my chest at seeing him. It isn't easy to face him again."

The scent of rose perfume surrounded her as her aunt shifted on the bed, smoothing the coverlet beneath her hand and giving Jane a sympathetic look. "No one said it would be easy, dear. I am sorry you have to face Mr. Revil again. It is unexpected. As for the ache in your chest...it will go away. It is only there still because the break was not so long ago. The embarrassment of the past lingers. The pain that he caused left a trail of smoke when the flame went out. Now, we just have to let the wind blow it away."

Jane raised an eyebrow. "The wind?"

A knock came at the door, and her aunt stood up and let the maid in to put down the tea tray. After the servant left, Aunt Agnes turned, a knowing expression on her face and her countenance light. "The wind of change, my dear."

Later that evening, Jane walked nervously down to dinner,

attempting to steady her breathing as her gloved hand skimmed the banister of the stairs. She'd dressed carefully tonight, wishing to appear as though nothing were amiss. She wore her rose-pink evening dress and matching slippers with a darker pink ribbon around her waist. She'd even asked her maid to arrange some small flowers in her hair, with curls artfully placed near her temples.

There was no way Laurence would look at her and think his absence had done a thing to harm her. She'd prove to him —and to herself—that she was unaffected by his presence here.

A footman opened the drawing room door, and she stepped inside. She was one of the last guests to arrive, it appeared.

Aunt Agnes moved forward to grab her hands. "You look lovely, my dear. That color suits you perfectly."

Jane lifted her shoulders. "Thank you, Aunt. I—"

Before she could say anything more, dinner was announced. She searched the room for Henry and found his gaze already on her. He looked dashing in his evening attire with his black coat and white cravat over a gold waistcoat. She began to make her way over to him when a tap on her arm paused her steps. She looked over her shoulder to see Laurence, a smile on his face.

"Jane." He held out his arm. "Might I escort you into dinner?"

Disappointment crawled through her. Henry was offering his arm to Miss Clarke now. She resigned herself to what was sure to be an awkward dinner conversation and took his arm.

He led her into the dining room and helped her into her chair before seating himself. The first course was served, and as Jane tried to enjoy her soup in peace, Laurence turned toward her.

"How have you been, dear Jane? I've missed you." He dipped his spoon into the white broth before him, clearly unaware that, for Jane, all the din around the table had just ceased to exist with his words. She nearly dropped her spoon.

She raised her chin. "Indeed?"

"Do you doubt it?" At his query, he raised an eyebrow, then he looked sheepish. "When you left me after the picnic and were no longer there to keep me company at balls and events and outings, I noted your absence. The longer you are away, the larger an ache I feel within. I regret what I said to you at the picnic, Jane. I shouldn't have. I hold your company above all others."

Laurence was apologizing? He had missed her? She brought another spoonful of soup to her mouth, her mind spinning. She swallowed, unsure of what to say. "Thank you, Laurence." But he'd also asked how she'd been. "I've been busy with the usual balls and soirees—now this party, of course. I'm quite enjoying myself here." Especially Henry and their pleasant outings—his warm expressions and joyous laugh.

"You're smiling, dear Jane, just at the thought. Pray tell, what about this house party is so enjoyable? Perhaps the idea of finding the lauded jewel? A fortune could turn with it." Laurence leaned closer to her with a smile, his shoulder against hers.

She hadn't realized she'd been smiling. "Truthfully, Lord Lendin is helping me rediscover what I enjoy, and it is that which has given me such happiness during my time here."

To Jane's surprise, Laurence frowned at her answer.

From his seat down the table Henry, too, remained unsmiling. Both men appeared to scrutinize each other, expressions grim. Clearly, Henry was also worried for her sake, but what would Laurence find distasteful in him?

*H*enry half listened to Miss Clarke's chatter about her family's estate in Devonshire as he pierced Mr. Revil with a stare. He really should be giving the girl more of his attention—she didn't deserve to be ignored, after all—but he couldn't ignore the intimate way Mr. Revil leaned toward Jane and spoke with her. A burning sensation crept into the depths of Henry's abdomen, lifting into his chest and tightening his ribs. He clenched the spoon in a rigid grip, Mr. Revil's stare meeting his diagonally across the table.

The man frowned. A muscle ticked in Henry's jaw. He didn't have time to interpret the source of the man's discontent. Why should Mr. Revil be unhappy? He was sitting next to the most beautiful woman in the room—the woman Henry had taken in to dinner the past evenings. The woman Henry had wished to take into dinner *this* evening as well.

"Do you not think so, my lord?"

Henry turned his head to look at Miss Clarke beside him, her dark eyebrows raised in question. The spoon loosened in his grip. "I'm terribly sorry, Miss Clarke. Could you repeat your question?"

Henry could've sworn a small huff escaped her, but she did as he asked. "I was speaking of parlor games, my lord. I find them to be entertaining, but I was asking you for your opinion. When my family holds house parties at our estate, we always play them at some point or other."

"Indeed, Miss Clarke, I enjoy parlor games." He flicked his gaze to Jane once more, and Miss Clarke, seeing that he would add no more in response, turned to speak to her other dinner companion, Mr. Langley.

In truth, whilst Henry did enjoy parlor games, he wasn't over fond of them as some of those in the *Ton* were. On occasion, he found the games to be rather too frivolous for his tastes. There were some he liked, however, and he wouldn't mind playing a few in Jane's company. Perhaps she'd enjoy them. It was another excuse to spend time in her company. The party hadn't spent any time at parlor games since it had commenced—likely due to the men's penchant for cards and port. Perhaps if Henry proposed the idea to Lord or Lady Sperrin, they would be amenable.

Port and cigars were a stilted affair that evening, with Mr. Revil taking up much of the conversation and speaking of himself. Henry didn't add anything, only listening to the man drone on as he leaned back in his chair. When they finally joined the ladies in the drawing room, Henry found Lady Sperrin in the corner of the room, talking to a servant about tea. The room was bright with candlelight, and the curtains were drawn, making a cozy area for their party, though it was still spacious enough for entertainment.

"Lady Sperrin, if I may have a moment of your time?"

She patted his arm. "Others may ask for it, but you need never do so."

"I thank you. I was wondering if—instead of cards—we might pass this evening with a game or two. It has come to my attention that others of this party are quite fond of them."

She tipped her head with a twinkle of contemplation in her eye. "That can certainly be arranged."

In short order, the woman had had the footmen push the tables to the sides of the room. She clapped her hands to garner the guests' attention. "This evening, we shall spend our time a bit differently. What does everyone say to a few parlor games?"

A murmur of agreement rose, and the excited guests whispered amongst one another. Henry felt a presence at his side and turned to see that Jane had separated herself from Mr. Revil. His heart lightened.

"I wonder what game we'll play first." Her whispered words brushed against his cheek in a soft breeze, her mesmerizing eyes dancing with excitement as they met his own. His pulse increased at her proximity, her violet perfume filling the space around him. Before he could speak, Lady Sperrin continued.

"Very good. We'll play a few different games this evening, but we'll first start with charades. We'll separate into teams—the men versus the women. Now, divide yourselves accordingly, if you please."

Sharing a commiserating expression with Jane that they had to part from each other so soon, Henry shifted with the men to one side of the room as Jane moved in the opposite direction.

Lady Sperrin dipped her head in approval. "The team who has given the most correct answers after everyone has taken their turn will win."

Her husband spoke up. "And what, my dear wife, will the prize be for winning?"

Lady Sperrin blinked for a moment, clasping her hands in front of her. "The winning team will decide the activity for tomorrow."

This was met with more murmurs of approval from the guests, and soon a thrum of nervous anticipation could be felt. What charade could he possibly choose? He hadn't played the game in a long while. Beside him, Mr. Langley muttered, trying to find a word to rhyme with *rain* that fit into his charade.

The first to stand up was Miss Wildon, whose cheeks reddened as she stepped to the center of the room. She cleared her throat. "My first is a briny, cold, expanse where captains on ships through spy glasses glance. The second is cracked to find inside a sphere so bright, but never dyed. The whole a thing upon the sands where water reaches out its hands."

Lord Windham's forehead creased as Miss Wildon finished her charade, but others seemed to be on the edge of discovering what the answer was.

"Is it a seashell?" Mr. Langley's question came from beside

him, and Miss Wildon nodded with a grin at him, bobbing a curtsy before she returned to the other side of the room.

Mr. Alton was the next to go. "The first is something that under I'll slink if I'm not feeling well after too much to drink. The second is something we use to make shirts, though I've always preferred the soft dresses and skirts." At this line, he glanced at Miss Wildon. Mr. Langley's hands tightened into fists as he stood at Henry's side. Mr. Alton continued. "The whole is something seen daily, when people gather to eat and drink and chatter rather gaily."

Miss Parblot inclined her head. "Is it tablecloth?" And with that, the teams were tied.

This back and forth continued for some time, with the women gradually gaining the lead over the men. Eventually, Henry moved to the center of the room, focusing on Jane. She smiled at him, and his lips raised in response.

"My first an organ in my chest that will not give me a moment's rest. The second a counter to melodies so we all may dance with ease. The whole a thing that grows stronger in a special someone's presence longer."

Jane tapped her foot, a finger pressed to her cheek. Her face lit up. "A heartbeat, my lord."

He kept his eyes on hers for a moment as the room seemed to still. "Indeed."

By the end of charades, the women had won and were eager to plan the next day's activity. Lady Sperrin paused them, however. "We've more games to play, ladies, and time to plan later. Our next game will be Blind Man's Bluff. Since the men lost at charades, one of them will be wearing the blindfold. Remember, if you do not guess who you caught correctly, then you must release them. If you guess correctly, then the person you catch is next to cover their eyes."

Fittingly, Mr. Revil elected to be the blind man, and the rest of the guests scattered about the drawing room as far as they could get from him. Henry didn't stand very far away, only watching the man as he held his arms out and stumbled across the room in a ridiculous fashion. The expensive carpet muffled steps, but Miss Clarke and Miss Appret had the disadvantage, their giggles loud enough to be heard from where they hid behind a potted fern. Mr. Revil stepped toward them, but they were quicker, fleeing on light feet.

Lord Windham stomped across the room to confuse Mr. Revil, who quickly turned in his direction. The man smirked and crossed his arms, turning his head around as though he could see past the cloth covering his face. When everyone had scattered, Jane had moved to the side of the room and pushed herself against the wall. She hadn't moved an inch since then, whilst others around her tiptoed about, even daring to step within inches of Mr. Revil.

Mr. Revil moved toward Henry, who remained in place. Mr. Revil passed Lady Caroline, who stood next to a small table. Was her mouth moving? Something seemed to be whispered and—in a curious change of tack—the man stepped back and to the side, nearing Jane's location. Mr. Alton strode toward him —daring to get close—and danced a short jig, but Mr. Revil's head didn't even turn toward the sound nor the guests' laughter that followed. In one swift move, he darted toward Jane. She attempted to jump out of the way, but he grasped her around the waist with a grin.

"Aha! I've caught someone! A fair someone, at that. Let me see if I can guess who."

Jane bit her lip, and the unpleasant burning sensation Henry had felt at dinner came back to haunt him. Mr. Revil placed a hand on Jane's cheek and moved his hand over her nose and chin. Henry crossed his arms and narrowed his gaze as the man pulled on a curl of her hair.

"Hmm. This woman is fair, indeed." Mr. Revil touched the

sleeve of Jane's dress, the fabric between his fingers. "I do believe this to be...Jane."

The party clapped as he removed his blindfold with a grin. "Ah, my dear Jane, I knew it was you! Rest assured, I'd know you even if I were a blind man."

She gave him a small lift of her lips, her face flushed.

It all seemed too convenient. Mr. Revil had completely ignored Mr. Alton's jig, even though the man had been right in front of him to grab. Furthermore, he'd managed to find Jane, who hadn't moved a single inch during the entirety of the game. It seemed as though the man had been looking for her specifically. As though—perhaps—he'd been told where she was. But why?

CHAPTER 18

Jane's face burned as Mr. Revil released her. She caught Lady Caroline's smirk from where the woman stood across the room. She stood tall—almost triumphant.

"You're next, dear Jane." Laurence murmured the words as he moved around her and covered the top half of her face with the blindfold. Her stomach lurched. She didn't want to be the one to stumble around a room of veritable strangers in an attempt to grasp one in her arms. After Laurence stepped away and the guests fled once more, she took a breath and began her search on unsteady feet. Her sense of hearing heightened at the loss of sight.

"She'll never catch you," a feminine voice whispered across the room.

"She certainly will if you keep chattering like you are." That sounded like Aunt Agnes.

Jane bit back a laugh and took a deep breath. She did know a *few* people in the room, at least.

Footsteps pattered at her side, and she turned to face them, but the person darted away with an exhale. Drat. Perhaps she should be bolder in her advances and move faster to get this over with. Maybe if she jumped at someone? Jane circled the room—she imagined that's what she was doing, anyway—and reached her arms out. A few giggles sounded around her and a gentleman's chuckle or two, but she grasped no one.

She didn't want to be doing this longer than necessary. More drastic measures were needed. Jane stopped abruptly and turned in a random direction. *Please let me not be facing a wall.* With a breath of courage and uneven steps, she ran directly forward, arms out and ready to receive.

"Ooof."

A few gasps sounded around the room as Jane hurtled into the mystery person, their arms going around her waist as they teetered on their feet. She might have caused a scene, but this was much better than being splayed across a card table with a bruise lining her middle. Whomever she'd run into, they hadn't expected this. The broad arms and chest suggested a man. The coat beneath her fingers agreed with this assessment.

He removed his arms from her waist as though fire had touched him, but she held onto his arm to keep him in front of her. Trailing a hand up his coat, she touched his cravat. "Simply folded. This person is no dandy."

A few chuckles came from behind her, but the man remained silent. She raised her hand to his face and brushed her fingers along his chin and cheeks. There was the sand of stubble there, likely grown only after this morning's shave. His face was warm—he must be as embarrassed as she. Jane moved her hand to his eyes and nose and tried to picture what his face might look like, then raised her hand to his hair to feel the texture. It was wavy, with a bit of a curl to it.

Jane's left hand remained on his arm, and the man did not so much as shift during her inspection. Was he breathing at all? At the thought of breathing, Jane inhaled and caught a whiff of the man's cologne. It was familiar. Bergamot and sandalwood. Henry.

Suddenly, her mouth dried. Her cheeks flamed. *She had touched his face.* She cleared her throat and clasped her hands in front of her, stepping away. The man exhaled as though he'd been holding his breath the entire time.

"I—I do believe this to be Lord Lendin."

There was a pause before Lord Sperrin's voice sounded. "Correct, my dear!"

Jane removed her blindfold. Henry's cheeks were as red as hers must be, and he looked somewhat undone. She'd wrinkled his cravat, and his hair was skewed to the side. What was far more interesting were his earthy eyes—so dark—fixed on her with such emotion behind them. What was it he wished to convey? Had she upset him? Been too forward with her actions? She had, after all, run into the man. Had he not steadied them, they surely would have fallen into a heap upon the floor.

Jane bit her lip and looked away, catching a glimpse of the fiery glare Lady Caroline sent her way. If the woman's mouth pulled down any farther, it might stick that way.

Oh, dear. When would Jane stop making such mistakes? When would she stop erring in society?

The games lasted well into the night, groups in separate corners with Lady Caroline seeming to become fast friends with Laurence—even Lord Windham joining their chat. Truly, their conversation was so involved, they didn't appear to notice what was going on around them.

Miss Apprett read in the corner, and Mr. Langley never strayed far from Harriet. Lord Sperrin watched over the proceedings and spoke with the guests of more middling age.

By the time they were done, everyone was rather tired of the shuffling of decks and feet. Some of the gentlemen ambled off to play cards and billiards, but Jane only wished to retire. Aunt Agnes had long ago claimed fatigue, leaving Jane under the watchful eye of Lady Sperrin, who was now looking worn out herself.

Jane stifled a yawn and brushed out her skirts, standing from where she'd settled next to Harriet on the settee. She caught Lady Sperrin's attention, who moved over.

"I think I'll retire, my lady. I'm feeling rather worn."

Lady Sperrin took up her hand and patted it. "I don't blame you, dear. It's getting late. Would you like me to send a maid up with you?"

Jane shook her head. "That's not necessary, but I thank you all the same. I shall be fine."

With murmured good evenings, Jane made her way to the door. She paused at the sight of Henry, standing beside it, and gave him a tired twist of her lips.

He bowed over her hand. "Good evening, Miss Talbot. Pleasant dreams."

As she made her way up the stairs, she frowned. Throughout the evening, she'd found Henry's solemn gaze on her more than once, and yet, he'd smiled just now and had been congenial. Perhaps he wasn't upset with her about the incident during Blind Man's Bluff? If that were the case, however, then what was Jane to make of his stare? And what was she to make of his subsequent reaction to the game? For after their collision, he'd been distracted—not only for the rest of that game in particular, but for the rest of the evening.

The carpet muffled the sound of her slippers as she walked down the corridor toward her room. Odd... Where candelabras would burn in bright arrays along the wall, interspersed with paintings, there were cold wicks and dark shadows. Jane shivered, wrapping her arms around herself. Perhaps the servants put them out after a certain hour.

As she neared her room, a floorboard creaked ahead. Jane paused. "Is someone there?" She spoke softly for fear of waking sleeping guests.

The sound did not come again. She bit her lip. It must have been the creaking of an old house. That was all. She took another two steps forward, the hair on the back of her neck standing up. Something didn't feel right. Her stomach was tight, her shoulders tense. She looked over her shoulder but could only see the dim outline of the corridor, illuminated from the sliver of moonlight that slid through the windowpanes.

She was being ridiculous. It was late, and her fatigue was making her anxious. She let out a great exhale and moved to her bedroom door. The tapestry beside it billowed, but there was no window to make it do so. Her stomach clenched.

"Who—"

Strong fingers pinched her arm. A figure emerged from behind the woven material, jerking her toward him. The man's other large hand covered her mouth. Her mind shouted at her to do something, but her body remained frozen. A scream gathered in her throat.

"Shh. No need for that." Her assailant's breath reeked of spirits. Dropping the hand over her mouth, he spun her to face him, then gripped both her shoulders. Though she struggled to identify his features in the dark, Jane knew that voice. Arrogant and cold—Lord Windham. "We'll just have a little chat, you and me. You know where the jewel is, and I know that you know. That's why they seek you out—your *admirers*."

Her body trembled as her veins filled with ice. Anxiety washed over her as though someone had poured a bucket of water upon her. "I don't—"

"Tell me where it is, and I'll let you go." He pulled her toward him, the moon caught in his eyes as though he'd stolen it and placed it there. It cried to be released. He didn't deserve to have the light there. He was too evil—his irises were too dark. He had a serpent's gaze. Black. Unfeeling. Unseeing.

Once more, her mind called out for her to act. *Do something!*

She thrashed wildly in his arms, fighting like a caged bird

flying into the metal wires of its enclosure. She breathed in a lungful of air to scream.

He smacked a hand over her mouth.

Jane blinked, lightheaded and dizzy. She stomped her foot as hard as she could on his.

He swore and loosened his grip, which allowed her to bring her knee up between his legs. He doubled over with a groan.

She threw her body weight against him to knock him down, her breathing shallow. Without looking back, she leapt over him and ran into her room, locking the door behind her.

Abigail sat on the bed looking bleary, but she shot up in alarm upon Jane's entrance. "What happened?"

Jane took another step into the room before grabbing one of the ornately carved bedposts and crumbling to the floor in a heap of sobs.

~

Henry had just taken off his boots when a knock came at his door. Rubbing a hand down his face, he moved to answer it. It certainly better not be Langley attempting to persuade him into a late night game of chess again. The Lord knew they had played way too far into the morning the last time. When he creaked open the door, it wasn't Langley who looked at him, but a maid—a vaguely familiar one, at that. He leaned back at her appearance, but before he could ask her purpose at his bedchamber door, she spoke.

"I'm sorry to disturb you, my lord, but Miss Talbot requires your presence. The matter is most pressing." The maid looked back and forth along the corridor as she murmured the words, and Henry's heart rate picked up. What had happened that Jane would send her maid to him at such an hour to request his presence? Such a thing was never heard of.

He ran a hand through his hair and opened the door wider. He'd already told Notham to retire, so he exited the room on the heels of the maid and closed the door behind him, following her down the darkened and deserted halls at a quick pace.

Henry's heart thumped in his chest as his mind raced with the possibilities of why he was being summoned by Jane.

Finally, they reached her bedchamber door, and the maid knocked. A shuffle sounded from behind it, and there was a pause before it opened, the candlelight from within illuminating the corridor. When the door opened enough for Henry to see Jane's face, he sucked in a breath. Her eyes were puffy and red, and tears streamed down her mottled cheeks. His heart fractured at the sight. Her pain was his pain.

The maid looked left and right down the corridor before ushering Henry inside. "Come, quickly."

The moment he stepped over the threshold and into the room, Jane fell into his arms, her crying muffled by his waistcoat. He'd discarded his dinner coat in his room. Henry wrapped his arms around her and held her to him in a tender embrace. She felt like she was meant to be there, just as she had when she'd run into him during Blind Man's Bluff.

Her shoulders shook with her shuddered breaths as she clung to him, her hands gripping tightly at the golden silk. He ran his hand down the back of her head, the soft clove-colored tresses flowing like water beneath his fingertips. He'd never felt her hair before. Half of it was still up in pins, and the other half was down around her shoulders. She still wore the gown she'd worn at dinner.

The maid stood in the corner of the room, head down, but Jane bid her to go wake her aunt.

After the girl left, Henry leaned closer to Jane. "What happened?"

Her sobs renewed, and she curled into him even more. He

whispered reassurances into her ear and continued to run his hand down her hair, holding her close. Eventually, her shudders subsided and her breathing evened.

"Are you hurt, Jane? Are you sick?"

She leaned back to look at him with pale visage and stricken stare, still gripping his waistcoat in a tight grasp.

He rubbed his hands up and down her arms to encourage her.

Haltingly, she explained to him all that had happened after she had left the drawing room that evening, and Henry's blood began to boil. What a cad Lord Windham had turned out to be—even more so than Henry had originally thought. An utter jackanapes, through and through. Never in his life had he felt more anger toward anyone. Never had he more desired to plant someone a facer—to call someone out, even. Lord Windham deserved it. But that was not what Jane needed. Jane needed him to be there for her. To comfort her. And Henry would.

He gazed into her beautiful eyes—so reminiscent of a milky cup of tea or a light autumn leaf. He lifted a hand to caress her jaw, and she blinked, taking a moment to settle into his palm. Her skin was as smooth as the petal of the calla lily he'd gifted her earlier in the week, though she smelled sweeter by far.

"I am here. I will keep you safe, Jane. You've no need to worry about Lord Windham. He will not hurt you again. I'll send him away."

Jane bit her lip and turned her head away. "You can't promise that, Henry."

He guided her face back to look at him. "You must believe that I will do my utmost to make it the truth."

"I believe you. But you mustn't tell Lord or Lady Sperrin. I am too ashamed." She mimicked his action and put her soft hand on his cheek, causing him to lose his breath.

He inhaled slowly. "I will not, but you must speak to your aunt."

"Thank you, Henry. Thank you for coming to me. I didn't know who else to talk to about this. I—I just...knew that I wanted it to be you who held me. I wanted it to be you who listened."

Henry's heart galloped at her words and her touch. Electricity seemed to spark within him as he was pulled toward her by a force unknown to him. If he didn't separate himself from her soon, he would do something unwise—like kiss her. As much as he wished to do so, now was certainly not the time.

He compelled his hand to drop from her face, and hers dropped accordingly. "You should rest, Jane. It has been a long evening. Sleep will do you well." He took a step toward the door. "Thank you for trusting me enough to tell me about this."

Jane moved toward the dressing table. When she reached it, she paused, looking back. "I'm not sure I've ever lacked trust in you, my lord—only myself."

CHAPTER 19

Three days after the attack, Jane spied Laurence from her bedchamber window with the gardener, cutting flowers from the rose garden. She glanced around her room at the two bouquets he had already given her—one on her dressing table and one at her bedside—and wondered, not for the first time, what his purpose was in sending them.

When he'd rejected her those months ago, he'd made it clear he'd no interest in her, but now, it seemed almost as though he wished for more. Could he still feel guilty about the cruel remarks he'd made? Perhaps that was what the bouquets were all about. He wished to clear the air between them. She couldn't erase the words he'd spoken to her from her mind, no matter how many vases of flowers showed up at her bedroom door.

Jane leaned toward the bouquet at her dressing table and inhaled the sweet perfume of the coral roses. It was a nice thought, to be sure. Laurence seemed to be making an effort. She'd do well to treat him in a warmer manner, she supposed. After all, he had expressed his regret for the way he'd reacted at their picnic, and did not everyone make mistakes at some point or another?

Exiting her room, she tucked her hands in the fold of her skirts as she took brisk steps toward the library. Henry was sure to be there this time of day. She could rest in the knowledge that Lord Windham had left the house party, and no one knew the true reason why except for Henry and her aunt.

As she walked along the hallway, she passed Aunt Agnes, who joined her with a subtle look of concern. "Good afternoon, my dear. How are you?"

As they rounded a corner in the hall, Jane wrinkled her nose, then said, "Better, now that *he* is gone." Henry had ensured that Lord Windham had left the Sperrin's home by that morning.

Her aunt's mouth turned down. "We could leave, you know. Return home, just to be certain of your safety."

Jane shook her head. "The jewel. I'm close to finding it." And it truly felt as though she was. Though she'd been spending much of her time with Henry, she'd been paying attention to the daily clues as well. She had an idea of where the jewel was. She only had to search the area.

"It's not that important, my dear. It's only a gem. You are putting yourself at risk." Distress laced Aunt Agnes's voice.

The problem was, the jewel of Parcathia was not the only reason she wished to remain at the Sperrins' country estate. The real reason was living and breathing. Henry. If Jane returned home, would she ever see him again? She couldn't help but think it unlikely. Their meeting in the first place seemed too good to be true. As much time as she could spend with him, she wished to.

Jane bit her lip. "I know, Aunt, but...I will not forgive myself if I leave just yet."

Aunt Agnes let out a heavy sigh as they reached the library doors. "If I see him again, my dear, I'll be getting out the dueling pistols myself. I'm something of a crack shot, I'll have you know."

Jane grinned and entered the library. Henry lounged in his usual chair. The sun shone on his wavy hair to make it look like spun gold, and her breath caught in her throat. One leg was crossed over the other as he gazed with interest at the leather-bound volume in his hands.

Jane moved toward him—her aunt opting to peruse the shelves of old tomes—and smiled as he glanced her way. He made to stand, but she swished her hand, signaling that he needn't stand on her account. She made her way to his chair and peered over his shoulder to catch a glimpse of what he was reading.

"*Hamlet*?"

He rested his head on the back of the chair and lifted his chin to eye her, the morning sun shining in from the large windows. The dark-blue of his coat contrasted the silver of his waistcoat, the fabric finely embroidered. "You don't enjoy Shakespeare, Miss Talbot?"

She held her hands together. "I do, but I would've guessed you'd much rather enjoy one of his lighter works. Perhaps a comedy."

He grinned, causing her heart to stutter. "Indeed, *Twelfth Night* is my favorite. I do find, however, that reading tragedies makes our own situations seem that much better. I, for one, am quite happy that my father is not a ghost to haunt me. I am also happy that my dearest love has not drowned in a river and that my uncle does not wish to kill me. It makes my life seem rather mundane—a thing for which I am fortunate. "

Jane chuckled and sat in the chair next to his. "I suppose that is true. We take for granted how good our lives are until we think about how bad they could be."

"Indeed." He frowned lightly, then lowered his voice. "An attack, however, is not so mundane. I do wish to look into Lord

Windham's background. Perhaps he's done this before. I could go to the magistrate—"

Just at that moment, Laurence burst through the library doors with a vase of flowers in his hands and an eager expression on his face. His black hair was combed as neatly as could be, and his coat was perfectly unwrinkled.

"Jane! Just the lady I was looking for." At the sight of Henry, his smile faltered. "Lord Lendin." He gave a short bow.

Aunt Agnes came out from behind one of the shelves of books. "What is all this ruckus about?"

"Ah, Mrs. Westby, you're here as well. I have brought some flowers for your lovely niece."

Jane stood and took the vase from Laurence, bringing the flowers to her face to smell. "How thoughtful. Thank you, Laurence."

Aunt Agnes crossed her arms and raised an eyebrow. "Indeed, that is very kind, Mr. Revil."

Laurence puffed his chest out. "Yes, well, Jane deserves them." He meandered toward the bookshelves, and Jane shared a look of surprise with her aunt. She turned to face Henry, but he had his book open once more, his jaw clenched. His shoulders appeared tense as he turned over the page. Was Laurence the reason for Henry's instant withdrawal?

Jane moved to ring the bell and had a maid bring the flowers to her room, then settled back into her chair. Not a few moments later did Laurence appear once more, this time with a book in hand. She didn't like where this was going.

He grabbed her hand and pulled her from her seat, leading her to a small settee near the corner of the room, where they were forced to sit much too close. She brushed her hands over her skirt and tried to shift farther from him on the cushioned seat. He brought her hand forward and placed a kiss there before clearing his throat and showing her the spine of the book he held.

"Byron." He tipped open the cover and flipped the pages to one in particular. Leaning close, he read the poem in a clear voice.

> "Away with your fictions of flimsy romance;
> Those tissues of falsehood which folly has wove!
> Give me the mild beam of the soul-breathing
>   glance,
> Or the rapture which dwells on the first kiss of
>   love.
>
> Ye rhymers, whose bosom with phantasy glow,
> Whose pastoral passions are made for the grove;
> From what blest inspirations your sonnets would
>   flow,
> Could you ever have tasted the first kiss of love!"

Laurence continued to read the poem, and all the while, Jane struggled not to wrinkle her nose in distaste. She found Byron's poetry to be most unpleasant. It tended on the side of vulgarity and often included underlying messages and meanings of—well—things not meant for polite company. Besides that, Byron himself was known to dally with women, and there were even rumors that he'd entered into an affair...with his own stepsister. He'd left illegitimate children on almost every corner of London, and yet, here was Laurence reading to her one of the man's poems as though the poet even knew the definition of love.

Henry, who sat not too far away, held the book he was reading in a white-knuckled grip. Lord Windham's attack really must have set him on edge.

Laurence brought her attention back to him. "Byron never fails to lift the spirits, don't you think? He uses words to paint such inspiring portraits of love and beauty."

"I suppose," Jane murmured.

"Of course, Byron pales in comparison to your presence. You never fail to improve my mood, dear Jane. Indeed, only this morning was I having a poor start when the thought of you entered my mind." He opened his hand. "Immediately, my heart was lightened, my troubles forgotten."

"And what was it that so troubled you, my lord?" Jane allowed a measure of curiosity to tinge her tone.

Laurence pulled at his cravat. "I lost at cards last evening, I must admit. A rather unsavory business."

A snort sounded from across the room where Henry was seated, catching the attention of both Jane and Laurence. He wasn't looking at them, however—still reading the pages of the book he held.

Jane returned her attention to Laurence. "Was it so very bad a loss?"

Laurence gave a sheepish grimace. "Not...so...very bad. I suppose it is thoughts of the estate that worry me more." He lowered his voice. "My father was not well when I left."

Jane frowned, confusion blossoming in her chest like the flowers in the vase he'd given her. "If your father remains ill—indeed, if his health is failing him altogether—then why would you come here, Laurence?"

A half smile pulled at his mouth. "To right the wrong I have done."

No waver was in his voice as he spoke the words. Was there any chance at all they were spoken in truth?

CHAPTER 20

*L*ater that afternoon, Henry watched Gerald as the parrot flew from one end of the billiards room to the other. He climbed up the plum-colored drapes with ease, using his large beak to grab onto the fabric. Then he swooped over Mr. Revil's head to land near Mr. Alton as they played a game, the latter ignoring the bird as he focused on hitting the ball before him.

"Blazes!" Mr. Revil crouched with a hand over his head. "Why does Lord Sperrin keep this bloody bird in the house?"

Henry hid his grin behind his hand of cards, signaling for Mr. Langley to go. They were stationed in the corner adjacent to the billiard table and had a perfect view of the disgruntled man.

Mr. Alton shrugged, blowing a piece of blond hair from out of his face. "S'pose he likes him, is all."

Mr. Revil scoffed. "Like? What's there to like about a bird? They're loud and obnoxious and are dirty animals. You never know where it's been." He leaned over the table to take his turn.

Mr. Alton looked at Gerald with admiration in his eye. "I think he's quite nice. 'Haps I'll acquire my own. I've heard the

Duke of Wharton has taken to bringing his parrot with him to balls. Quite well-behaved, they say."

Henry played his hand. "The duke or the bird?"

Mr. Langley chuckled across from him.

Mr. Alton pursed his lips, looking out the window. "You know, Lendin, I can't say."

Gerald flew overhead again, and Mr. Revil missed his shot, letting out an oath. This was almost better than seeing the man's expression of irritation when he'd noticed Henry in the library, this morning.

When Mr. Revil had brought Jane flowers and begun to read such drivel as Byron to her, that burning had started in Henry's stomach. The man had leaned too close to her, his grin too wide. His kiss on her hand had been too long, his hair too neat. The problem was, he was...not Henry—and that rankled —for Henry was no longer falling in love with Jane. He was *in love* with Jane. There was no denying it. She had stolen his heart as easily as Gerald had stolen a green bean off of the dining room table, but he couldn't yet tell her. Surely, he'd scare her off with the suddenness and ardency of his feelings. Still, he *would* tell her before they parted—certainly before Mr. Revil could intervene.

And should that man's attempts at courting Jane continue, Henry would not hesitate to resort to relearning a few of the things he'd been taught at school. After all, all was fair in love and war, and Henry intended to win Jane's heart.

Gerald flew over to Henry and croaked at him. "Lendin."

Henry ruffled the feathers of the bird's head and gave a small smile. Yes. If Mr. Revil continued, Henry knew just where to start.

*T*he next morning, Henry gaped as Jane entered the dining room looking radiant in a light-blue dress. Her hair was pulled into a knot at the back of her head with small ringlets framing her face. He closed his mouth and stood up, just remembering to bow.

But...she was not alone. Mr. Revil entered on her heels and was all too pleased to fill a plate for her with items from the side table. Henry suppressed a smirk, though, as the man put items on the plate which Henry knew Jane disliked. Such was the evidence that Mr. Revil didn't know Jane as well as he made a show of doing.

Miss Clarke and Miss Apprett sat at the other end of the table, chatting in quiet tones, and Miss Wildon's father hid behind a copy of *The Times*. Mr. Revil, having breakfasted in his bedchamber the past few days, had not yet been made aware that Lord and Lady Sperrin, very affectionate of their dear Gerald, allowed him to roam the house where he wished, and he could be called with a simple whistle. Indeed, the bird must have slept late this morning, for he was normally here by now of his own volition.

He would be soon. Henry grinned, refilled his cup of tea, and started to whistle—a little louder than normal, but not loudly enough to cause suspicion. Jane looked over her shoulder at him with a raised eyebrow and an amused expression on her face. He only met her look with a quirk of the lips.

Mere moments passed before a scuffle occurred at the door, and the footman muttered something that sounded like, "Oh, very well." The door to the breakfast room opened, and Gerald was presented on the footman's arm. At the sight of the feast before him, the bird gave a happy squawk and flew to Jane's shoulder as she stood next to the victuals.

Mr. Revil backed away, holding the plate of food in front of him as a shield as a look of disgust spread across his face. "Dear Jane, you'll let that thing step on you? Think of where it's been!"

She chuckled, raising her hand to cover her mouth. "I'm sure Gerald's been exactly where I have—the drawing room, the dining room, the—"

"Strawberry." Gerald walked with careful steps down Jane's arm. She held it out to make the journey easier for him. The bird tilted his head to eye the plate Mr. Revil was holding, once more croaking, "Strawberry."

Henry watched in delight.

Backing away with slow steps, Mr. Revil frowned. "No. No, that is not for you to eat."

"Strawberry." Gerald perched on the end of Jane's hand now, leaning as far toward the plate as he could, attempting to use his beak to grab the fruit.

Mr. Revil moved the plate a bit nearer, but just as Gerald made a grab for the strawberry, tugged the plate away, a smirk on his face. "Stupid bird. I've always believed they were unintelligent creat—"

Gerald took off from Jane's arm and landed on Mr. Revil's in the blink of an eye, cutting off the man's words. The bird made another reach for the strawberry, but Mr. Revil shook his arms in a fit of panic, attempting to get Gerald to fly away and—in turn—sending the food on the plate careening in every direction. "Someone get this devil off of me!"

Gerald flapped his wings to keep steady, remaining unperturbed when such a prize was still in sight. He hopped forward, his scaly feet planting into the kippers, and plucked the strawberry off of the fine dish, flying in a victory circle around Mr. Revil's head.

Henry choked on a sip of tea. Miss Apprett covered a giggle, whereas Miss Wildon's father behaved as though this was something he witnessed on a regular basis—merely turning another page of the newspaper. Jane stood back, her mouth opened wide as Mr. Revil swatted at the bird.

"Bloody pest! Where's my gun? I'll shoot the blasted thing!"

Gerald landed near Henry's plate with his strawberry, picking it apart and making an utter mess of the tablecloth. He was certainly no favorite of the maids. Mr. Revil would not be either. Eggs and kidneys littered the floor. A kipper had even managed to stick to the wall.

"Surely, you cannot blame Gerald for the mess you've created, Mr. Revil." Jane held her hands on her hips.

Mr. Revil threw his hands out, still holding the plate. "The bird's a menace! He—"

"—only wanted a strawberry. And I would gladly have given it to him, had you handed me my plate to do so. You taunted the poor creature for no reason but your own pleasure, sir. That, I cannot abide."

She pivoted to ring the bell for a maid, leaving Mr. Revil standing there, open-mouthed and anger coming off of him in waves. Henry went to the breakfast table to fix Jane a new plate, quite happy with the outcome of Gerald's appearance.

The men went out to hunt that afternoon, with the ladies remaining behind to take tea and paint. As Henry's hunting skills were lacking and the men should—perhaps—be allowed to bring back a buck or two this time, he opted to refrain from the hunt. Fortunately, this allowed him time to do a little digging into Lord Windham's past.

He'd written a letter to one of his friends the morning after Jane's encounter with the man, inquiring as to Lord Windham's background and other possible incidents of the same nature. According to his friend, there was a maid living in a neighboring county who had experienced something similar to Jane at Windham's hands—though she'd fared worse and been sent from his home without a reference when the consequences of his actions were made known.

Henry walked to the stables and there called for a horse to be saddled. It would be quicker to ride on horseback than in a carriage, and he didn't have time to spare. After all, he was supposed to be making sure Jane was safe. With Mr. Revil in the house, she might be in even more danger than before.

With a flick of the reins, he was off toward Hampshire and the woman's cottage, the stones of the drive crunching beneath the horse's hooves. He wouldn't be gone for long. If anyone found the jewel while he was away, so be it. Jane was worth more—far more—than any gem.

~

Where was Henry? Jane hadn't seen him since yesterday morning, and it was now afternoon. She turned another page in the book she was reading, the words a blur as much as the library around her. She'd come here to seek him out on the off-chance he might be hiding, but the room was empty. Had he given up the search for the jewel without telling her? Had he found it and left, prize in hand?

She frowned. He wouldn't have done that, surely. And the Sperrins certainly would have told the guests if the jewel had been found. There was no point continuing the party and the clues otherwise. She sighed and closed the book, placing it on a table beside her. She might as well do some searching of her own if Henry was nowhere to be found. Perhaps that's what he was doing this very minute, and she was only acting the ninny, waiting like a dog for its master to return.

She propped her hands on her hips, frustration growing within the pit of her stomach. Was this what she'd become? Someone who waited on another for protection? Someone who relied on another to be happy? Indeed, it would not be so.

Even with Lord Windham gone, she wasn't going to be foolish enough again to traverse the darkened halls at night.

She could protect herself, as long as she made wise choices. And Henry? It made sense that Henry wished to spend a bit of time searching for the jewel. That must be why she couldn't find him. After all, he hadn't spent much time searching for it up to this point—not to her knowledge, anyway. Truly, Jane should be looking for it herself. It was one of the main reasons she was at this house party in the first place.

She brushed her hands down her skirts and moved to the doors of the library, peeking out to make sure Laurence wasn't in sight. The Lord knew he'd been attempting to make up for his cruel words at the picnic at her estate, but she couldn't have him at her side whilst she searched for so priceless an item. She crept down the hall toward the servants' stairs, taking them two at a time to the center of the manor.

She thought of the day's clue and how it fit with the previous days' clues.

> 'Tis in a place of voice and sound,
> And placed not very high.
> It's plain in sight all to be found,
> Near place to cool a pie.

The jewel simply had to be in the kitchen. The sounds grew louder as she neared that room. The banging of pots, scraping of knives, and hum of voices flooded the air. It would be odd to search when there were occupants in the same room, but it had to be done if she were to reach the jewel before another guest. It was in a box—she knew as much from another clue.

She stepped over the threshold and onto the stone floor, the cook eyeing her over her shoulder. Scullery maids moved in and out, this way and that way, like ants in a colony.

Jane straightened her shoulders. "This may be a strange question, but where do you cool your pies?"

~

*H*enry knocked thrice on the solid wooden door, worn from the sun and weather. After a few moments, it creaked open.

"What do ye want?"

Henry's jaw dropped at the young woman before him, her cheeks sunken and face pale.

"I..." How did one broach such a topic as an attack from years before? Most people might state their name first, but Henry's manners were lost in the moment—as a cow away from pasture. None of his persuading would get them back within the fence posts of propriety.

The door of the run-down cottage began to close in his face. He stuck the toe of his boot in the frame, preventing it from shutting completely. "Er—wait! Please. I mean you no harm. I've come to ask you a few questions, is all—assuming you're Miss Sarah Tern, that is."

"Who's askin'?" The woman's tone had turned suspicious. "Only trouble comes from the likes o' those who dress and speak like you."

He mentally slapped his forehead. He should have figured she'd be wary of noblemen—perhaps even men, in general—after what had happened to her. He gave a low bow, attempting to appear non-intimidating. "My apologies for not introducing myself, miss, and for interrupting your day. I am Lord Lendin. I think you may be able to help me with something."

The sky was grey above, and a raven sounded somewhere nearby. Henry peered at the cracked boards that made up the front of the home and the small dusty windows, sorrow building in his stomach.

Curiosity flickered in the woman's countenance, and the door opened slightly. "What is it ye think I can help ye with? I don't have no money."

Henry shook his head. "And I would never ask for it from you. All I wish for is for you to tell me exactly what happened to you. What happened to...to put you here."

Her face reddened. "I cannot talk of that. The last time I spoke to a lord, I was sent away."

Henry gave her his most earnest look. "He cannot do anything to harm you now, Miss Tern. You are safe here. I have a friend who Lord Windham has attacked. He is seeking to do her harm as he has harmed you. If I do not get your story, he will not be brought to justice. With your story and the story of my friend, there is a good chance he will be put in prison and sent across the ocean. Then you truly will be free."

A gentle drop of rain dropped on his topper, one falling on his shoulder. Miss Tern gave a shaky sigh as she clutched the doorframe.

"Ye'd better come in, then." Her voice held a quaver of hope.

~

Jane sat in the carriage across from Laurence, her knees brushing against his with every bump they rolled over on the drive. She looked out the window, watching as the grassy hills passed, wildflowers of every color dotting their surface at intervals. Two days had passed since she'd seen Henry, and she'd been Laurence's dinner partner for each of those evenings. Henry, it seemed, had opted to take dinner in his chamber, so occupied was he with the jewel.

Last night, Laurence had asked her to take an afternoon drive with him along the country roads the next day—which she'd accepted with hesitance. Lately, he'd been monopolizing all of her free time. Whenever she walked down a hallway, she happened to run into him, and whenever the men entered the drawing room after port and cigars, he was the first at her side, no matter if Henry was the first to enter the room. He'd paid her marked attention since arriving at the house party, and Jane hadn't the foggiest idea as to why. At first, she'd suspected that he only wished for forgiveness for what he'd said upon their last meeting, but now...now...it seemed as though—perhaps—Laurence wished for what Jane had once dreamed of. A courtship.

"Jane?" Laurence looked at her askance, one eyebrow raised in question as he eyed the maid next to her.

"Oh, sorry, Laurence, I'm afraid I was quite caught up in the scenery. What was it you were saying?" Her cheeks heated at her runaway thoughts, and she gripped her hands tight in her lap.

He settled more comfortably on the bench. "Not an issue, my dear—I only wondered if you might like to stop to stretch our legs for a bit. We can enjoy the picnic I've had prepared."

This picnic could only go better than the last one they'd had together. "That sounds wonderful." At least it would prevent her thoughts from straying to the fact that Laurence had interrupted her search for the jewel yesterday. She'd just walked in and asked her question to the cook when Laurence paraded downstairs with a curious expression on his face, distracting everyone and keeping Jane from her answer.

Laurence knocked on the roof with his fist, and the carriage pulled over to the side of the road, slowing to a stop. He hopped out and extended his hand for Jane, helping her down the steps and onto the flat ground. The midday air was warm, but not overly so, and the clouds above provided a welcome respite from the rays of the afternoon sun. Jane inhaled the fresh, earthy scent of leaves and fragrant blossoms.

Laurence took the basket of food from Jane's maid as she alighted from the carriage and held out his arm to Jane, leading her to a shaded area beneath a cluster of oak trees, not far from the road's edge. The coachman stayed with the horses and carriage, seemingly content to have a bit of time to himself.

Jane's maid settled herself a short distance away as Jane and Laurence sat in the grass, eyeing Laurence with misgiving. Apparently, Abigail hadn't forgotten the outcome of the previous picnic either.

"Here you are, my dear." Laurence uncovered the basket and filled a plate for Jane, handing it to her with the reverence a queen warranted. Bread, cheese, cold meats, and berries made her mouth water. She hadn't realized how hungry she was.

"Thank you, Laurence, and thank you for inviting me to this outing. It is very kind of you." She removed her gloves and nibbled at a piece of cheese.

"I know how much you love picnics, and—well—I wanted to replace the memory of the last one." He tugged at his cravat and looked away. "I know it did not go as either of us expected."

Jane's cheeks burned, but she forced the embarrassing memory away, clearing her throat. "Indeed."

Laurence reached for her hand, the skin of his palm soft against her own. His hands were the hands of a gentleman—they hadn't known a day of work in their life. "Jane, you know how I regret what I said before. It has tormented me ever since the words have been spoken." He pierced her with a stare. "I need to know—do you forgive me?" His expression looked so pleading, his lips drawn into a desperate curve.

Did she forgive him? She'd been so affected by his terrible words. Could she find it in her heart to close that wound? Jane searched her heart for an answer, finally realizing the surprising truth—she already had. She no longer took his previous words to heart in such a way. He was no longer someone she longed to court, nor was he someone she longed to marry. He was a friend only. Why should she let it torment him? The Lord taught to forgive, and so she would.

"Yes, Laurence. I forgive you." She squeezed his hand and let go, breaking off a piece of bread from a slice on her plate.

He beamed at her. "Dear Jane, thank you. I was hoping you would. I wish to be friends as we once were. To be truthful, I wish to be...even more."

Jane coughed, almost choking on the bite she'd been chewing. She swallowed it, blinking quickly. "You what?"

He looked at her with a tender expression, the birdsong around her quieting. "Somerset wasn't the same without you, my dear. I went to the balls and card parties, but you were never there to keep me company. Instead, I danced every set with one chit or another, all of them green young things with one foot in the schoolroom. I even danced with Miss Castleborough at the Wrenthams' ball, but she proved to be rather dull, after all. I always wished you might appear to save me from the monotony —that I might see your beautiful face again and that we might dance until the early-morning hours."

Jane's heart stuttered. "I—I don't understand, Laurence. What is it you want, exactly?"

Was that a flicker of exasperation in his expression? In the next moment, it was gone. He plucked a piece of grass from the ground and twirled it between his fingers, looking thoughtful. "It might be somewhat of a surprise to you, Jane, but I wish to court you." He tossed the piece of grass over his shoulder and tilted his head to the side, giving her a grin. "Indeed, that's what I've been trying to do since I arrived at Lord Sperrin's house party. It's why I discovered where you were from your parents and requested an invitation here in the first place."

CHAPTER 21

Jane blinked. "A courtship?"

Laurence stretched out his arms. "Why do you think I've been sending you flowers daily? You are a dear friend, Jane, but friends don't send friends flowers every day. And why do you think I've been constantly escorting you in to dinner? It's been dashed difficult getting to you before the others." He frowned. "And I didn't expect to have competition when I arrived at this house party, though it appears I do."

"Of course, you'd have competition. We're all searching for the jewel."

Laurence's mouth pulled into a thin line. "Not of that sort."

Did he mean *courting* competition? He mustn't. She leaned back. "Who?"

He huffed. "Lord Lendin, of course!"

Jane waved her hand. "Lord Lendin's not competition. He merely thinks of me as a friend and I, him. I told you he's been helping me to remember the things I find enjoyable—that's why he's often in my company."

Laurence scratched the back of his neck. "Is that so?" He

grunted. "Well, then, I suppose that means no one else is vying for your hand?"

"No one else."

Laurence looked well pleased as he lifted a strawberry to his mouth. "Very good."

Jane brushed out her blue skirts. "Why, Laurence?"

He swallowed the bit of berry and crossed his arms. "Why, what?"

Jane hesitated. "Why do you wish to court me?"

"I've already told you." He shook his head. "Once you left Somerset, I missed your company. The balls and parties were dull without your presence."

Jane wrung her hands. "But—well, before we parted at our last picnic, you seemed so determined that I was beneath your notice. You—"

He frowned. "I thought you had forgiven me."

She rushed on. "And I have! I only wonder at the change between then and now. You were very...clear...before, that I was not someone you were looking for in a life partner. You told me, in no uncertain terms, that I was 'deficient' in your view. Why the sudden change? Why am I no longer so?"

Laurence hesitated before shrugging one shoulder, blinking a few times. "When I spoke those words, I knew not what I was saying." He brushed invisible crumbs from his coat. "I was so thrown off balance by your admission of affection for me that I didn't know what to say, and I'm afraid I only said the first words to come to mind. I didn't know what to do with an affection so freely given, so I batted it away as a cook might a fly." He looked away from her and rubbed a hand over his mouth, suddenly grinning. "But now, I am here and have realized my affection for you. Now, there is nothing to stop us from a courtship."

Jane stuffed a piece of bread into her mouth so she wouldn't have to say anything. She'd just thought she no longer desired to be courted by Laurence, but she didn't have any other options, and she was sick of being paraded about London by her parents. They would only continue to do so if she returned home from the house party without a beau, and Laurence was the only man here who'd declared interest in her romantically. Maybe a courtship with him wasn't the worst idea.

When they arrived back at the manor, Lady Caroline and an unfamiliar man strolled to the side of one of the paths, her maid a bit farther behind than was typical. Lady Caroline's head was bent quite near to the man's, as though she were imparting a secret. His clothes weren't of the latest fashion. Indeed, they were rather worn. As the wheels of the carriage crunched along the gravel of the drive, the two sprang apart and looked over their shoulders, masks of politeness pasted to their faces. A dark mustache fell over the man's upper lip. His eyes were small.

Laurence waved from the window, a smile lifting his lips. Lady Caroline nodded, and the man tipped his hat.

Jane blinked at the odd interaction. "You've become fast friends with Lady Caroline, I've noticed." Laurence had also been fast friends with Lord Windham, when that man was still at the house party.

Laurence cleared his throat. "Indeed, I have. She is an enticing conversationalist."

Surprising. She'd never heard of either of them to speak of deeper topics than fashion or self-aggrandizing. "Is she? Tell me, what do you speak of with her?"

The carriage slowed, and Laurence nearly leaped out whilst it was still in motion. He answered as he handed her out. "Oh, we each have our own...problems, I suppose you could say. We converse in the evenings after dinner and give each other advice on how to solve them. That is all. Others' perspectives are very beneficial."

"Oh." Advice? From Lady Caroline? Well, Jane certainly

wouldn't take advice from her, but if Laurence was benefiting from it—who was she to question its validity?

~

As Henry rode back toward Wiltshire and Lord Sperrin's secluded estate, his success at collecting Miss Tern's story couldn't keep his spirits from dwindling. A frown marred his face, however, and he couldn't seem to banish it, knowing Jane was currently in the same house as Mr. Revil and that Lord Windham might still be in the area. Lord Windham was a known danger, but Mr. Revil was something else—something Henry couldn't quite decipher.

The mere idea of her spending any amount of time in the company of that man made his hands tighten into fists and his jaw lock. Something wasn't right about Mr. Revil, but Henry wasn't sure what just yet. Was Henry biased because of his love for Jane? Probably. But there was more to it than that. Ever since the man had come to the house party, it had seemed as though his sole purpose was to court Jane, and given how Jane and Mr. Revil had last parted, that didn't quite make sense.

According to Jane, the man hadn't wished to accept her affection when she'd freely given it, so why was he seeking it now? Was he attempting to get close to her in order to find out where the jewel was, as Lord Windham had when the house party began? Whatever it was, Henry would keep her out of danger.

Now that he was sorting out this mess with Lord Windham, it was finally time to tell Jane of his feelings. Before now, there had been too many factors getting in the way—the attack on Jane, Mr. Revil's arrival—everything. Now, however, he was ready. When should he tell her? Would she accept his feelings when he did?

Upon his arrival at the manor, the sun was just dipping

below the horizon. It would soon be time for dinner. Unfortunately for Henry, that also meant that he'd have to wait to take his findings to the magistrate. That man would certainly be in a poor mood if Henry were to knock on his door in the middle of some delicious repast. Callers were not expected at this time of day unless the news they held was urgent. Henry's wouldn't be deemed as such, considering Lord Windham had already left.

He sighed, his shoulders lowering. Henry would just have to bring Miss Tern's and Jane's stories to the magistrate tomorrow and hope that, in the meantime, Lord Windham remained in England.

Mr. Revil was late to dinner that evening, so Henry was able to escort Jane into the dining room, her gloved hand on his arm as though it was always meant to be there.

She turned her head toward him as she settled in her seat. "Have you found the jewel, then?" Her tone was lacking in its usual warmth.

He sat next to her and frowned as he pulled his gloves from his hands. "You will be the first to know when I do. I must admit, I expected a bit of a warmer welcome after two days away."

Jane huffed. "My search bore no fruit either. I—" She pushed out her chin. "What do you mean, 'two days away'?"

Henry chuckled, surprise lightening the tension in his abdomen. "Are you telling me you haven't noticed my absence? I left the manor for Hampshire whilst you were painting the other day and have only just returned."

"You mean..." A small gasp emitted from her mouth, and she lowered her voice. "I thought you were secreting yourself away, in search of the jewel."

The corner of his lip quirked up of its own accord. "How could I have moved about the manor without being seen for such a time? Do you believe me to be so stealthy? I assure you, my dear, even I could not accomplish such a feat for so long."

Jane leaned back in her seat. "I suppose I've been harboring a bit of unfounded irritation toward you." Her tone turned repentant. "I thought you'd been ignoring me, without a word —suddenly throwing my company over for a jewel."

He shook his head, captured by her gaze. "Never even think it so. Nothing so frivolous as that. I did forget to leave a note about my leaving, but I assure you that the trip was most necessary."

He peered around the table to ensure no one was listening before making known to Jane the reason for his journey to Hampshire and the successful outcome of it. She nodded all the while, a light of hope brightening her face as he shared his plan of bringing his finding to the magistrate.

When Mr. Revil finally arrived a few minutes after the guests had seated themselves, the man's expression was thunderous. His movements stiff, he apologized for his tardiness and sat in the empty chair near the middle of the lavish table next to Miss Clarke and Miss Parblot. The air was savory with the smells of the venison that the men had succeeded in felling the days previous and the herbs the cook had dressed it with.

Jane leaned toward Henry and spoke in a whisper. "I wonder what happened to so upset Mr. Revil. Our outing went well today."

Henry raised an eyebrow, spearing a green bean with his fork while his insides turned at her words. "Did it, indeed?"

"Yes. He was all that was congenial. I don't know what could be the cause for his agitation."

Henry eyed the man and his restless movements. He wiped his mouth on his napkin. "I do wonder. I cannot like him for what he's done to you."

"Oh." Jane pushed around a piece of potato.

Henry's brow furrowed at her lack of response. He'd thought she'd be pleased with his words, given her tumultuous past with Mr. Revil. "What's wrong?"

Jane exhaled and tilted her head to the side. "On our outing today, he apologized for his previous actions. It doesn't seem right to punish the man for something he regrets. I told him I forgave him."

It was Henry's turn to remain quiet. He was suddenly starting to regret the thoughts he'd had about the man and the trick with Gerald he'd played.

While Henry still didn't like Mr. Revil, that didn't mean that the man deserved Henry's tricks—especially if Revil regretted his actions from before. After all, he seemed to suffer from the same illness Henry did—love for Jane. Henry was letting his jealousy turn into suspicion of the man, which was unfair. Yes, Revil had some undesirable qualities, but so far, Henry's suspicions had proven unfounded. Truly, he didn't even know what he ought to be suspicious of.

Henry caught Jane's eye. "I will cease my antagonism."

Jane's shoulders relaxed, and she reached over to pat his hand. "Thank you, my lord. It would mean a great deal to me. You see, Mr. Revil has—just this day—expressed his intention to court me. I wish him to know that there is no ill will between us."

Henry almost choked on the piece of venison he'd just popped into his mouth. Downing his wine to wash the piece away and to fortify himself, he turned his body in his seat to face Jane more fully. "He *what*?"

Jane inclined her head, clearly oblivious to Henry's inner turmoil. "According to him, he's been attempting to court me since he arrived at this house party, though I only thought he was trying to garner my forgiveness. He told me that when I left Somerset, he realized his affection for me and how much he wished me nearby."

Henry's head spun, his chest tightening until it felt as though he could no longer properly breathe. How did one inhale, again? The torrent of emotions this new information caused threatened to drown his mind. He met Mr. Revil's eye across the table, the man wearing a smirk—his eyes triumphant as though he'd won some sort of battle between them.

Henry looked back at Jane. "And you...you have accepted this proposal of courtship?"

Jane took a sip of her wine. "No, I have not."

With her words, Henry felt as though he had just broken the surface after being plunged into a freezing underwater abyss. She hadn't accepted Mr. Revil's proposal of courtship— not yet, anyway. That was something Henry could hold onto. He still had time to tell her his feelings.

"But I think it might be best if I do."

And just like that, Henry was dragged back under, kicking and screaming, with flailing arms and lungs burning for air. He got the attention of a nearby footman and signaled for his wineglass to be refilled.

Jane continued. "Think about it, my lord. This is what I've been waiting for—a man who loves me, an end to the constant progression of seasons. I'll no longer be a wallflower. I'll no longer be seen as a spinster. My parents will no longer lament my unmarried existence."

With each of her reasons, Henry felt more and more ill. *He* was the one who wanted to marry her and love her. *He* was the one who wanted to dance with her for every set at every ball. *He* was the one who wanted to continue to show her the joys in life —joys she'd forgotten existed or had never experienced. It was supposed to be Henry and Jane.

He pulled at his cravat. "Do you not think another man could provide the same?"

Jane chuckled. "Mr. Beaton certainly won't be sweeping me off my feet, I can assure you."

Henry frowned. "I'm serious. There are other men who could give you the same things."

Jane ripped off a piece of her roll and buttered it, eyeing him skeptically. "Don't you think that after five seasons, someone would have done so already? I am tired of waiting. I may not be some large catfish like Miss Eugenia Castleborough, but I am a fish worth keeping if caught, and Mr. Revil knows my worth."

Henry had no idea who Miss Castleborough was, but Jane must think this decision through. "Will he treat you well? Will he provide you with the kind of life you deserve? What about his family—do you like them and they, you? You might be tired of waiting, Jane, but I assure you that there are more men than just Mr. Revil who would be very happy to have you as a wife."

She pierced him with a look. "Who?"

He swallowed, his cheeks heating. Before he could respond, she continued.

"Mr. Revil will treat me well. I've spent much time with him this past season, and he's the son of a baron, so I know he will be able to provide me with a comfortable life. It's not as though I desire riches, anyway, for I would marry a pauper if he loved me. I've only met his sisters, but they seem very nice. They're quite popular among the Ton, I've heard. Unfortunately, I've never had the pleasure of meeting Laurence's father, for the man has an illness that keeps him at his estate in a poor condition."

Henry picked up his glass of wine, taking a large sip. "Are you so certain of this path?"

Jane shrugged lightly. "I haven't any other options at the moment, really. I could go back home, unmarried, and have my parents prepare me for another season. That, I have no interest in." She shuddered. "I suppose I could marry the elderly vicar, but this option seems preferable." She gave a little huff of laughter.

Henry nodded. He couldn't even summon a smile at her joke.

Jane poked at a piece of meat with her fork. "So you see, my lord, why it is in my best interest to accept Lord Revil's proposal of courtship. There is much to be gained by it. I do believe it will make me happy."

Henry didn't speak, merely shoving another piece of venison in his mouth. How could this house party be going so awry? It wasn't long ago that Henry dared to think Jane might harbor an affection for him, but now she spoke of accepting Mr. Revil's proposal. He looked down at the long table of smiling guests and glowing candles, the golden candelabras shining and setting light over the feast before them. He wasn't hungry anymore.

The time to tell Jane of his feelings for her had passed. He'd missed his chance and would suffer the consequences. To tell her now would only complicate matters.

CHAPTER 22

As soon as Jane entered the drawing room that evening, someone grabbed her arm—tightly. Lady Caroline led her to the corner of the room and away from the others. There she dropped Jane's arm and turned to face her with an expression of outrage.

"I don't know what you think you're doing, but you won't be marrying Lord Lendin. Not if I have any say in the matter."

Jane exhaled reflexively and took a step back, bumping into the wall behind her. "What—"

Lady Caroline pointed at Jane's chest. "You're trying to use your wiles to trick him into a marriage with you, acting as though you know exactly where the jewel is—but you don't! You don't know a thing about it. A man only leaves a house party like this for a special license, but I won't have it, I tell you. He'll only marry you for the jewel, you know. Once he has it, you might as well return to your parent's house." Her mouth pinched. "I've known him far longer than you have and far better than you ever could. There's nothing in you that could attract such a man." She bit out the words in a hushed voice. "If you accept his proposal, there'll be dire consequences, and don't you forget it. You don't know who you're in competition with. Remember Miss Parblot?"

She certainly did. Jane's mind was reeling. Come to think of it, she hadn't seen the woman in the past few days.

Lady Caroline sneered. "See how fast I'll make *you* disappear."

Jane shivered. Where was Miss Parblot? Why was Lady Caroline so intent on having Henry for her own? He wasn't even interested in Jane, so why was she talking all this drivel about a marriage license? Was it really so difficult to believe he could have taken a trip for another purpose?

Lady Caroline moved a step back, and Jane fled past her, a chill sweeping her. She joined Lady Sperrin, who was just finishing a conversation with Harriet. "Lady Sperrin, where is Miss Parblot?" Jane had to know now that the question had been raised. "I haven't seen her in a few days."

The woman shook her head and murmured, "She had to return home, my dear. Fell ill, the poor thing. It was quite similar to your illness the other day. Couldn't resume the search for the jewel."

Jane thanked her and stepped to the side, her stomach turning. Was it true that Lady Caroline had had something to do with Miss Parblot no longer being at the house party, or was it a mere coincidence? And, given that the illness was so similar to Jane's, could Lady Caroline have been responsible for making Jane sick in the first place?

Someone cleared their throat at her side. She jumped.

"I didn't mean to startle you, dear Jane." Laurence grinned and bowed, a bit more subdued than on previous evenings.

Apparently, the men had finished with port. She glanced around the room, quickly spying Henry. Pushing thoughts of both him and Lady Caroline's threat away, Jane refocused on Laurence. "You seemed upset at dinner. What is bothering you?"

Laurence's smile fell, and he waved his hand. "Nothing to concern yourself with—only a disagreement with someone. He is intent on making the plan complicated for me, that is all. I have had to sway him to remain with it."

"And what plan is that? Something relating to your father?" Hopefully, that man wasn't worsening in his illness.

Laurence's mouth pulled down. "It is not. Truly, you need not ask me more about it, for all will untangle itself soon." Lines formed in his forehead, and a muscle twitched in his jaw. Clearly, he was still stewing over it, whatever it was.

Jane sought after some other topic she could bring up. The other guests were forming groups at the card tables. Perhaps she could entice him to play a game or two. She looked for an open table. All of them were occupied. "Fancy a game of chess?"

He lifted his chin with a smirk, his shoulders easing. "I would."

They moved to the chess table and sat across from each other, Jane situated behind the white pieces. She moved one of her pawns forward, then reclined back. This so reminded her of the many enjoyable evenings spent with her parents, before she had to care about finding a husband or fretting over her dance card that only held a few names.

Laurence leaned toward the board and moved his own pawn forward. "How was dinner?" He raised an eyebrow. "You spoke often with Lord Lendin."

Jane moved her bishop diagonally a few spaces, meeting his eye. "I did. He is my friend, and one must not ignore one's dinner companions."

"And yet you ignored Mr. Langley on your opposite side for the entirety of the second course." He pushed forth his queen.

Jane frowned lightly, moving another pawn forward. "I didn't want to monopolize the man, Laurence. Harriet—Miss

Wildon—has an affection for him, and I wanted to allow them to speak to each other."

Laurence grunted, pushing his pawn forward again and threatening Jane's bishop. She moved it back a space, wary of his queen.

"I don't trust Lord Lendin." Laurence murmured the words, carrying his knight to the front of his array.

Jane had picked up her bishop but paused. "Don't trust Lord Lendin? Why ever not?" She took the pawn in front of his left bishop, setting the piece to the side on the table.

She realized her foolish mistake too late, for the corners of Laurence's mouth quirked up, and he was quick to move his king diagonally one space and capture her bishop, setting the piece on the opposite edge of the table as her captured pawn. Jane wanted to groan at her lack of thought but repressed that desire. She'd been too caught up in his words and had become distracted.

Laurence answered her question as she moved her queen diagonally across the board.

"There's something about him I dislike. He seems too clever by half. It seems as though he dislikes me as well."

"Check." Jane placed her queen down, and Laurence moved his king one space forward.

"Dislike you?" Jane forced a chuckle. Did it sound as fake as it felt? "Surely not." She moved a pawn forward, her palms beginning to sweat. The board was no longer as clear as it once was as she tried to remove Henry's name from this conversation.

Laurence shook his head. "Oh, but you've not seen the looks he gives me, dear Jane, when I'm at your side." They each moved a piece. "He looks quite eager to have me sent away, you know."

Jane waved her hand, the game continuing with each moving multiple pieces. "I'm sure it only appears that way because you don't really know him. I assure you, Lord Lendin is a very kind person." She cleared her throat. "How was *your* dinner this evening?" She moved a piece, Laurence sliding his queen swiftly thereafter.

He shook his head. "I don't believe it, Jane. You'd do well to stay away from that man."

In two more moves, Laurence had her in check. She hadn't played well for the entirety of the game, unsettled by the confusing conversation. Why was Laurence so against Henry? Why must he continue to utter his name? Couldn't he just drop the subject?

"He's harmless, I assure you." Jane put a hand to her head, the beginnings of a megrim coming on. She scanned the board, her pieces in random places without reason—or perhaps with reason, but she'd forgotten it. She moved her remaining knight forward, for he'd captured the other one at some point, and frowned.

"Checkmate!" He crowed the word, slamming a fist against the table and calling the other guests' attention to their little corner of the room.

Jane's head throbbed at his exclamation, and she blinked her eyes closed for a little longer than normal to abate the pain. "Congratulations, Laurence." She forced her tone into something pleasant.

Henry stood from a chair across the room, appearing as though he was about to come over. She shook her head as subtly as possible.

Laurence grinned. "Don't look disappointed, Jane—for I was bound to win." He guffawed. "I am, after all, well known for being very good at chess. At Cambridge, my friends used to call me 'The Sneak' for my ability to lull my opponents into a false sense of security."

His laugh grated, but Jane kept quiet, merely nodding at his words. She caught Aunt Agnes's eye from where she sat in a nearby chair next to Lady Sperrin. Her aunt's arms were crossed and mouth pulled into a tight line. Clearly, she had heard every word of Laurence's boasting.

"Another game?" An eagerness tinged his offer.

Jane shook her head. "Forgive me, but I think I'll retire. My head—"

Laurence scoffed. "Is your pride so fragile that one loss will send you away?"

Jane bristled. "Not at all. I happen to feel a megrim beginning and—"

"Ah, well..." Laurence leaned back with a casual air. "Only few can bear losing at chess more than once in a day. It seems you know your personal limits." He spoke as though if they were to play again, it was an undeniable fact that he would win.

Jane frowned. "Something like that." She stood, and Laurence followed suit, grasping her hand in his to press a kiss upon the back of it.

"I do hope we can share many more games of chess in the future, dear Jane." Laurence released her hand, his blue stare locked on her. "Perhaps, in the future, I might even teach you a few things about the game. Of course, a woman like you can't be expected to know as much as someone like myself, though it's quite surprising you've come as far as you have." He chuckled. "I even heard from Mr. Alton that you beat Lord Lendin at chess sometime during the beginning of the house party, so that tells you something about that man's skill. I'll have to play him sometime. I'd trounce him in a moment."

Jane took a step back, her irritation mounting. Who was this man that stood before her? This wasn't the Laurence she remembered. Then again, she'd never played chess with Laurence. If she married him, would he continue to be this way?

She raised a gloved hand to her head, the ache there becoming stronger. She was simply tired. It had been a long day. That was what this was. Her nerves were a bit frayed with all of the circumstances, including the outing with Laurence, Henry's trip, and Lady Caroline's threat. It was too much to think of. She must rest.

Seeking out Aunt Agnes, Jane gave her apologies to Lady Sperrin, catching Henry's concerned look as she fled the drawing room, her aunt right behind. She only had time to give him a subtle shake of the head, signaling that she didn't want to talk about it, before she headed up the grand staircase and down the corridor to her room.

"I don't like that Mr. Revil." Aunt Agnes shut the door behind them and helped Jane out of her dress, waving off Abigail, who'd been waiting as she sat on the end of the bed.

Jane sighed. "He regrets how we parted, Aunt, and I've forgiven him for what he said."

Aunt Agnes shook her head, lifting Jane's plain nightgown from the bed. "Even so, he should not be speaking to you as he is."

Jane pulled the nightgown over her. "He doesn't usually, and he has asked to court me."

Her aunt raised a wary eyebrow. "Has he, indeed?"

Jane inclined her head and moved to the dressing table, pulling pins from her hair as she did so. "He is not a bad man, Aunt. I could grow to love him again. It wasn't so long ago that I did."

Aunt Agnes helped her with removing the last of the pins and picked up the hairbrush from the table, beginning to brush Jane's hair with gentle movements. "I wish you'd have set your cap at Lord Lendin. Even Mr. Langley would be preferable. That's why I introduced you to that man in the first place." She huffed.

Aunt Agnes's brush strokes became harsher, and Jane took over brushing her own hair, eyeing her aunt in the mirror.

"Laurence has been very kind since he arrived. These bouquets are all from him." Jane gestured around the room.

Aunt Agnes clicked her tongue. "A shame. I thought Lord Lendin might finally be showing you more outward affection."

Jane dropped the hairbrush on the table, jumping from her seat with arms outstretched. "Why does everyone seem to think there's some sort of affection between us? It's absolutely ridiculous! He's so much higher in rank than I am. He's a viscount—vibrant and handsome, always up for an adventure. I'm just—I'm just...plain Jane! I don't even know what I find enjoyable, Aunt. How pathetic is that? Even Laurence seems to be hinting at something between Henry and me, but why? How could there ever be?"

Her aunt pierced her with a look, her expression fierce. "If you truly believe there is no affection between yourself and Lord Lendin, Jane, then I fear for your future. Cannot you see past this foolishness? Cannot you see that not all is as it seems?"

"Call me a fool, Aunt, for I cannot!"

Her aunt stood there, unmoving. "I wish to help you—"

"Aunt, I can help myself." Jane exhaled, her shoulders drooping. "This is the path I wish to take. I don't need your interference."

Her aunt's arms dropped to her sides. "Very well. I shall watch you from afar, then, and act solely as a chaperone would, if that is what you desire." She moved to the door and looked over her shoulder. "This is a mistake, Jane. It is plain to see—"

"I apologize, Aunt, but I don't wish to hear it. I'm tired and must rest." Jane *was* tired, but she also wished to escape hearing anything more about a possible affection Henry had for her or anything about Laurence's behavior. Her heart couldn't take it.

With a nod, her aunt was gone, shutting the door with a quiet click. Jane climbed into bed, her limbs heavy. Abigail returned to ask if Jane needed anything before she retired, and then Jane was alone with her thoughts, wishing she might fall into sweet oblivion and avoid the worries of the day.

She already regretted arguing with her aunt, but there was nothing to be done for it at the moment. Jane was being truthful when she'd said she wished for her aunt to cease with her interference. She rolled over under the covers, burying her face in her pillow. At least, things would be easier tomorrow after a good night's rest. She finally had a man who cared for her. A boorish man. And not the man she would choose—but Henry was beyond her reach.

CHAPTER 23

*H*enry didn't know when, but Lady Caroline had situated herself next to him on the settee in the middle of the room after Jane had retired early. Her shoulder brushed his as she leaned nearer, her floral perfume overly sweet—some mixture of roses and lilacs, or maybe lavender?

She clasped her hands in her peach skirts, decorated here and there with embroidered vines, and peered at him through her lashes. "How are you this evening, my lord?"

He shrugged, looking away. "As well as can be, I suppose."

She laughed as though he'd just made some great joke. "How droll you are, my lord." She sighed contentedly. "I'm quite glad that Miss Talbot has left the room."

Henry turned to look at her, an eyebrow raised, so she continued.

"I find her company to be very stifling, don't you? And what poor manners! She couldn't even stay around after Mr. Revil had beaten her at chess."

Henry straightened in his seat, shoulders tense. "I do not believe she was feeling well, Lady Caroline. As for her 'stifling behavior,' as you say, I have never felt it to be thus. I believe she is all that is pleasant and light."

Lady Caroline shook her head and her blond ringlets along with it. "She's only a baron's daughter. There are women here with far greater titles, if a wife is what you seek." She angled her head. "And much better features, as well."

Henry leaned away as far as he could, almost hanging over the armrest of the settee, his mouth pulled into a frown. Why couldn't she find some other viscount to hound? Why had she chosen him as her prey? He inwardly groaned. "What makes you think I am seeking a wife?"

Lady Caroline straightened, blinking a few times. "Are you not? The *Ton* seems to think you are. I've heard from many members that you've been on the lookout for a marriage partner."

He grunted, which she seemed to take as an affirmation.

She smiled a cat's smile. "Ah, so they were correct." Placing a gloved hand on his arm, she lowered her voice. "You know, my lord, we are not so dissimilar."

He eyed her warily.

"You are looking for a wife, and I am in search of a husband." Her tone was calculating.

Henry removed her hand from his arm. "Lord Gillingham wouldn't do?"

Lady Caroline wrinkled her nose. "As much as my father wishes for that match, I find the man much too brooding."

Henry almost scoffed. Lord Gillingham? Brooding? Pompous, yes, but brooding?

She continued. "I'd much prefer my husband to be... blonde. With brown eyes." The corner of her lip lifted up in a flirtatious manner. "And, above all, I'd like for him to be the Viscount Harroway."

That was specific. Henry adjusted the cuffs of his coat. "I appreciate your candor, Lady Caroline, but you and I have very different personalities. We would not be well suited. We—"

She grabbed onto his arm with both of her hands. "Do not make your decision now, my lord, for what if something happens in the next few days to change your mind? You can never know what the future may hold."

With those parting words—her tone almost ominous—she released him and stood, brushing off her skirts and giving him a tight-lipped smirk that made him uneasy. The farther she moved away, the lesser the weight on his shoulders became. With her presence came a sort of heaviness. It was ironic, since Lady Caroline spoke of Jane being the one with the stifling presence.

"Ahem." Someone cleared their throat beside him, and he looked up to see Mr. Revil at his side, appearing piqued. Henry hadn't paid the man any attention since his chess game with Jane had ended, so why was he here now...and looking so vexed?

"Mr. Revil." Henry nodded in greeting, trying, for Jane's sake, to be cordial.

"My lord." The man gave a shallow bow and sat on the settee beside Henry, taking the seat Lady Caroline had just left.

Henry forced his sigh back down. He would have no peace this evening. He waited for the man to speak, which didn't take long. Henry had a sneaking suspicion that Mr. Revil was in love with the sound of his own voice—as much as Narcissus was in love with his own image.

He pierced Henry with a look. "You spend much time with Jane, is that not correct?"

Henry scratched his chin, feigning surprise. "Miss Talbot? I would say we spend a moderate amount of time together."

Mr. Revil seemed to take umbrage at this. "Moderate?" He snorted. "You spend nearly every day with her, my lord, and you call that a moderate amount of time?"

Henry brushed a nonexistent piece of lint from the shoulder of his coat and met Mr. Revil's icy stare again. "And? What do you have to say to it?"

Mr. Revil's face turned red, and he huffed a breath. "What do I—" He paused, closing his mouth. "I, *my lord,* say that you spend far too much time with a woman who is about to enter into a formal courtship." He leaned closer to Henry, his voice low. "You'd do well to desist."

Henry lowered his voice as well, narrowing his gaze. "And *you* would do well to remember that I am watching you, Mr. Revil. Something isn't right with you, and I'll find out what it is."

The man paled but threw Henry's accusation back at him. "Me? Ha! You are the one Jane should be wary of. Why should a viscount take such interest in *her,* a baron's daughter? Unless..." Revil pinned him with a stare. "What is it you know?"

Henry clenched his jaw and shook his head, his chest tightening in irritation. "You speak nonsense. There is nothing to know. Why shouldn't I wish to spend time with a lovely young woman?"

Mr. Revil appeared, at first, to be relieved, but the expression disappeared in an instant. He stood from the settee with a glare. "Stay away from her."

"I certainly will not." Henry glared right back, not letting Mr. Revil's intimidation tactics work. He'd seen far worse at Oxford.

Mr. Revil stepped forward and jabbed a finger in Henry's direction. "Then face the consequences."

Henry clenched his jaw, thoroughly done with this man and his belief that he could order others about. "So be it."

CHAPTER 24

The shot of a pistol rattled the windowpanes of Jane's bedchamber, followed by a shrill scream. She tossed the bedcovers aside and stumbled to the window where morning light filtered through. Her heart beat at a rapid pace, threatening to break right through her ribs. What had happened?

Pressing her hand against the warm glass of the window, Jane held herself upright as relief filled her body. On the back lawn, multiple targets were set up. Four gentleman stood a distance away from one with a pistol in hand, taking their aim. Apparently, Lord Sperrin had decided to host a shooting match this morning.

Miss Clarke hovered in the garden nearby with one hand held to her chest. She must've been the one to scream. Jane didn't blame her. Not everyone was accustomed to the deafening boom of a gun, especially at such an early hour.

Henry took aim, his back perfectly straight as he held his arm out in front of him. He wore a coffee-brown coat that stretched across his broad shoulders, a moss-colored waistcoat peeping out from beneath. His buff trousers contrasted his dark waistcoat, a snowy cravat wrapped around his throat. Lady Caroline was standing about as near to him as she could be without being in harm's way, her hands clasped dramatically to her breast. Jane leaned her forehead against the glass as Henry cocked the hammer of the pistol with his thumb, his gaze never wavering from the target.

He pulled the trigger, and a loud bang rang through the air. The pistol smoked while the other men stood still. Jane squinted. Henry, from what she could tell, had hit the target at dead center. She silently cheered for him from where she stood at her window, watching as the other men clapped his shoulders and congratulated him.

She blinked, swallowing. She ought to be looking for Laurence. Where was *he* among this crowd?

~

"Why couldn't you have shot like that when we were out hunting?" Langley chuckled, eyeing Henry after the match was over.

Henry lifted the corners of his mouth and gave a small shrug. "I suppose I just wasn't feeling myself that day."

Langley ran a hand through his dark hair, grinning. "Well, I hope on future hunts that you are. You should visit my estate sometime. With your aim, we'd be sure to have dinner for at least a few nights."

Not wishing to spoil the man's assumption that Henry enjoyed hunting, he returned Langley's grin. "Indeed."

Mr. Beaton and Mr. Alton sidled up, the former with an upturned nose and thinned lips as he examined Henry. "Where'd you learn to shoot like that, Lendin?"

Henry inwardly groaned, putting the pistol back into its box, then closing the lid and latching it. "My father taught me."

Mr. Alton appeared thoughtful. "Right'o, Lendin. Fathers are the best kind of teachers. Mine taught me how to wager. 'Tis why you'll always find my name in the betting books."

Mr. Beaton ignored his comrade's comment. "Your father, eh? Good man, he was."

"Thank you."

"My father ne'er taught me to shoot," Mr. Alton said to Mr. Beaton in a matter-of-fact tone. "'Twas a skill I learned from my mother."

Mr. Beaton harrumphed. "How scandalous! A woman shooting? The day I should see it, I should keel over."

Mr. Alton shrugged. "You can come over to my estate next month, if you'd like."

Henry held back a laugh at Mr. Beaton's red face.

Henry's eyes caught movement over Mr. Alton's shoulder. Mr. Revil stood in his grey jacket across the lawn, deep in discussion with Jane. When had she gotten out here? The muscles in his jaw tightened. "Excuse me, gentlemen."

Mr. Beaton scoffed, puffing his chest out. "I should not like to visit your estate if your mother is performing such vulgarities."

Henry didn't care—his only concern was Jane. He'd written a note to the magistrate that morning and now awaited the man's arrival. Until then... "Excuse me, gentlemen." This time, his voice brooked no argument.

Henry headed to where he'd just seen Jane with Mr. Revil near the hedge maze. They were no longer there. "Blast." At a steady pace, he moved across the lawn, weaving around groups of ladies and gentlemen chattering about the shooting match and other topics of interest.

Jane's aunt stepped in front of him. "Have you seen Jane?" Concern laced her tone.

Henry frowned. "I just saw her with Mr. Revil near the maze. I intend to go there myself."

She looked grave at his words. "Please find her, my lord." She spoke in a low voice. "I do not wish for there to be a scandal. I'll follow you not far behind."

He nodded, and she moved away from him, pasting on a mask of ease for the other guests' benefit.

Once Henry reached the entrance of the maze, he glanced around to make sure he went unnoticed before he stepped inside. The hedges that surrounded him were taller than he was, so he couldn't see above them to find out where Jane and Mr. Revil were. It was darker and cooler within their walls, for the sunlight was blocked from view by the multitude of leaves and branches on every side.

He moved forward, the grass pillowing his footsteps. On a whim, he took a left turn, only to reach a dead end. Spinning around, he hurried to where he'd been and turned right instead, anxiety creeping up within him. His palms began to sweat, and his heart began to race faster, his blood pumping within his veins as a sense of urgency overcame him. Henry had no idea where Jane was, but she was with Mr. Revil, and that wasn't good. At that very moment, anything could be happening to her. If Mr. Revil touched a hair on her head—

Henry strode forward and took another right, the faint sound of voices increasing his pace. He raised his hat and ran a hand through his hair. After one more left and another right, the voices sounded adjacent to whatever room-sized area he'd found himself in. The space he was now in held a simple iron bench and chairs, but the voices were coming from behind the wall of hedges right next to him.

Henry didn't have time to go back and find the correct path to whatever area they were in. What if Jane was in distress? He took off his hat and tossed it on the bench. Hopefully, the gardener wouldn't be too angry at him for what he was about to do.

Stepping a few paces back from the hedge, he straightened his shoulders and took a breath. After one moment of hesitation, he was running forward and diving through a wall of branches and tight-woven leaves. He would have to apologize to Lord Sperrin for the man-sized hole in his hedge maze later.

"What the de—" Mr. Revil's voice filled the air, interrupted by Jane's.

"Henry?"

Henry crawled through the hedge, pulling his legs after him and ending up in a heap on the ground at Jane's feet. "Good morning! I didn't expect to see the two of you here."

Jane pulled the leaves from his hair. "Whatever are you doing? You do know the point of a maze is to find the middle without crossing the hedges." Her voice was full of humor.

Henry stood up and brushed off his person, many leaves stuck to his clothing. He met Jane's eyes and grinned. "Indeed, I do. I figured I'd jump a few steps."

In the middle of the space, water flowed from the top of a circular fountain down to a middle tier and then to the basin beneath. Iron benches and chairs sat nearby, with rose bushes in the corners giving the area color.

Revil grunted, folding his arms in front of his chest. "What is the meaning of this interruption?"

Henry raised an eyebrow at the man. "What is the meaning of you bringing Miss Talbot to such a secluded place?"

Revil shifted on his feet. "I—er..." He sounded less certain of himself now.

Jane waved her arm. "Laurence had just invited me to explore the maze, Henry—that is all."

Henry looked around, his concern growing. "Unchaperoned?"

Jane's gaze flicked around the space, gaze widening as though she'd just realized she and Mr. Revil had been alone.

"Laurence, where is the maid that was following us? You told me she was just a little way behind."

Henry hadn't seen a maid with them when they were speaking on the lawn. He looked to the man in question, who pulled at his cravat.

"She must have gotten lost on her way, my dear."

He was clearly lying. There had been no maid. He must've told Jane there was in order to get her to follow him, and she'd trusted him enough not to look behind her to see if there ever actually was.

"I see." Henry forced his stare away from Mr. Revil and turned to Jane, softening his gaze. A strong urge to protect her burned through him. "Your aunt wishes to speak with you. She's only a little way behind me. Will you find your way all right? I would escort you, but I must have a word with Mr. Revil."

Jane nodded, a hint of worry in her eyes. He lifted her hand and kissed it before she curtsied to them and left, finding her way back through the maze.

Henry clenched his jaw at the sight of the man before him, his fists tightening. Now that they were alone, he wouldn't hesitate to say exactly what he wished to Mr. Revil. "I'm not sure what your game is, Revil, but you must cease playing it."

Revil huffed. "My game is chess, my lord, but I doubt you'd know anything about *that*." He smirked. "I heard you're not as good at that as cards."

Henry scoffed. "You know of what I speak. What was this maid's name—the one you asked to accompany the both of you into the maze?"

Revil shrugged. "I'm sure I don't know. I don't make a habit of asking *servants* their names." He wrinkled his nose as though the very idea was distasteful.

Henry made a show of examining his fingernails. "What did she look like, then?"

This place was much too charming for the tension created by this conversation and the animosity between them. It was almost laughable, really. All around them were roses and intricate iron benches, yet here they were, staring each other down.

Revil lifted a hand to his chest. "About this tall. Bl—Brown hair...maybe a small nose." During his description, he found the ground and hedges very interesting all of a sudden.

Henry grew tired of his lies. "Stop with the acting. You and I both know there was never a maid."

"There most certainly was! You simply do not like the idea of Jane and I together." Revil took a step toward Henry, his fists balling at his sides.

"You're taking advantage of her trust, and that, I cannot allow. What is it you're here for? Why have you come?" Henry moved forward as well.

"Miss Talbot—Jane. I told you to stay away from her or face the consequences. You keep getting in the way, Lendin, and I don't like people getting in the way of what I want." Revil lunged, throwing a punch that Henry quickly dodged.

Henry put his arms up in front of his face and bent his knees, circling the man for a minute. Without warning, Henry reached out and struck the man's cheek, throwing Revil off balance.

Revil swung at Henry once more, but Henry avoided the hit, retaliating with a solid fist to the jaw that resulted in a cut where Henry's signet ring had caught at the flesh. Revil yelled and charged at Henry. Henry sidestepped at the last moment, and Revil careened over the fountain's edge and into the murky water.

Blood dripped from his chin, and he spluttered as he righted himself. "Don't think this is over, Lendin." Revil spat the words. "You may have won the battle, but you haven't won the war."

Henry waved off his threat, leaving through the hole he'd

made so he might retrieve his hat from the bench. Revil was a liar and a conniver, and in no way could Henry allow a man like that to marry the woman he loved. Perhaps he would tell Jane how he felt, after all.

~

"Jane, you mustn't go places without a chaperone." Aunt Agnes propped her hands upon her hips moments after they'd exited the maze, her mouth pulled into a stern line as they stood away from the other guests.

Jane lowered her head and spoke in a murmur. "Laurence said there was a maid behind us, Aunt. I was safe the entire time."

Her aunt sighed, lifting Jane's chin with a finger to meet her gaze. "What if he lied, my dear?" She softened her tone to a maternal concern. "You could have been ruined."

Jane's pulse sped up as the possible outcomes of actions fell upon her. Aunt Agnes was right. She had blindly trusted Laurence, never once checking to see if what he'd said was true. They'd only just become friends again. Should she be so quick to restore her trust in him?

Jane's shoulders drooped. "I understand, Aunt. I'll not do so again."

Her aunt patted her cheek, her gaze following the other guests. "Let's go inside to have some tea with the others."

As Jane followed her aunt, Henry emerged from the maze, brushing leaves from his shoulders. He scowled and adjusted his cuffs as he moved toward the back entrance of the manor. Her gaze locked with his, and she raised her arm in a wave. He returned the gesture, a small smile on his face, before she had to hasten to catch up with her aunt. He had something on his face, though she could not tell what is was from this distance.

She hadn't thought he'd sustained a cut from climbing through the bushes. Had something happened after she left?

Her heart quickened its beat. What had he spoken about with Laurence? Had Henry been there to defend her honor? And, if so, dare she hope that meant he had feelings for her?

<h1 style="text-align:center">CHAPTER 25</h1>

"**J**ane."

On her way to change for dinner after parting company with her aunt, Jane almost stumbled in the hallway. Anxiety streamed through her veins. She knew that voice. How could it be? He had left. How had she managed to find herself in this situation again?

She looked around the dimly lit hallway. Where was he? She pressed herself against the wall, edging into a darkened corner behind the statue of a bird. Her palms began to perspire, damp within her gloves.

A dark chuckle sounded from somewhere nearby. "I can see you, Jane. You need not hide from me."

His voice sent a shiver down her back, making the hair on her neck stand on end. She stepped back into the half light.

Lord Windham appeared from an alcove, a smirk on his face. "There you are. I was wondering when I might be alone with you again."

Jane's hands trembled. How had he managed to get back into the manor without her notice? It wasn't particularly late, but everyone was dressing for dinner in their rooms. He'd picked the perfect time to find her alone, with all guests preoccupied.

"My lord." She tried to straighten her shoulders and hide the quiver in her voice. "What is it you want? How did you get here?"

He chuckled again. "My Jane, but you've quite a fire in you." His mouth twisted. "How did I get here? Lord and Lady Sperrin let me in, of course. You never told them why I left, did you?" He scoffed. "There was no reason for them to bar the doors on an esteemed guest such as myself."

She squirmed under his intense gaze. "Pardon me, my lord, but I must be going."

Jane turned on her heel and took a step forward, but his words stopped her in her tracks.

"Not so fast, Jane. I haven't sought you out merely to compliment you."

"Why have you stopped me, then, my lord?" Jane crossed her arms in a protective stance, her breathing shallow. "I must dress for dinner, and there isn't much time. My maid will wonder where I am." She tightened her grip on her arms and bit her lip. If she put any more pressure on it, she might draw blood.

Lord Windham took a step forward, nearly suffocating her with his presence. "Dinner can wait, and my valet has seen to stalling your maid. What I have to say is far more important." The corner of his mouth raised. "I have been watching you, Jane, since the first day of this house party. At first, you bored me, with your simple story of Somerset and your proper missish behavior." He leaned closer. "But witnessing you with Lendin...your behavior was different. No longer so dull. I realized you were clever. Revil wants you for his own reasons, but I can see more...potential."

Jane backed up a step. "I—I don't know what you're telling me this for, my lord."

In the blink of an eye, his hand darted out to grab hers, not letting go even when she pulled back. Jane swallowed, panic seizing her. Was this meeting to go the same way as the previous one? The scream that climbed up her throat stuck there.

"Think, you silly girl." Lord Windham's voice sent skitters down her back. "I could give you everything. I'm a duke—there are not many of us to be had, you know. I am offering you marriage. You'd be foolish not to accept. You need only tell me where the jewel is."

"I—I don't know—"

"Five long seasons you've had, with not one proposal." He moved closer, his breath upon her cheek. "Here I am—a duke—offering for you. Your spiritedness draws me. With my title and the money from the jewel, we'd have everything. I assure you, we'd be *very* happy together."

Jane shivered at his words and the vile set of his lips. She had no desire to be married to this man and, frankly, why was he offering? He must be in worse straits than she'd believed. Henry had spoken of his debts, but... "I don't believe it's my spiritedness that draws you to me, my lord, but my dowry and your belief that I know where the jewel is."

He dropped her hand as quickly as he'd taken it up, his eyes flashing though his cheeks paled. "There's that fire." He gave a dark chuckle. "I will so enjoy taming it."

Jane shook her head. "I fear there's a misunderstanding. I've no wish to be *tamed*, and certainly not by one who's proved more beast than man. Perhaps next time you discover a maiden with a sizeable dowry, you should try to win her affection, not steal it."

His expression turned dangerous. "Ah, but I haven't observed other women as I have you. I've spent time attempting to get to know you, Jane. I've watched your vitality increase with everything you've done that is new to you. Our marriage will only enhance that. I will introduce you to everything I know. I will take you to countries you've never been to and introduce you to people you've never met." He took a step closer. "And experiences…"

She suppressed a shudder. She'd known from Henry that Lord Windham had been eyeing her for the jewel but had no idea he'd been watching her with such unwavering resolve.

"When I noticed Lord Lendin taking an interest in you, I resolved to make you mine. He cannot offer what I can." He scoffed. "He reminds me so much of my brother. So perfect. Always the favorite. Well, who ended up with the dukedom? And who will end up married to you?" He gave a grunt. "Father can roll in his grave for all I care. You and I will find the jewel together, then we can begin our lives as husband and wife."

Jane began to back away. "I already told you, I don't wish to marry you. I'm sure there's some woman you could find to marry you within the hour. Their dowry will settle your debts as well as any gem. As you said, you *are* a duke."

He scowled. "Holding out for him, are you? That self-righteous prig wouldn't have a notion of what to do with a woman like you."

Jane looked down the hall. Would anyone pass by? "I will not change my answer, my lord."

He grinned, the sight turning Jane's stomach. She placed a hand over it as he pulled back his shoulders. "There are ways of changing your mind. I don't intend to let you escape this time."

She turned to flee. He grabbed her shoulder and spun her around, eliciting a yelp as he opened the door to his room just across the hall. Jane sucked in a breath to scream, but Lord Windham slapped her, sending her sprawling with a small cry.

He stood over her, no regret in his cold stare. "Once you're ruined, you'll have no other option but to marry me or remain a shunned woman for the rest of your days."

She'd heard of such things happening to other women…but

never imagined being in such a position herself. No. She would not let him have his way with her. The floor and walls blurred as she put her hands on the floor to push herself up. "I'd rather be cast out upon the streets than married to a monster like you."

The door in the corridor next to the bird statue flew open, and Laurence stepped out. "What is this?" He hurried to her side. "Dear Jane, are you all right?" He helped her up, putting a hand on her arm to steady her as she teetered dizzily from side to side.

Lord Windham eyed Jane as though daring her to tell the truth and find out what consequences he had in store for her. "Miss Talbot fell, and I was inquiring if she was all right. In darkened corridors like these, it can be hard to see in the evening. Don't you agree, Mr. Revil?"

Laurence eyed him, a firm set to his mouth. "Indeed, and it's good to have you back, my lord. Thank you for helping Jane. You can continue with your search for the jewel. I presume that is what you returned for? That has been your plan, after all."

Lord Windham nodded, setting his shoulders.

Laurence's grip loosened on Jane's arm. "I've much to do myself to that end."

With a grunt, Lord Windham peered at Jane. "It is a shame you've hurt yourself. But with not only Mr. Revil but your aunt and your dear friend Lord Lendin here to look out for you, I leave you in good hands." With those parting words, he spun on his heel and left.

His message was clear—she wasn't to tell anyone of what happened, or they would get hurt as well. But if she stayed quiet, that would only spell more trouble for her in the future, would it not? And what was with Laurence's odd speech?

"Jane?"

"Hmm?" She looked up at Laurence. Apparently, he'd been speaking.

Concern tightened his features. "I asked if you wished me to bring you to your aunt."

She dipped her head. "Please, but—before we go—I must tell you, Laurence. He lied."

Laurence's forehead creased. "Who?"

"Lord Windham." She grasped his hand, her own trembling as she did so. "I didn't fall, Laurence. He proposed to me. Then when I refused—."

Laurence stepped back, ducking his chin. "Proposed to you? Why in heaven's name would he do a thing like that?"

Jane exhaled. "Because he thinks I have the jewel. When I refused him, he was going to ruin me, Laurence."

Laurence scowled. "Look, Jane, I understand I treated you poorly, but there's no need for you to make up stories. Windham is a *duke*. Obviously, I find you quite fetching, but why would he do such a thing? The very idea is ridiculous."

Her mouth fell open, and she stepped away. "You don't believe me?"

Laurence sighed as though the conversation was tedious. "Come now, Jane, that's a serious accusation. Have you any evidence behind it?"

Jane jabbed her finger toward her cheek. "Surely, the red mark upon my skin is evidence enough for you."

Laurence shrugged. "You could've hit your face when you fell."

Jane flung out her arms. "Why would I lie to you, Laurence? He hit me! He was angry that I refused his proposal. He was going to ruin me. Does none of this matter to you?"

Laurence moved closer, grabbing her hands. "Oh, dear Jane, don't get hysterical. You know you've already won my affection."

Jane ripped her hands away from his, too shocked to speak. He thought she'd fabricated the entire story just to make herself appear more appealing to him? That she'd said Lord Windham had proposed in order to—what—entice Laurence to propose sooner? Because, surely, if a duke wanted her, then a future baron should be happy to have her?

Tears began to flow down her cheeks as she rushed down the corridor to her aunt's room, Laurence calling after her. Although, perhaps Aunt Agnes wouldn't even want to hear her woeful tale after Jane had argued with her the other day. Jane *had* told her to limit her interference. How she regretted that.

She switched directions and headed for her room. She would eat there tonight, for she certainly wouldn't be going down to the dining room after all she'd just experienced.

Since her last encounter with Lord Windham, Henry had been diligent in accompanying her throughout the corridors and ensuring she felt safe in the house, keeping an eye on her. He was her protector. If only he could be with her at all times. Laurence hadn't understood what had happened, but Henry would. Dare she go to him and tell him of this second encounter?

But given Lord Windham's talk of Henry being his enemy and the man's veiled threat, would speaking to Henry of this put him in danger?

Jane shook her head. She couldn't risk seeking him out right now. Not when Lord Windham might still be prowling the halls. Better to go to her own room and keep this to herself until later. For all she knew, Henry might already be in the drawing room, awaiting dinner. She'd tell him after, when enough time had passed that he'd be sure to be in his room. He knew how to comfort her. He'd know what to do.

Abigail awaited Jane in her bedchamber, moving frantically upon her arrival. "Come, miss, you're bound to arrive after the entire first course if we don't get you into your gown now. I got held up belowstairs—some valet askin' after something or other." She moved to the armoire. "I was thinking ye could wear yer blue dress tonight, with the white embroid—" As

Abigail turned around with the dress and noted the expression on Jane's face, she stopped.

"I'll be dining in my room this evening, Abigail." Jane's words came out just above a whisper. "Please have a tray sent up."

Abigail put the dress back. "Right away, miss. Are ye feeling ill? Should I ask fer a special tea to be made? Some broth?" She wrung her hands together.

Jane shook her head, wrapping her arms around her abdomen. "No, thank you. A dinner tray will suffice."

Abigail hesitated as though she wished to ask more questions. Fortunately for Jane, the maid's mouth remained closed, and she left the room with swift footsteps, heading toward the kitchen for the requested tray.

Jane sat on the edge of her bed and kicked off her slippers, lifting her legs onto the soft mattress. Her limbs felt heavy and her body ached from the tumble she had taken. She touched her cheek where Lord Windham had struck her, tears wetting the raw area where the back of his hand had made contact with her skin. She wouldn't be surprised if there was a large bruise there upon waking in the morning. How had things escalated to this?

She hadn't done anything to try to appeal to the man. Indeed, she'd completely ignored him. She wasn't clever at scavenger hunts. Why had Lord Windham singled her out? Was it simply a matter of proximity?

But there were other ladies here with larger dowries. He could've set his cap at Lady Caroline—she had a very large dowry and was beautiful. And spirited, which Lord Windham seemed to so admire. He'd even been talking to her the other day, and they'd seemed to have a good conversation. Was this truly all about revenge now, as he'd inferred?

A few minutes passed before Abigail reentered the room with a tray filled with delicious-smelling foods and a glass of wine. She set it in Jane's lap with a smile, though her expression still showed a hint of concern. "Here you are. Is there anything else you need?"

"No thank you, Abigail." Jane took off her gloves and made her tone light, attempting to set Abigail at ease. "There is nothing else I need at present. I will ring for you when I'm finished."

Jane ate her meal in solitude, puzzling over Lord Windham's behavior and his odd desire to marry *her*, of all women. She still trembled at the thought of what had occurred, but a curiosity burned within her that begged to be sated.

As the hours ticked by on the clock above the mantel, she grew more and more restless. She called for Abigail to take her now-empty plates away and swung her legs over the side of her bed, sliding her feet into her slippers. It was time to find Henry. By now, he would have seen that Lord Windham was back in the manor—he'd probably even met the man at dinner.

Jane waited for Abigail to return from the kitchen. When she came back, they left to go to Henry's chamber, their movements as quiet as they could make them.

The hallway was quiet, most of the guests having already gone to bed. Jane dearly hoped Henry was still awake. He must normally go to sleep rather late, for he'd found her in the library in the early-morning hours before.

They stopped in front of his door, and Jane knocked gently. After waiting a few moments without an answer, she knocked again. Nothing. He must be sleeping, after all. Jane sighed. She'd waited too long to find him.

She and Abigail had just turned to return to Jane's chambers when a shuffle on the floorboards sounded from behind the door and it creaked open. A middle-aged man peeked through the crack.

His bushy eyebrow rose over a bleary eye—the only one

that could be seen through the small opening. "What's this? Has something happened?"

This must be Henry's valet. Jane stepped forward, her voice low. "I'm sorry to bother you, sir. I was just looking for Lord Lendin. Is he awake?"

The man shook his head, the hinges creaking as he opened the door a little wider. "My lord's in the library."

"Oh." Jane looked down the hall, ensuring they were still unseen. "I guess that's where we'll have to go, then. Thank you, sir."

He gave a bow, closing the door as they left.

Jane changed her direction for the library, Abigail following just behind. She should have known he'd be there.

The halls were eerie as they made their way to the staircase. The marble statues of foreign animals seemed as though they might come alive at any minute. When they reached the ornately carved doors to the library, candlelight flickered from beneath. Her heart began to beat faster at the knowledge that Henry was behind those double doors.

She pushed them open and scanned the room for the head of golden hair that had become so familiar. Instead, she found Laurence, perched in a wingback chair near the empty fireplace, a glass of amber liquid in his hand. He looked up at her entrance.

"Dear Jane, it is late for you to be awake." He stood, moving toward her.

She stepped forward to look around him, gazing past the shelves of books. Where was Henry?

Laurence took her hand and kissed it. "I will say, you were missed at dinner." His tone was carefree as he squinted at her face. It was as though nothing had happened between them earlier to raise her ire. He dropped her hand and lifted his to her cheek, caressing the place where Lord Windham had hit her. He made a *tsk*ing sound. "What a shame. Your skin is still red. A bit of powder should cover that. No one will be the wiser about your fall."

"It wasn't from the fall."

Laurence took a sip of his drink, his face impassive. "Let us not argue, dear Jane."

"I'm not your *dear*." Jane ground out her words.

"Come now, we're both tired. Let's put this behind us." He set his drink aside on a nearby table. "I'm glad you're here, truly, for what happened earlier has served to affect me."

Jane crossed her arms, her foot tapping on the rug. "How is that?"

Laurence opened his mouth to speak but, before any words came out, he glanced toward Abigail—who was standing not far away and watching all that occurred with interest. "Before I say anything further, might we have some privacy?"

Jane looked over her shoulder at the maid and hesitated. If she dismissed the girl to the hallway, she'd be at Laurence's mercy. Was Jane willing to put her full trust in him...after the incident with the maid missing from the maze? Would he truly take advantage of her, though?

She met Abigail's eye, then turned back to Laurence. "I insist she stay. Whatever you need to say to me may be said in her presence."

Laurence gave a great huff but stepped forward, taking both of Jane's hands in his. "You know I would never harm you, Jane."

She shrugged a shoulder, avoiding his gaze. "That may be so, Laurence, but a woman must never be too careful."

"You have made this difficult for me. You are like a bird I am attempting to catch, and every time I try to get close, you flutter a little away." He winked, his voice low. "It is one of the things I have grown to love—the chase."

She froze, her limbs as frozen as though she was one of the

carved marble statues in the hallway. Her breathing grew shallow, and her chest tightened. She tilted her head. "Love?"

Laurence nodded. "Love."

Jane grew cold, beginning to shiver.

Laurence pulled on her hands, drawing her forward a step. "But it is not the *only* thing I have grown to love. I have grown to love *you*, Jane. I don't know when it happened, but at some point during this house party, you stole my heart. Your gentleness and easy forgiveness have reached out to me. I've hesitated in sharing my feelings, but your charade today has only proved that you wish to marry me as much as I wish to marry you. Say you'll be my wife, dear Jane."

Before Jane could stutter out an answer, Laurence wrapped an arm around her waist and pulled her against him, pressing his mouth against hers. His other hand, he placed on her shoulder, running it along her arm. His lips were unyielding as she stood, shocked, in his embrace. What in heaven's name was happening?

$\mathcal{H}$enry hurried away from the library doors, the scene he'd just witnessed turning the smooth stone in his hand to something jagged. He'd stopped by the kitchen for a strawberry tart and to do a bit of searching for the jewel. It turned out to be about the size of a strawberry itself, nestled inside its small wooden box. It no longer felt warm in his palm, but cool. The box itself had been at about eye level, wedged between some jars in the larder. Not in the tea chest, as he'd thought. The excitement he'd experienced at finding it was nothing compared to the pain that seared him at the image of Jane in Revil's arms.

He stumbled into the wall as he took a corner in haste, the darkened halls masking his error. His stomach churned, his head light and dizzy. He might just cast up his accounts. To see Revil's lips against hers in such a way... He shuddered. Henry had certainly never been the cause of such a blush on her cheeks—almost a plum color.

Had they come to some sort of understanding? Had Revil convinced her to accept his courtship—or worse—a marriage proposal? Abigail had been there, after all, so Jane mustn't have been in danger. She must have accepted.

Jane didn't believe she had any other options, but she failed to realize Henry had been here the entire time, waiting for her to notice him. He'd planned on telling her this evening, but then Lord Windham had arrived and she hadn't shown up to dinner. Now, it seemed, his plans were thwarted once more.

He slumped against a wall in the corridor. He'd lost track of how many steps he'd taken. He barely even knew where he was in the house anymore.

Crossing his arms, he bent over, searing pain in his chest. It pierced him with a blade as sharp as any sword. The pain was so intense that he couldn't breathe. All he'd hoped and wished for was gone, for the woman he loved, loved another.

The magistrate had failed to arrive at the manor today—business in another county, he'd written—but with any luck, he'd come tomorrow. Then, all there'd be left to do would be to return home, forgetting all about this woman whom he could never tell that she'd won his heart.

≈

A moment's confusion passed before Jane wrenched herself away from Laurence, her palm connecting with his cheek. "How *dare* you!" Tears welled in her eyes as Abigail flew to her side. Jane backed away, pointing an accusing finger at him. "You claim to be a gentleman, but all you are is—is a—a cad!"

Laurence rubbed his face and scowled. "It's only a kiss, Jane, and we're about to be married. Would you have me wait until the evening of our wedding?"

Jane's face flamed. "I haven't said yes to your proposal, sir, and did you ever ask my father to court me?"

Laurence tugged at his cravat. "Well—"

"Exactly as I thought." Jane shook her head. "You do not think of my feelings, Laurence."

He swung his arms out as though he had done no wrong. "But I do, my sweet—otherwise, I wouldn't have come to this house party in search of you. Think of how happy a union we could have. You love me, and I, you."

Jane headed for the door. "Come, Abigail. As Mr. Revil said, it is late for me to be awake." Tonight, she could take no more.

～

"A letter fer ye, miss." Abigail handed Jane a missive and left the room.

Jane had asked for solitude ever since the previous evening's tumultuous proposal from Laurence. Things had changed so much between them in such a short amount of time, and she didn't know how to make heads nor tails of it. Why was he so interested in marrying her when he hadn't been only a few months ago?

Her mother's looped handwriting marked the front of the letter with her father's seal molded into the dollop of wax on the back. Jane's heart fluttered. She hadn't heard from them in weeks, and it would be pleasant to hear any news they had to share. She slid her thumb under the red wax and popped it open, unfolding the foolscap.

> *July 19, 1817*
>
> *Dearest Jane,*
>
> *Your father and I hope you are doing well at Lord Sperrin's house party. We are doing well at home and are busy with calling upon Lady Towbridge and Miss Susan. The latter will be making her debut soon and is excited, as any young girl is. I remember how excited you were for your first season.*

In order to make your time seeking a match at Lord Sperrin's house party easier, your father and I have decided to increase your dowry.

Jane's breath caught, her heart stopping in her chest at the words written before her. They had increased her dowry? By how much? Her gaze flitted through the rest of the letter.

This decision, we feel, will increase your chances of making a match during this vital time. Given your father's successful investments this year, we were able to increase it rather significantly. We hope you are as excited as we are at this prospect.

Isn't this wonderful news, dearest? You might finally be able to make the match you wished for all along. We also wish you success in the scavenger hunt. Your father and I are praying for you. We remain

Your ever loving parents,

Mama and Papa

July 29, 1817 - P.S. - Apologies for this late letter, as your father had it hidden under a stack of correspondence in his study and forgot to send it out until today. We're sure Mr. Revil has informed you of your increased dowry by now. We told him to do so when we learned he was attending Lord Sperrin's house party. By now, hopefully, someone has caught your eye and you've learned the whereabouts of the jewel.

Jane stared at the letter in her hands, question upon question forming within her mind. This letter had been sent from her home only two days ago, but her parents had increased her dowry almost two weeks ago. Jane brought her hands to her face. Laurence had shown up a week ago, and he'd never told her of her increased dowry, despite her parents asking him to. Was that the reason for his sudden interest in her?

She must find out.

She left the room, the afternoon sun flooding the corridor as she closed the door behind her. Aunt Agnes had visited this morning and told Jane the guests would be outdoors today, playing more lawn games. The woman had inquired why Jane was upset, but Jane had kept mum. Eventually, her aunt had left, the crevice Jane had opened between them growing even larger as Jane refused to talk.

She didn't wish to burden her aunt with news of Laurence's proposal, and her aunt still didn't know about Lord Windham's proposal...or second assault...either. Jane sighed, her insides tightening. There was too much between them now. Jane had built a fence somehow, and she didn't know how to take it down.

Cheers erupting outside drew Jane to a window. Mr. Langley stood tall with Harriet clapping beside him, a grin on her face. He was one of a few gentlemen holding shuttlecocks, including Laurence. If Jane could get outside quick enough, perhaps she could catch him before a new game began.

Jane's slippered feet barely touched the stairs as she dashed down them, making her way to the back door. She darted outside and waved quickly at Harriet before grabbing Laurence's arm.

He'd been in conversion with Mr. Beaton, but at her touch, he turned his head. She gave both gentlemen her best apologetic smile, adding in a curtsy for good measure. "I'm terribly sorry to disturb your conversation, but I've something pressing I need to discuss with Mr. Revil. Would you allow me to steal him away for a moment?"

Jane expected Mr. Beaton's face would turn as red as the vegetable he so disliked, so it was surprising that he lowered his chin and nodded. It seemed she'd found her way into the man's good graces, for some reason. She thanked him, tugging Laurence to the side without a care for if it caused him a nip of discomfort. She *needed* to know.

He followed her, swinging his racket at his side. "What's all this about, Jane? Are you finally coming to your senses?"

When she'd drawn him far enough away from the others not to be heard, she turned to face him. "Perhaps so, but not in the way you might think."

She peered over his shoulder at the other guests playing games. Strangely enough, Henry wasn't among them. That was odd. Had he taken ill?

She shook her head. Never mind that—she was questioning Laurence right now. She pierced him with a stare. "I got a letter from my parents today."

He swallowed. "A—And how are they?"

Jane jabbed a finger into his chest. "You've been here an entire week, Laurence—an entire week—and not once have you told me that my parents increased my dowry."

He looked away, sniffing. He turned toward her again and planted his hands on his hips. "They—They what?" His voice hit a higher octave. "Well—I never would—" He put a hand to his cheek and ceased speaking, ducking his chin.

Anger bubbled within her at his acting. She would have laughed at the ridiculousness of it if not for the pain it caused her. She crushed the letter in her hand. "I know you know, Laurence!" She lowered her voice, seething. "They mentioned in this very letter that they *told* you to tell me. But you haven't."

He shook his head, pinching the bridge of his nose. "I—I forgot, Jane. I forgot."

"You forgot?" She waved the letter in her hand. "How could you forget a thing like this? You've claimed to have wanted to court me since your arrival at this house party." Jane dropped the hand holding the letter and raised her opposite one, gently removing his hand from his face and forcing him to look at her. "Tell me, Laurence—with your father ill at your estate, how bad are your finances?"

He blanched, taking a step back from her.

She moved forward. "Has all of this been a lie, Laurence? A ploy? You knew my parents increased my dowry, and you knew that I did not. Did you come here to convince me to marry you so you would have my dowry?"

Laurence remained quiet, his gaze not meeting hers.

She reached out to touch his arm. "Laurence, tell me. Do you truly regret saying those words in March? Or was asking for forgiveness just one of the many steps in your plan?" Her stare begged for him to answer her and to tell her the truth.

Laurence had arrived at the house party so suddenly, acting as though they had never parted the way they had. Had he hoped she'd forgotten his words? Had him asking for forgiveness been an alternate plan?

The corners of his lips turned downward. He tapped the racket against his leg. "Congratulations, Jane. You've found me out." He looked into the distance. "The estate's finances are not what they should be, no. Father will be dying soon, and then it's up to me to set everything to rights. That's where your dowry comes in."

Jane sighed as a heaviness settled deep into her bones. She had been used again by Laurence. How naive she'd proved to be. She closed her eyes, the sting of tears behind them. "Did you ever feel even friendship for me, Laurence?" Her voice came out in a waver.

He tilted his head, picking a piece of lint from his coat sleeve. "You amuse me, Jane. That must count for something."

A large tear rolled down her cheek. No wonder he'd made friends with the other two people in the manor who were her enemies.

She took a step back, folding the letter back into a rectangle. "You are no friend, sir."

～

*J*ane took dinner in her room again that evening, trying to come to terms with Laurence's lies. She took a small sip from her wineglass. She'd forgiven him, and yet, he'd betrayed her again. She raised her hand to her head, heaving a sigh. The Lord always called for one to forgive others, and she had, but she must remember that didn't mean the others wouldn't betray one again. She had been slapped and had turned the other cheek. Now, the second slap had come. Unexpected, but it had come, nonetheless.

Disappointment drenched her insides, leaving no space untouched. She was a sheet plunged into a laundress's boiling kettle, pushed and pulled this way and that in the suffocating water. Not an inch of her was dry. She'd truly thought Laurence was her friend.

The image of Henry came to her mind, and her heartbeat picked up its pace, as though it was a fox being chased in the hunt. Henry was so different from Laurence. Besides their looks being almost completely opposite from each other, their personalities were too. Where Laurence was methodical, Henry was spontaneous. Where Laurence was dour, Henry was mischievous. While Jane didn't feel a thing for Laurence, she felt a great many things for Henry.

Her face flushed as the realization took hold of her. She pierced a piece of chicken on her plate and cut it with more force than necessary. She'd tried for so long to keep her heart from becoming attached, but it had grown roots like a stubborn vegetable and now refused to be pulled out of the earth that was Henry.

Throughout her time at Lord Sperrin's house party, Henry had been the one to keep her steady. He'd been the one who she went to when tears streamed down her face. He'd been the one she'd shared her happy moments with—and the one who knew her history. The more she'd wrapped her arm around his, the less she'd wanted to let go, no matter how likely it was that she'd have to.

Only today, she'd seen him talking with the magistrate—a thing he did for *her* sake. To keep her safe from Lord Windham. After interviewing Jane, the magistrate had ordered Windham to remain in his room until the magistrate could speak with Miss Tern. Jane would be safe—for that time, anyway.

Jane plucked a piece of chicken and chewed, deep in thought. When she'd thought herself in love with Laurence, that hadn't been love. Her feelings had been mere infatuation. Over the course of her five seasons, Laurence had been the only man to pay her so much attention, and she'd been reasonably affected by it.

What she felt with Henry...

Jane blinked, swallowing. She set her fork down. That was another thing entirely.

She missed him when she hadn't seen him, if even for a few hours. The thought of his smile always brought about her own. She bit the inside of her cheek, her fists tightening. A fate had befallen her—one far worse than being infatuated with Laurence. She loved Henry.

"Miss?" Abigail entered the room, a carefully wrapped handkerchief in her hand.

Jane set her fork aside and leaned back. "What is it? Is something amiss?"

Abigail only moved toward the bed, holding out the wrapped-up handkerchief. "Lord Lendin's valet bid me give this to you. Said his lordship wishes for you to have it."

Jane's curiosity was piqued as she took the fabric. There was something in it. Something rather heavy for its size. She set the object in her lap and carefully unwrapped the cloth. Abigail watched, seemingly as curious as Jane as to what the gift could be.

Abigail emitted a gasp and covered her mouth as the candlelight gleamed off of the object. Jane could only hold her breath in awe.

The jewel of Parcathia.

It was a deep red like a garnet or ruby and as large as an apple tree's young fruit, or perhaps a large unshelled walnut. It was spherical, though it had many cuts made to it—each of which shined dazzlingly in the flame.

He had found it. Where? Had it been in the kitchen, as Jane had supposed? Or had it been elsewhere? How long had it been in his possession—for days or mere hours?

And he's given it to me?

She couldn't make heads nor tails of it. She folded the jewel back up into the cloth and set it on the bedside table.

Abigail must have sensed her turmoil, for she left not long after, taking Jane's dinner tray with her.

Jane fell against her headboard and pillows, her emotions strung tight. Even with her increased dowry, it was unlikely that Henry would ever love her, so why would he give her the jewel? She was a spinster with five seasons to her name, a plain woman. If Laurence found fault with her, certainly Henry would as well. It was for that same reason that Henry could never know her feelings had developed.

But it still begged the question—why her? Out of all people, why had he given it to her? Truly, why had he given it away at all when he'd talked of it being a benefit to his estate?

Sometime later, a key twisted in the lock, waking Jane. She turned over under the covers at the creak of the doorknob. It would be Abigail tending the fire. Jane exhaled and nestled into her pillow before a wave of anxiety pounded into her.

It was August. There was no fire to tend.

The sound of footsteps heading toward the bed froze Jane in place. What should she do? She had no time to ponder. Jane sat up in bed and eyed the person standing only feet away.

She had trouble seeing their face in the darkness, but their figure was large. She swallowed. "What are you doing?"

A pistol's hammer clicked as it was drawn back. "Only taking what is mine. Scream, and it'll be the last sound you ever make."

CHAPTER 27

ord Windham stepped into the moonlight coming through her window, his pistol pointed in her direction. Jane quaked with fear.

He moved toward her and grabbed her arm, yanking her out of the bed. "Put on a dress. Quickly. We're going on a trip." His tone brooked no argument. He peered out the door and down the hallway, shutting it behind him as Jane attempted to pull on her stays and tie them up over her nightgown. She'd never done so without a maid before. She threw her blue dress over her head and tried to button it up but could not reach the buttons at the top. Her cheeks flamed. She didn't want to ask this monster to assist her, but she couldn't walk around with an unbuttoned dress. Where was he going to take her, anyway? How could she escape this?

Jane cleared her throat, catching Lord Windham's attention. "I—erm—I require a maid for the buttons."

He grunted and moved behind her, his large fingers fumbling on the delicate closures. "What the dev—" He huffed and set the pistol aside, mumbling curses under his breath.

Now was the time. Jane could run—

"Done. Now where is it?"

Her pulse sped. "Where is what?"

"You know of what I speak—what I've been searching for this entire time." His tone took on an edge. "*Where is it?*"

"I'm not telling you." Jane shook her head, though her tone wavered. She couldn't give up the jewel. Not when she'd just received it. It had been a gift from Henry. He wouldn't want to see it in Lord Windham's hands.

"Ah, so you do know where it is." He leveled his pistol at her. "You've no choice in the matter, my dear. Tell me, or you're dead."

"If I'm dead, you won't ever learn its location." But how could she keep it hidden?

His pistol dropped to aim at her shoulder. "How about a wound, then? Something painful to help you speak?"

She swallowed. She could be vague. "It's nearby."

He grunted. "Be more specific, or you'll never dance again. How would you like to have a limp for the rest of your life?"

He was serious. She was about to suffer a grievous injury if she didn't give it up. Her shoulders drooped like a wilting flower, defeat falling over her like a burial shroud. *I'm sorry, Henry.* She gestured toward the folded napkin on the bedside table.

Lord Windham stepped over, unfolded it, and revealed the jewel within. A sneer came to his face. "I knew you had it. That wasn't so difficult, now, was it?" He pocketed the jewel and shoved her toward the door. "Walk toward the stables."

Jane stumbled forward and made a left down the hallway toward the servants' stairs, angry with herself for having missed her chance at escape—and for losing the jewel.

Lord Windham followed with the cold tip of the pistol pressed into her back. As they exited to outside, the night air was warm, with the singing of crickets and frogs all around. It would've been a beautiful night—if she weren't being kidnapped.

The large brick stable building loomed in front of them, dark except for one lantern the candle of which guttered, about to go out. Lord Windham turned Jane around to face him and pulled something out of his pocket.

"What's that?"

"Keep quiet." He muttered the words in a harsh tone and pocketed his gun, then wrapped the fabric—a handkerchief—around her eyes and tied it in a knot behind her head.

No. She couldn't let herself be kidnapped. And would he truly shoot her? Her legs moved of their own accord, and she jumped away from Lord Windham, attempting to run back to the manor, her pulse thrumming.

"Oh, no, you don't." He grabbed her around the waist. Something heavy hit her head.

She crumpled to the ground, darkness consuming her...

When Jane next awoke, she saw only blackness. Where was she? Memories of the kidnapping returned as she caught her bearings. She was lying on the seat of a carriage—at least she thought that was where she was. Her head split as though someone had driven multiple nails into it, and each time the carriage bumped over some hole in the road, another one was added.

How long had she been unconscious for?

A noise sounded opposite her. Snoring? Perhaps that was Lord Windham. Jane tried to lift her arm to take the blindfold off, only to find that her wrists were bound together. She huffed.

Someone yawned in front of her. "Ah, so you're finally awake."

Jane frowned. She was growing tired of being scared. Now, she was becoming angry. "Likely, due to your snoring. I'm sure it could raise a bull even if you'd given him fifty spoonfuls of Valerian root powder."

"Don't forget who's holding the pistol, *dear Jane.*" His cold voice made her want to wrap her arms around herself.

She changed the subject, attempting to stretch her arms as best she could. "Where are we going?"

"Gretna Green, of course. Aren't spinsters supposed to be intelligent? I thought that's why they were unwanted. Perhaps you're just one of the ugly ones." He chuckled at his own joke as Jane prayed for God to help her out of this situation.

"I'll never marry you." She gritted her teeth.

"You missed your chance for that, my dear." His voice was smooth.

Her stomach clenched. Who was she marrying? Then it hit her. The planning. The conversations Laurence had had with Lord Windham and Lady Caroline. The advice they'd been giving him.

Given how far Wiltshire was from Gretna Green, it would take them at least three days to get there. That should be plenty of time for someone to catch up with them and rescue her. That was something. They'd have to stop regularly to change the horses, so maybe she could even notify one of the innkeepers that she was in danger. Maybe help would come sooner than she thought. She could only pray.

She swallowed. "Who's driving this carriage?"

❧

A pounding came at Henry's door early the morning after he'd witnessed Jane and Revil embracing in the library, jolting him awake. He pulled on a pair of trousers and stumbled to the door, opening it before another round of knocks could begin. On the other side was Lord Sperrin with Jane's aunt—Mrs. Westby—at his side. Her face was ashen. She wrung her hands together before her as she stared at him with a desperate look.

"Jane is gone."

What? "What do you mean, gone?" He clasped onto the doorframe with a tight grip as his stomach dropped.

Lord Sperrin spoke up. "She's disappeared. So have Lord Windham and Lord Revil. The latter's written a note saying that they've gone to Gretna Green to elope."

Mrs. Westby shook her head. "She never would've done such a thing."

Henry wasn't so sure. He scratched the back of his head. "She loves him, doesn't she? Perhaps—"

"No." Mrs. Westby's tone was unmoving, earnest. "She does not. No matter what you may believe, my lord, I can tell you that Jane does not love that scoundrel—even if he has come to win her hand. I know my niece."

Lord Sperrin's gaze flicked between the two of them before he seemingly took note of Henry's state of undress. "Meet us in the drawing room as soon as you are able. We need to discuss what our next steps will be."

His host shut the door, and Henry finished getting dressed, not stopping to shave or comb his hair. Notham could barely get him to throw on a coat before Henry was in the drawing room with Lord Sperrin, Lady Sperrin talking in the corner with Mrs. Westby. Thankfully, no one else was present.

At Henry's questioning look, Lord Sperrin explained, "The other guests are unaware of the matter. They believe the three in question to be ill in bed today. Now, what can you tell us?"

Henry shared what he knew regarding Lord Windham's interest in Jane and how the man had cornered her in the hallway. He told them how he'd believed the attack to be singular and that he'd been keeping Jane safe ever since. He also spoke of the shared kiss between Revil and Jane in the library.

Lord Sperrin dropped his head in his hands. "And we let Lord Windham back into our house. You should have told us."

Henry shook his head. "Jane made us swear not to, my lord."

Lady Sperrin scowled. "We should never have invited him, James. I know his father was your friend, but..."

"I...found the jewel yesterday. I gave it to her." Henry's shoulders dropped at his confession. Would Lord Sperrin be disappointed that he hadn't told anyone?

Lord Sperrin slapped his knee. "We knew someone had. It wasn't in its box this morning."

Mrs. Westby's mouth dropped open. "You gave it to her?"

Henry nodded. "I did. All along, I have been attempting to help her find the joys in her life, but she has helped me to find the joy in mine. I wanted her to have it."

Lord Sperrin flattened his mouth. "If Lord Windham believed she had it, he could've kidnapped her."

"But what of Mr. Revil?" Lady Sperrin spread her hands.

Henry straightened his shoulders, determination flowing through him. "I'm going after her."

Lord Sperrin glanced at him. "Not alone, you aren't. What if the man has others working with him? You'll need allies."

Mrs. Westby stood tall, her mouth drawing into a thin line. "I'm her aunt. I'll be coming too." She looked out the drawing room window at the cloudy sky, the same turmoil in her demeanor. "Before we go, allow me to fetch my things. I'm sure the both of you will need to ready yourselves, as well."

Without an answer, she strode from the room, her pink gown swaying. Henry didn't want her to get hurt, but there was something about her countenance that made him believe there was more a possibility of him getting injured than she.

He dipped his head to Lord Sperrin. "I shall fetch my pistol."

Lord Sperrin kissed his wife on the cheek and moved toward the door. "I'll have the carriage brought around."

The three of them were soon ensconced in the fast-moving carriage, Henry and Lord Sperrin facing backward and Mrs. Westby facing forward with a basket of victuals beside her. They had some ground to cover, especially considering that they hadn't a clue when the kidnapping had taken place. For all they knew, Windham could've taken her right after midnight, or it could've occurred in the early morning. The difference of those hours could be a matter of Jane's marriage taking place or being stopped.

Henry clasped his hands to pray. *God, please let me reach her in time. I can't live my life knowing she is attached to so monstrous a man. Let her be unharmed, and allow me to save her from this situation.*

The countryside blurred by in greens and browns, the sky darkening with every minute that passed. Unease pooled in the pit of his stomach at the looming clouds overhead, the land around them taking on hues of grey as though someone had dropped a spot of ink into a teacup. His leg began to bounce as the first drop of rain splattered against the window.

Lord Sperrin eyed him. "Nervous, are you?"

Henry tried to loosen his jaw. "Not for the upcoming quarrel with Lord Windham."

Mrs. Westby tilted her head in question, but Henry remained silent as childhood memories flitted through his brain. He hadn't been lying when he'd told Jane of his dislike of riding in carriages in the rain. He blinked, thunder and the frightened screaming of horses echoing in his mind from a distant time.

The rain was only a light drizzle now, but it showed no signs of stopping. Indeed, it looked as though it would get worse as the day dragged on.

Lord Sperrin reached into the basket and withdrew a boiled

egg, content to break his fast on the road. Mrs. Westby placed a napkin on her lap and helped herself to a currant muffin, the top a golden brown.

Henry rested his head against the squab and closed his eyes, attempting to regulate his breathing. Perhaps he could rest a bit on their journey, for learning of Jane's absence had made him lose his appetite. He had no desire to seek anything in that basket, though he probably should eat *something*. If he were to rescue Jane, it would be better to do so with something in his stomach.

A few hours later, the slowing of the carriage urged Henry's eyes to open. At least he'd been able to rest them, though not to sleep. He peered out the window as they stopped in front of an inn called *The Oak and Ash*. It seemed a pleasant sort of place, with flowers planted in front. The outside was painted white, and several windows dotted the facade, their curtains drawn to let the light in—what light was left of the day, anyway, for it was still raining.

As soon as their carriage pulled up, they were met by ostlers who were instructed by the coachman to change the horses for fresh ones. Henry and Lord Sperrin jumped out and walked to the door of the inn, while Mrs. Westby remained within the carriage, staying dry.

The owner, a large man with greying hair and beard, met them at the entrance. He grinned and gave a bow. "Gentlemen. I'm Mr. Garmer. What ken I do fer ye?"

Lord Sperrin dipped his head. "Greetings, Mr. Garmer. This is Lord Lendin, and I'm Lord Sperrin—"

The man's face flushed, and he wrapped his hands in the dirtied apron around his waist, straightening his shoulders. "Terrible sorry, milords." He bowed again, a bead of sweat on his brow. "I didn't know—"

Henry waved his hand. "'Tis no matter, Mr. Garmer. We are wondering if a young lady and man stopped by your establishment today or last night. The lady has hair the color of mahogany, her eyes like amber, her skin fair. She's about this tall." He gestured. "The man in question has dark hair, almost black, and eyes that are the same. He is around my height."

Mr. Garmer put a hand to his chin and drew it down his beard. "Well, I can't say I know what amber looks like, but I did see a sister and brother 'round 'ere with that description. They 'rrived in the early hours—say, four—and left around eight. Her betrothed was 'ere too. Were in the private dining parlor a long time, you see." Mr. Garmer stretched out his arms. "The fellow said they was to be married. Said they 'ad to talk about where they was ta live."

So Revil *was* with them. Henry frowned and his fists tightened, but he thanked the man. "Did they say anything else?"

Mr. Garmer shook his head. "Only as much as I've said."

He tossed the man a coin and turned, Lord Sperrin on his heels. They hurried back out through the rain and into the carriage, brushing droplets from their shoulders as they shared the information with Mrs. Westby.

"They left at eight? But that's when we left the estate!" Mrs. Westby raised a gloved hand to her forehead.

Lord Sperrin knocked on the roof of the carriage, sending it into motion once more, now that the horses had been changed for fresh ones. "Don't worry. We'll catch up to Miss Talbot in no time, Agnes. Sacrifices will have to be made." The corner of Lord Sperrin's mouth quirked up. "Is everyone all right with missing tea?"

CHAPTER 28

Jane entered The Coxcomb, this inn not as nice as The Oak and Ash. Laurence's arm held her tight to him as they stepped through the narrow doorway of the dilapidated building. He ran a hand through his hair and straightened his damp jacket as the thin innkeeper came to greet them.

Lord Windham, following just behind, was the epitome of the inn's name. She still couldn't believe it was true—that Laurence was in on this plan. When they'd arrived at the first inn and she'd stepped out of the carriage, Laurence had turned out to be the driver. *He* was the one who was planning to marry her, as Lord Windham had gotten what he wished for in the jewel. Laurence wanted her dowry.

Laurence nodded at the innkeeper. "My betrothed and I and her brother will need use of your private dining room for a midday meal. We've traveled from Wiltshire and are rather famished."

The innkeeper twitched his thin mustache and bowed, getting the attention of a nearby maid. "Nancy, show these guests to the private parlor an' get them somethin' to eat."

The short girl with stringy blond hair stopped what she was doing and bobbed a curtsy, her gaze on the ground. "Right away, sir." She turned in their direction. "Come wit' me, please."

They followed her to the medium-sized room, a square table in the middle with an empty hearth on one side. Equally empty bookshelves lined one wall, and a dirty window at the far end allowed in a bit of light.

"Today we've beef stew or chicken pie. Which'd ye like?" The maid looked from Lord Windham to Laurence to Jane, the cap on her head slightly askew.

After they gave their orders, the maid left, closing the door.

Jane swallowed and took in a deep breath. Her plans to escape had gone awry at The Oak and Ash, for Lord Windham hadn't let Jane speak to any of the staff. If they asked a question, he was always the one to answer it. She hadn't been allowed to even look at the maid. Laurence had fabricated an entire story that he told to the previous inn owner—something about them meeting in an ice shop and loving each other from the start. If only that were true.

What was true...her meeting with Henry was as beautiful as the fabricated one—even more so. She'd no longer deny her feelings for him. She had to allow herself to be vulnerable, regardless of the risk. She was going to tell him, even if he rejected her. The possibility of a lifetime with Henry was worth much more than the possible months of grief she would face should he deny her.

That meant, however, that she'd have to figure out a plan to get herself out of this situation.

Laurence grabbed her arm and turned her to face him. She bit her lip to keep from crying out in pain.

"Don't try *anything*." His severe voice came out in a whisper, his mouth pulled down into harsh lines.

She moved back from him. "I didn't at The Oak and Ash, did I?"

He grunted, seeming to agree with her there. Releasing her arm, he glared, his face transforming into a tender look of adoration as the maid returned with a tray of their food and two tankards of ale.

"Here ye are." She placed the tray on the table. "Call for me if ye be needin' anythin' else." She bobbed a curtsy and left the room.

Jane's chair made a scraping sound as she pulled it toward the table. She seated herself while the rain pelted the dirty window, filling the silence of the dusty room. Lord Windham sat also and dug into his pie without delay. Laurence sipped at his ale before he began to eat.

Jane pushed her fork through the crust of her pie and into the gravy and chicken, then slid a small bite into her mouth. The meal was actually good. She took several more bites, stopping every now and then to have a sip of ale and to wipe her mouth with her napkin. All the while, her gaze roved the room, seeking a means of escape.

Likely, a window so smudged and grimy would be difficult to open, possibly not having been opened in years. There was a good chance the seams had been painted over. What about the hearth? She could threaten them with a poker, but it seemed a silly thing when Lord Windham had a gun at his disposal. Wouldn't he just shoot her before she could get near? The pistol hidden in his waistband really limited her options.

After almost an hour of Windham's inane chatter about how he planned to spend the money from the jewel—using the majority of it to clear his debts—he called for the plates to be cleared.

She held her hand out in Lord Windham's direction. Perhaps she could play on his ego. "My lord, won't you tell me about the horses at Tattersalls?" The longer she could keep the men stationary, the more whoever was coming after her could shorten the distance between them.

Laurence frowned. "Now is not the—"

Nancy came in again to take their plates, and Jane bid her to refill their mugs. The girl was back in a trice, and the alcohol was flowing once more. Perhaps it would help to keep the men in this place for a bit longer.

"Perhaps the hunt, then." Jane softened her tone into something innocent. "How many pheasants did you shoot this year, again?"

A smug expression crossed his face, and Lord Windham settled back into his chair. "Two-and-thirty."

Almost another hour passed before Lord Windham began to shift in his seat. He stood after finishing one of his stories, and Jane could've sworn Laurence sighed in relief. "Come, we must leave now." Lord Windham's tone brooked no argument. She had held them here as long as she could.

Jane followed them out of the parlor. The innkeeper appeared once more, and Laurence threw a few coins into the man's hand. "Thank you, my good man. We'll be on our way now."

The innkeeper raised an eyebrow. "In this weather? The roads are terrible, sir. Ye're sure to get stuck."

"We're sure." Laurence smile appeared like a grimace, his tone decidedly less congenial. "Our carriage is the finest." With that, he yanked on Jane's arm and pulled her into the rain.

She shivered as the droplets hit her skin, irritation building within her. Lord Windham had not given her time to collect her pelisse when he'd ordered her out of her room last night.

Their carriage was brought around with fresh horses, and her booted feet sank into the mud as she stepped off the stone pathway. She took a step forward, tripping as she struggled to pull her foot out of the mire near the base of the carriage. Lord Windham didn't hesitate. He hoisted her up from the muck and pushed her inside the conveyance, climbing in after her. Without even a knock on the roof, Laurence set the carriage in motion, driving at a slower pace, however, than before. Lord Windham retied her wrists together and leaned against the seat.

The rain pounded against the windows, and he pulled the curtains shut once more, sending the carriage into darkness and his figure into a faint outline. He swore under his breath. "Can't this blasted thing go any faster?"

Jane crossed her arms, thanking God for their slow pace. "You heard the man, my lord. The roads are in poor shape. It will take us longer to reach Gretna Green than expected. What do you get from ensuring I marry Laurence, anyway? You've already gotten the jewel."

Lord Windham leaned closer, his voice near. "A portion of your dowry. Laurence wouldn't let me marry you as I wished. He revealed your increased dowry one night after imbibing too much—and you can only imagine how that increased my wish to marry you. I'd get the jewel *and* your dowry." He sneered. "Laurence said I couldn't get everything and he nothing. He'd come all this way for your dowry. So in exchange for helping me get the jewel, I'd help him bring you to Gretna Green where you could be married."

Jane's stomach turned, but an odd sense of bravery crept up within her. "And what if I tell my parents that I did not agree to the marriage? My father will not grant Laurence my dowry."

"You won't dream of doing that, of course." The sound of metal clinking against metal reached her ears over Windham's hard voice. "For if you do, you won't survive very long. A spinster finally finds love and marries, only to die days later—how tragic that would be."

Her chest tightened. There seemed to be no way out. Droplets of water continued to beat down against the outside of the carriage, filling the silence after his threatening words, though he spoke again.

"I'm sure you're pleased at that thought of the rain, eh?

Don't let your hopes out of their cage, Miss Talbot, for I don't intend to be thwarted. A little rain won't wash away our plans."

Jane's heart sank. The carriage moved back and forth as the horses pulled it through the mud. She shifted with the movement, her eyelids heavy. She fought to stay awake. Minutes passed. A crack of thunder rent the air. She bolted upright, limbs tense. The carriage picked up its pace.

"That's more like it." Lord Windham's comment held a note of pleasure.

Jane tucked her hands in her lap, squeezing her fingers tight together. This was faster than they should be going, considering the muddy state of the roads. Could Laurence even see properly? Another roar of thunder came, and the carriage seemed to gain speed. Jane's heart galloped as quickly as the horses' hooves.

She tried to catch a glimpse from in between the curtain and the wall to see how fast the countryside moved by, but the fabric was pulled too far over for her to see anything. Lord Windham didn't make a sound, though she heard his steady breathing. Could he have fallen asleep? By Jane's estimation, they'd been traveling for less than an hour, and that time hadn't been spent in comfort. If the man could sleep through the carriage's rough movements, he could likely sleep through anything.

Suddenly, a cracking sound split the air, and the carriage pitched to the right, sending Jane flying across the seat and onto the door. Her head smacked against the wall, and she groaned.

A curse flew from Lord Windham as he tumbled along with her, scrabbling for something to hold onto.

The carriage had stopped, the cabin in a precarious diagonal position. Lord Windham grunted and pushed open the door, almost falling out into the mud. His boots sank into the wet earth, puddles all around, and a cold breeze whistled through the open door. Jane's eyes adjusted to the grey light that filtered through the opening, the rain still pouring from the sky as though God were emptying a ewer.

Lord Windham yelled a few things to Laurence, but she couldn't make out what he said. She lifted her hands to her head, the rope scraping against her skin and making it sting. The place where she'd hit her head was warm and wet. It stung as soon as her fingers brushed it. Jane winced. She held her hands toward the light, noting a dark splotch on her palms.

Jane planted her feet on the carriage floor and pushed toward the left side of the bench, pressing herself into the corner. She was hurt, disoriented. The rain and darkness forbid any attempt at escape. She bit her lip, forcing tears back. All she could do was pray someone caught up to them before the men concocted another plan.

CHAPTER 29

They were getting closer. As Henry and Lord Sperrin exited The Coxcomb and hastened to the carriage, rain coming down in droves, Henry's hope stirred.

"What have you learned?" Mrs. Westby leaned forward as he slammed the door.

Lord Sperrin took off his hat, allowing the water droplets that had accumulated on the brim to pour off onto the floor. "They left here two hours ago. The innkeeper warned them not to go out in this weather, but the woman's betrothed was determined, the man said." He knocked on the roof, and the coachman set off.

Henry grunted. "They must've thought they could lose us if they continued."

Mrs. Westby eyed him. "If they suspect anyone is following them in the first place."

Henry twisted his signet ring around his finger as he looked out the window. By continuing to travel, Revil put Jane in danger. Carriages could be perilous in this sort of weather. The fact was not lost on Henry as he sat in one, lightning flashing across the sky in vein-like streaks. No matter how much he feared being in a carriage in such weather, he wouldn't let it stop him from rescuing the woman he loved.

After half an hour, the carriage pulled over to the side of the road. Lord Sperrin pulled his coat tight. He exited and spoke with the driver. When he returned, his face was grim. "The coachman says the weather's made his hands stiff. He's having a difficult time controlling the carriage. Something about the storm affecting his arthritis."

Mrs. Westby frowned out the window. "We cannot stop now. Not when we're so close."

Possible options flew about in Henry's head. In an instant, he knew what he must do. Henry pushed open the door of the carriage, his booted feet vanishing into the mud as soon as he placed them on the ground. He settled his hat more firmly onto his head and braced himself against the wind, moving toward the front of the carriage.

"Come down, man!" He called up to the hunched coachman, who was flexing the fingers of one hand, getting his attention. "I'll take your place."

The man straightened, then he climbed to the ground, reins in hand. "I can't let ye do that, milord."

"It's not up to you." Henry took the reins and gestured toward the door of the carriage. "Go inside and make yourself comfortable. I'll take it from here."

Rain dripped down the coachman's slackened face. "What shall I tell Lord Sperrin, milord? He'll not like that one of his guests is doin' me job."

Henry swiped the rain from his eyes. "Tell him this is the best option we have."

The man dipped his head and entered the carriage.

Henry stepped up onto the box seat, nerves tingling throughout his body. In his Oxford days, he'd raced curricles against other students—surely, driving a carriage could be no different. He licked his lips, tasting the water that had dropped there. He'd never driven in the rain.

In his mind flashed the image of Jane's desperate face—the look she'd given him after Lord Windham's first attack. Henry tightened his grip on the leather and straightened his shoulders, angling his head down to shield his face.

With a flick of his wrists, the horses were moving at a quick clip, the clinking of metal fasteners and attachments filling the air. He imagined he was racing Lord Windham to Gretna Green, seeing which one of them could reach it first. He skirted around holes in the road and large stones that threatened the wheels, his hands pulling on the reins with deft movements.

He thanked God for his Oxford foolishness, which had actually served a purpose, in the end. A crack of thunder boomed through the sky, but the horses remained calm. He rolled his shoulders back, easing the stress there.

More time passed until a carriage came into view some way in the distance, the diagonal set of it indicating that it couldn't possibly be in motion. A wheel must have been broken.

As Henry neared it, the sleek design became apparent, and the man who knelt in the mud wore fine clothing. What was this? Henry was about to pull the carriage over to inquire if the party needed assistance when the carriage door slammed open and Lord Windham jumped out.

"Devil take it, Revil, can't you fix that any faster?"

"I can't fix it, Windham—that's what I'm trying to tell you. We'll have to send for help." Revil threw his arms out, his hands caked in mud.

Henry's heart leapt. He'd found them!

As he pulled their carriage to the side of the road, Lord Windham squinted. "What the de—"

Henry jumped down from his perch and spread his arms wide, grinning. "'Tis I, your old friend!"

The coachman leaped out of the carriage behind him, and Henry handed the man the reins.

Lord Windham jumped back into the carriage.

Henry laughed as Lord Sperrin got out of the carriage behind him and said, "So we've caught up with them, after all." He leveled his pistol at Revil, who immediately held his hands up.

"Where is Jane?" Henry approached the carriage with slow steps, withdrawing his pistol from his waistband. He held it in front of him, moving toward the carriage door.

Before he could reach the handle, the door burst open once more, this time with Lord Windham holding Jane in his arms, his pistol thrust against her chin.

Henry's blood turned cold. He cocked the hammer on his pistol and pointed it at Lord Windham. Jane's face was pale as she struggled in his arms, a smudge of blood across her forehead. She looked like a rabbit that had been captured—just one of the many prey that Lord Windham hunted for sport.

"Let her go, Windham." Henry's voice came out in a hard tone, his chest tight. "Think about this. You're a duke—you might even get out of this unscathed." The words were untrue considering that the magistrate was already on his tail, but Henry would let the man believe what he liked.

Lord Windham gave a harsh laugh. "You believe you have the upper hand? What has a man to lose when he has debts as deep as I?" He pierced Henry with a dark stare, a chilling smile on his face. "No, Lendin. You'll pay, in the end."

The man's finger moved on the trigger, and Henry didn't hesitate. He pulled the trigger of his own gun, but no explosion occurred. A boom expanded through the air as he looked down at his pistol, but the sound hadn't come from there. Jane and Lord Windham fell in tandem. Blood soaked into the fabric of her dress. Had Lord Sperrin managed to shoot the man, or had it been too late?

Ears ringing, Henry dropped his gun and rushed forward, diving to the mud at Jane's side. He examined her for wounds, brushing his hands down her arms and across her face. "Jane?"

Eventually, she blinked. Then she grabbed something from Lord Windham's pocket before reaching toward Henry with her bound hands. He pulled a knife out of his boot and cut her wrists free, then took her into his arms. He picked her up from the ground and cradled her to him, her head nestled into his shoulder.

He turned around to find the smoking gun not in Lord Sperrin's hand, but Mrs. Westby's. She still pointed it at Lord Windham's body, as though he might get up again. Her shoulders were set, her grip steady.

Lord Sperrin's mouth hung open. "You never told us you could shoot!"

She shrugged as she tucked the small pistol back into her reticule. "My dear husband taught me quite a lot of things before he passed."

Lord Sperrin moved to Lord Windham, his pistol still aimed at Revil, and felt for a pulse. He shook his head. "Good aim. He's dead."

Henry nudged his gun with the toe of his boot, frowning at the useless thing that had failed in its most important moment. "I'm glad you took the shot, Mrs. Westby. Turns out, my gun got wet from my hour and a half as a coachman. It wouldn't fire—the powder was damp."

Lord Sperrin scratched behind his head, looking down. "I'm embarrassed to say I hesitated with taking the shot. I was too afraid I'd hit Miss Talbot."

At this, Jane pulled her head out of Henry's shoulder. He immediately missed the warmth of her there.

"I am very grateful you didn't shoot me, Lord Sperrin." She looked around at all of them. "I am grateful to all of you who you saved me." Tears slid down her face. "You've rescued me from a truly terrible fate. I did not wish to marry Mr. Revil. He was only going to marry me for my dowry."

Just as he'd suspected. A tiny worry in the back of Henry's mind that he hadn't even known existed immediately ceased to be. She hadn't gone willingly, nor eloped. Some part of him had wondered if she *had*—not with Lord Windham, of course, but with Revil.

Henry carried her to the carriage and set her inside.

Mrs. Westby entered and sat beside her niece, wrapping her arms around Jane. "I'm so glad we reached you in time, my dear." She wiped her cheek. "If you had married that scoundrel, I don't know what I would've done."

Henry sent a prayer up, thanking God for letting them reach Jane in time.

Revil still stood in the rain, shifting from foot to foot.

"What shall we do with him?" Henry asked.

Lord Sperrin climbed into the carriage. "The rain is abating." He turned to their coachman. "John, please stay here and keep watch of Lord Windham's carriage and horses. We'll be back shortly with the constable." He pointed at Revil. "You, step up to the box seat. You'll be driving us to The Coxcomb. No tricks, mind. The better you behave, the better we'll speak of you to the magistrate."

The man nodded, and after taking the reins from John, climbed up to the perch.

The drive to The Coxcomb seemed to pass in seconds, with the party fussing over Jane's wounds and asking numerous questions about her journey and what had taken place. It wasn't long before they arrived at the inn and the magistrate was there, listening to their testimonies and requesting to be taken to Lord Windham's body.

Released at last, their small party headed back toward Lord Sperrin's estate. The rain had let up, so John was able to drive once more, but with the sun fast setting on the horizon, they decided to stay the night at The Oak and Ash. They were all exhausted and in dire need of a hearty meal and restful night of sleep.

Sometime later, Henry stepped into his small, dusty room. He shrugged out of his coat and hung it over a nearby chair. Sitting on the edge of his bed, he pulled off his boots, then dropped them on the floorboards with a *thunk*. He ran a hand through his hair, his shoulders easing. Jane was safe. She was no longer in danger of Lord Windham. That didn't, however, mean he could tell her how he felt. How could he be sure she reciprocated his feelings? Revil might have wanted her for her dowry, but that didn't mean she hadn't harbored feelings for him. Henry had witnessed that awful kiss, after all.

As he allowed his weary limbs to relax, he told himself that all that mattered was that he had done what he'd sought to do. It would have to be enough.

CHAPTER 30

When they arrived back at Lord Sperrin's estate early the next afternoon, Jane breathed out a sigh of relief. It felt good to be back where she'd spent the past few weeks. It was familiar. Pleasant, even, despite her encounters with the man who'd kidnapped her. But...

"What is happening?" Jane leaned toward the window.

Carriages lined the drive as their own rumbled over the pebbled circle, pulling up in front of the stairs leading into the manor. Footmen carried trunks out and loaded them onto the backs of the conveyances while fellow guests embraced and bowed to each other.

Lord Sperrin shrugged. "Lady Sperrin must have told the guests that the jewel has been found, my dear. The guests are leaving."

Her gaze met Henry's, who sat across from her. Would today be the last day she saw him? Her heart broke at the very idea.

As though reading her thoughts, Lord Sperrin continued. "You and Mrs. Westby are more than welcome to stay longer, considering the events that have just taken place. I believe Lord

Lendin will likely be staying as well." The man glanced at Henry, the corner of his mouth lifting.

Aunt Agnes answered for her, a knowing look on her face. "That is very generous of you, my lord. We would be thankful to."

For once in her life, Jane was grateful for her aunt's intervention. It would allow her the chance to tell Henry how she felt about him. She tried to meet Henry's gaze, but he was looking out the window.

They exited the carriage, and Jane was immediately embraced by Harriet, her blond curls bobbing. "Jane! How fortunate it is that you are well."

Jane returned her hug, smiling. "Yes, I'm not sure what you've been told, but the past few days have been...eventful."

Harriet leaned closer, drawing her arms closer to her. "We were told that you, Mr. Revil, and Lord Windham were sick in your beds, but with Lord Sperrin, Lord Lendin, and your aunt gone...well, none of us believed it. I'm sorry to say that your reputation might be a bit damaged after this." She bit her lip. "Perhaps more than a bit. Especially with Lady Caroline spouting to everyone that you've been seducing Lord Windham."

Jane gasped. "I certainly have not!"

Harriet patted her hand. "Certainly, *I* know that, but others don't know what to believe."

Jane set her jaw, determination flowing through her. "Well, let them believe what they wish. They took no notice of me for five seasons. If they choose to do so now because of this, then let them. I know what the truth is, and so do those who matter to me."

Harriet linked her arm through Jane's as they walked forward. "That's the best way of looking at it, I think." She brightened, clasping her hands together. "While you were away

—not of your own volition, of course—I formed some news of my own to share."

Jane tilted her head. "And what is that?"

Harriet stopped and whirled to face her, a grin on her face. "Mr. Langley has asked me to be his wife!" The woman squealed, bouncing up and down on her heels.

Jane clapped her hands, Harriet's excitement infectious. "Oh, congratulations, my friend. How wonderful! You must tell me all about your preparations as you plan the wedding and—"

"Harriet, come along! We must leave now if we're to reach home before evening," Harriet's mother called, interrupting their conversation.

Harriet's cheeks flushed. She looked over her shoulder. "I suppose I have to go. Write to me. I'll tell you all about it." She lowered her voice. "You must tell me what happens between you and Lord Lendin. I foresee another engagement in the near future."

Jane's cheeks heated, but before she could say anything, Harriet turned away, striding to her parents and their carriage.

Lord Sperrin walked up the steps to greet his wife, who was seeing to the needs of her departing guests. He kissed her full on the lips, and Jane looked away, wishing to give them a private moment. She greeted Wheaton, who welcomed her back with a polite bow, and searched the chaos for Henry. Where had he gone? She finally had a moment to tell him how she felt, and he had disappeared. She moved around to the side of the manor and away from the guests, curiosity pricking at her mind. Was he hiding from the guests?

"*Miss Talbot.*"

She stifled a groan as the voice sounded from behind her. It was a pity her nemesis hadn't left yet. Straightening her shoulders, Jane wiped the frown from her face and turned around. "Lady Caroline."

"I told you to stay away from Lord Lendin." Her voice was low and as sharp as a butcher's knife.

"*He* came to find *me*."

Lady Caroline raised a dainty finger to her cheek. "And who do you think was the person telling Lord Windham you knew where the jewel was? I mean—the man had to think *you* had it for some reason."

Jane's stomach flipped.

She continued. "Miss Apprett, Miss Wildon, Miss Clarke— any of them might have known where it was. I wonder who told him to seek you out. Someone who wished, perhaps, for your time to be spent in his—and not another's—company."

Lady Caroline was the one who had been encouraging Lord Windham to seek Jane out? Jane's pulse increased.

Lady Caroline tugged at the wrist of her glove, a disturbingly unhinged look on her face. "How simple it was to get them to agree to my plan. Lord Windham would get the jewel and Mr. Revil your dowry. You would be out of the picture. Lord Lendin would be mine."

Jane licked her lips. "How did you know I found the jewel?"

Lady Caroline's smirk became even more mocking. "I did not have to know that you did—only convince Lord Windham that you would. How lovely it turned out. A kidnapping, an elopement..."

"You're evil. You care nothing for anyone but yourself."

She shrugged. "All of this would have worked out far better for you if you'd decided to leave when you'd gotten ill. Most would, you know. Eel is not for everyone." She molded her face into an expression of false sympathy. "Mr. Revil fancies himself good at chess, but there is only one queen."

Jane scoffed. "And I suppose you fancy that is you."

"Indeed." She opened her reticule, tone icy. "It's a shame those silly men couldn't accomplish what they sought to do. I'll have to protect my king now." With a smirk, Lady Caroline pulled out a small pistol and aimed it at Jane. "I'll not let you have him."

Jane's heart seemed to stop. From around the corner of the house, the grey-haired magistrate appeared—apparently done with his dealing with Laurence. He stiffened as he took in the scene before him. Then he began to run toward them.

Jane stood frozen as Lady Caroline pulled the hammer and took a step back. As the woman did so, however, she moved directly into his path.

With a spryness that belied his age, he seized her shoulders, then wrestled the gun from her hand.

"Unhand me! I must finish what's been started!" Lady Caroline's shrill words and shrieks of injustice surely only condemned her in the minds of her fellow guests, who had heard the commotion and gathered at the corner of the house to ascertain the cause.

"There will be no chance of that, my dear. Come with me." The magistrate's tone was stern.

Lady Caroline blanched, and the satisfied feeling of justice served flowed through Jane. The evil woman had gotten what she deserved. The magistrate, with the help of a few of Lord Sperrin's footmen, took Lady Caroline away, her parents at their heels with shocked expressions and words of outrage on their gilded tongues.

Oddly enough, the shock of the moment didn't even last long. Perhaps the more a gun was pointed at a person, the less frightening it became. After a few moments of breathing deeply and Lord and Lady Sperrin asking her if she was all right—as well as a long hug from her aunt—Jane's heart rate returned to normal.

Now, to find Henry.

A few moments later, she entered into the library with muffled footsteps, the sun shining through the windows onto the carpet. The room was empty. She walked past the shelves of books, their old leather smell filling her nose and reminding her of the time she'd spent here with Henry—the time he'd startled her at night, the time he'd snorted while Laurence spouted poetry, the time they'd met here before going strawberry picking...

"What are you doing here?" Henry's murmured voice came from over her shoulder.

She shivered as it cascaded over her. Turning around to face him, her lips pulled up into a small smile. "Searching for you."

His arms were crossed in front of him. "Indeed?"

Jane matched his expression. "Why shouldn't I be?"

He scratched the back of his neck. "I just thought you'd be elsewhere."

She took a step back in surprise. "Where else but here?"

Henry seemed to stop moving. His chest didn't even rise or fall with breath as his eyes met hers again. "Did you ever love him?"

Jane leaned back. "Who?"

"Mr. Revil."

"No." She spoke in earnest. "I do not believe I ever truly did. It was not love, whatever it was."

Henry looked away, fidgeting. "I saw you kiss in the library—"

Jane's face heated. "*He* kissed *me*. I had no willing part in it, I assure you. It wasn't enjoyable in the least."

He went still again. "Truly?"

"Truly."

He covered his face with his hand and leaned next to her against the bookshelf. "I have been a fool."

She started to reach out to him but stopped herself. Perhaps now wasn't the right time to tell him of her feelings, after all. He needed to think through this newly revealed information first. Her heart ached to unveil all to him, but her mind told her no. She could do so later. This evening, even, if the time proved right. "I'll leave you to your thoughts, then. There are a few things I must attend to, but I'll see you at dinner."

Henry lifted his hand. "If you must go now, then meet me in the drawing room this evening, after everyone has gone upstairs."

"I will." She spoke on a whisper, then fled from the room, hoping he couldn't hear her pounding heartbeat.

She wore her lilac dress to dinner that evening, asking Abigail to arrange her hair in careful curls. The evening meal proved a quiet affair, given the lack of guests. It was also a great deal more comfortable, considering that Jane knew and liked the people surrounding her. They played cards and talked after dinner and retired rather early, still fatigued from their stressful adventure.

Half an hour later, Jane returned to the drawing room, a candle in hand. She'd made the effort to look her best for Henry. Tonight was the night she would tell him she loved him —that she'd loved him for some time now. The light-purple skirt of her gown swished around her legs as she strode along the corridor and turned down the hall.

When she arrived at the drawing room door, voices came from within. Was someone else there besides Henry? Jane placed her hand against the wood and pushed the door open, peeking inside.

Gerald perched on the edge of the settee, and Henry was nowhere in sight.

Jane greeted the bird, stepping nearer to him. "How do you do, Gerald? I didn't expect to see you here."

"Will you..." The bird croaked the words, squawking after them.

Jane raised an eyebrow. "Will I what, Gerald?"

"Will you...be merry?"

Jane tilted her head. "I consider myself a fairly merry person."

Gerald stretched his wings. "You...will...merry...be."

She glanced around the room. What on earth was happening? Where was Henry? Gerald was starting to sound like Nostradamus, and she wasn't sure she wanted to be the only one to hold this secret.

Henry burst out from behind the velvet curtains across the room. He reached them in a few long strides. He huffed out a breath of exasperation and held out his arm to the bird, who stepped onto it. "No, Gerald, you've got it all wrong. We've been over this many a time now. *Will you marry me?* Not *you will merry be.* I really don't know why you like that variation so much."

Gerald croaked again, bobbing his head. "You...will...marry...be."

Henry heaved a sigh and scratched the back of his neck. "I really thought it would go better than this." He turned his gaze toward her, flushing. "Will you marry me, Jane?"

Jane went perfectly still. Her tongue was dry—her whole mouth like the desert. He was still saying something about Gerald, but she couldn't hear. She needed to understand. "Stop." Her voice sounded foreign to her own ears.

At that one word, his eyes widened, a look of wariness coming to them. He set Gerald back on the settee.

She had to brush that wariness away, so she spoke the very thing that was on her mind. "I love you."

He sucked in a quick breath. "May I kiss you?" he asked in the softest voice.

She nodded.

In one stride, he had her wrapped within his arms, his lips pressed to hers with a sweetness she'd never known. One hand caressed her cheek, the other pulling her closer to him at the waist. Her hands molded against his chest as her mouth moved under his, his intoxicating scent of bergamot and sandalwood dazing her almost as much as his kisses. She clutched at the fabric of his lapels, pulling him as close as she could.

When they finally separated for air, he brushed a stray hair from her face, looking at her in adoration. "I love you, too, Jane." The words on his breath made her sag farther against him. He leaned his forehead against hers. "I have loved you since you beat me at chess—perhaps even before that. I just didn't know it yet. You accept me for who I am. You don't try to change me." He kissed her once more. "You're gentle and kind, fun and humorous. You joke with me but know when I need serious. You are everything I could dream of in a wife."

Jane played with a curl of his blond hair, twisting it in her fingers. She looked into his soft eyes. They'd always been so warm a brown—so welcoming. She wished to see them every day for the rest of her life. "I don't know when I fell in love with you, Henry. I tried very much not to." The corner of her mouth pulled up. "I feared you would break my heart, as Mr. Revil had. I never dreamed that someone like you could love someone like me."

He brushed his thumb over her lips, eyebrows pulling down. "You speak as though I am some king."

"To me, you might as well have been, but I think like that no more. God saved you for me." She placed a soft kiss on his cheek.

The crease between his brows faded. "And you for me."

Jane leaned her head into his shoulder and whispered. "You are the man I love, Henry. You are everything I've dreamed of. You are my prayers brought in human form. Without you, I could not be happy. I love your stories and your mischievous side. I love your chocolate-colored eyes and your glances that ask me if I'm all right. I love when you show me the joys in life."

Henry lifted her chin to look at her. "I'll show you more joys in life, love. I'll tell you stories every day. I'll challenge you to as many blackberry-eating contests as you wish—just say you'll marry me."

Jane's vision clouded with unshed tears as she beamed. "I will."

Henry lowered his mouth to hers again, this kiss slower than the first. It was a promise of their future bliss and the happiness to come. He took his time in pulling the pins from her hair and let it fall about her shoulders in silken waves, pushing his hands through it.

Jane wrapped her arms around his back, tugging him close. Henry would forever be her home. He would forever be the person who caused her to find joy, because he *was* her joy. He was the man who had taught her to be vulnerable. He was the man who had taught her to truly love, and now she'd spend her life loving him in return.

EPILOGUE

Henry hid behind the door to the library at his estate, keeping an eye out for his wife to come down the hall. It had been four months since they'd been married, and what a pleasant four months they had been. Henry regularly showed Jane the little joys of life, and Jane continued to brighten all his days with her joy and laughter, causing him to fall even more in love with her with every one.

He adjusted his stance behind the door, making sure he was hidden. He eyed her green skirt swaying along the edge of the hall and ducked his head back behind the door, his heart beating quicker in his chest.

Her footsteps got louder. She stepped into the library. Now was the moment.

He leaped out from behind the door—his arms outstretched—and wrapped them around his wife.

She yelped. "'Something is rotten in the state of Denmark!'"

He laughed, pulling her tight. "'The lady doth protest too much, methinks.'"

She turned in his arms, closing her hands around his waist.

"What a wicked trick to play upon your wife." Her tone attempted irritation, but the corners of her mouth edged up.

He kissed her brow, grinning. "Forgive me, dearest. I couldn't help it." He wrapped her arm around his and pulled her to the chair in the corner of the room, bathed in sunlight. He sat down and settled her on his lap, enclosing his arms around her waist. "How was your letter from Harriet?"

Jane beamed. "Wonderful. She is increasing! As you can imagine, Charles is simply thrilled."

Henry squeezed her. "Is she? How exciting. Soon, they shall have a little Langley running around." He kissed her temple. "I cannot wait until we might have our own little Jane or Henry running these grounds, causing all sorts of chaos." He leaned his head back against the chair.

Jane put her head on his shoulder, a hand on his waistcoat. "I know, my dear. It won't be long now. Only seven more months."

He nodded, then paused as the words caught up with his mind. *What?*

His head jerked upward.

Jane kissed his jaw. "Seven more months, my darling."

He turned his face toward her, his breath stuck in his throat. "Are you increasing, as well, my dear?" His heart raced, his blood pumping through his veins.

A grin broke out on her face. "I am."

He placed his hands on her cheeks and pulled her face near, pressing her lips to his, their softness like a flower's petal. Elation raced through him.

He broke away, murmuring to her, "My darling, I love you so much. You'll make me a father." He ran his knuckles down her jaw. "You'll be the perfect mother." He kissed her again, lingering until he remembered. "But I startled you!" He looked down at her still-flat stomach. "Do you think the baby's unharmed?"

Jane giggled, placing a hand to his cheek. "Yes, dear, I'm sure the baby is fine." She snuggled into the space where his neck and shoulder met. "Your fatherly instincts are already appearing, it seems. This baby of ours—and any that come after—will be perfectly safe."

Henry held Jane close, thanking God for all of the blessings he'd been given. He'd found his wife and now would start a family. As Jane filled the space within his arms, Henry knew he'd never want for more.

THE END

Did you enjoy this book? We hope so!
Would you take a quick minute to leave a review where you purchased the book?
It doesn't have to be long. Just a sentence or two telling what you liked about the story!

Love Christian Historical Romance?
Looking for your next favorite book?
Become a Wild Heart Books insider and receive a FREE ebook and get exclusive updates on new releases before anyone else.
Sign up for our newsletter now.
https://wildheartbooks.org/newsletter

ACKNOWLEDGMENTS

Thank You to my Heavenly Father for all of the help you have given me and all of the abundant gifts You bless me with and rain down upon me. I am forever grateful to You and love You with my whole heart and soul. I would like to thank my publisher, of course, for their endless help throughout the publishing process. I would have no idea how to go about this without them. I would like to thank also my editor, Denise Weimer, for all of the help and encouragement she has given me throughout the editing and rewrite process. Her insight has been tremendously useful at all stages, and I cannot recommend her enough to other writers in need of her editing skills. Last, but not least, I'd like to thank my friends and family for their kind words and help as I have gone through the ups and downs of this process of writing and publishing. I appreciate you all.

AUTHOR'S NOTE

I really enjoyed writing this book, and I hope you enjoyed reading it! Ever since I came up with the character of Lord Lendin in *His Grace's Governess*, I've wanted to make him his own story. He's such a fun, mischievous, spontaneous character that was a lot of fun to write. Jane was a bit more complicated but also fun. I hope you can relate to them and find them as loveable as I do.

I definitely had to research a variety of fun things for this book, including but not limited to: lawn bowls, brag, fishing during the Regency period, Regency charades (they are very different from modern charades), how strawberries grow, etc.

In case you were wondering, Mr. Alton is a character based on one of the characters in Georgette Heyer's books, and he is sort of a lovable/not very bright/strange character only meant to add humor. If only I could pull off her type of characters. I tried, anyway. He makes me happy. My favorite scene in the book is probably the scene over dinner where Jane tries to tell Henry that she wants to go fishing and he misinterprets what she's saying. What do you think he thinks she says? And what's your favorite scene?

I hope you've enjoyed reading my novel and would be ever so glad if you could leave a review on Amazon or wherever it is you prefer to leave your reviews. I delight in reading every one.

If you wish to follow my progress with books and keep up to date on new releases, please follow me on Instagram on my page: @authorjackiekillelea or on my Facebook page: @AuthorJackieKillelea. I also have an author website, https://jackiekillelea.weebly.com/, and you can find me on BookBub at @authorjackiekillelea. If you are interested in other books I've written, you can find them on Amazon. Thank you!

ABOUT THE AUTHOR

Jackie Killelea is a born and raised small-town girl from Connecticut with a degree in English and Creative Writing. She started off her writing journey with poetry, soon shifting into novels and becoming hooked. On days when she's not busy with her nose in a book, she can be found typing away with a piece of chocolate in hand.

If you love historical romance, check out the other Wild Heart books!

Rumors and Promises by Kathleen Rouser

She's an heiress hiding a tumultuous past. He's a reverend desperate to atone for his failures.

Abandoned by her family, Sophie Biddle has been on the run with a child in tow. At last, she's found a safe life in Stone Creek, Michigan, teaching piano. But when a kind, yet meddling and handsome, minister walks into her life seeking to help, Sophie is caught off guard and wary. When her secrets threaten to be exposed, will she be able to trust the reverend, and more importantly, God?

After failing his former flock, Reverend Ian McCormick is determined to start anew in Stone Creek, and he's been working harder than ever to forget his mistakes and prove himself to his new congregation—and to God. But when he meets a young woman seeking acceptance and respect, despite the rumors swirling about her sordid past, Ian finds himself pulled in two directions. If he shows concern for Sophie's plight, he could risk everything—including his position as pastor of Stone Creek Community Church.

Will the scandals of their pasts bind them together or drive them apart forever?

A Summer at Thousand Island House by Susan G Mathis

She came to work with the children, not fall in love.

Part-nanny, part entertainer, Addison Bell has always had an enduring love for children. So what better way to use her creative energy than to spend the summer nannying at the renowned Thousand Island House on Staple's Island? As Addi thrives in her work, she attracts the attention of the recreation pavilion's manager, Liam Donovan, as well as the handsome Navy Officer Lt. Worthington, a lighthouse inspector, hotel patron, and single father of mischievous little Jimmy.

But when Jimmy goes missing, Addi finds both her job and her reputation in danger. How can she calm the churning waters of Liam, Lt. Worthington, and the President, clear her name, and avoid becoming the scorn of the Thousand Islands community?

~

Revealing the Truth by Lorri Dudley

His suspect holds a secret, but can he uncover the truth before she steals his heart?

When Katherine Jenkins is rescued from the side of the road, half-frozen and left for dead, her only option is to stay silent about her identity or risk being shipped back to her ruthless guardian, who will kill to get his hands on her inheritance and the famous Jenkins Lipizzaner horses. But even under the pretense of amnesia, she cannot shake the memory of her sister and Katherine's need to reach her before their guardian, or his marauding bandits, finish her off. Will she be safe in the earl's manor, or will the assailant climbing through her window be the death of her?

British spy, Stephen Hartington's assignment to uncover an underground horse-thieving ring brings him home to his family's manor, and the last thing he expected was to be struck with a candlestick upon climbing through the guest chamber window. The manor's feisty and intriguing new house guest throws Stephen's best-laid plans into turmoil and raises questions about the timing of her appearance, the convenience of her memory loss, and her impeccable riding skills. Could he be housing the horse thief he'd been ordered to capture—or worse, falling in love with her.

www.ingramcontent.com/pod-product-compliance
Lightning Source LLC
Chambersburg PA
CBHW070529310726
48976CB00002BA/576